About the Author

I live in Stoke-on-Trent, where I have lived my whole life, with my husband and our two beautiful daughters. I am very close to my family and my favourite time of year is Christmas!

Photograph by Jodie Brennan Photography

A Love Torn Apart

Amy Pugh

A Love Torn Apart

Olympia Publishers
London

www.olympiapublishers.com
OLYMPIA PAPERBACK EDITION

A CIP catalogue record for this title is
available from the British Library.

ISBN: 978-1-80074-658-9

First Published in 2022

Olympia Publishers
Tallis House
2 Tallis Street
London
EC4Y 0AB

Printed in Great Britain

Dedication

I dedicate this book to my loved ones in the sky xxx

Acknowledgements

Thank you to all of my fantastic family who have shown me no end of love and support xxx

Chapter One

Sarah Bailey's eyes rested on the framed photograph of herself and her father as she pulled her brush through her light brown, shoulder-length hair. Feeling a little deflated, she dropped the brush onto her bed and picked up the frame. She studied her father Stan's face each time she looked at photographs of him. Her eyes were exactly the same as his, from the rounded shape to the baby blue colour. Sarah had always loved this photo of them, herself sitting on her father's knee and him sitting on the new swing set that he had built for her in the back garden. She was only seven years old at the time, and the new swing set had been a present from her new baby sister, Katy.

Even now, at twenty-eight years old, Sarah could still remember how she had reacted when her mother, Suzanna and her father had told her she was going to be a big sister. She screamed angrily, cried, then stomped off to her bedroom. She hadn't wanted to share her parents, especially her dad. *Daddy's little princess*, he'd always called her. She felt that she would no longer get everything she had wanted for Christmas and she wouldn't have a gigantic pile of presents on her birthday, or even a party, in fact! She had come out of her room hours later, muttering about being replaced and making it perfectly clear to both of her parents that she would not be sharing any of her things with the new baby. That memory still made her chuckle. What a spoilt child she was and how wrong she had been before Katy had arrived.

As soon as Sarah had laid eyes on her new baby sister, she was besotted. The tears she cried as Katy was placed gently in her arms were happy ones. She whispered a promise to Katy that she would be the most perfect big sister to her. Throughout the years, she had firmly kept true to her promise and had grown up as Katy's most fierce protector. She still shared everything with Katy, from secrets and stories to clothes and jewellery.

Not believing it possible, Sarah and Katy had grown closer together after the death of their father when he sadly passed away only ten years after Katy was born. Sarah herself was left fatherless at only seventeen years old. Sarah had taken on a second mother role to Katy as Stan's death had completely broken her mother. The cries that escaped Suzanna every night for months after his death sent shivers down Sarah's spine. She lay awake most nights waiting for her mother's wails to start through the bedroom wall, even though Suzanna had insisted that she was okay, at which point Sarah would make her way to her mother's bedroom and squeeze her tight until her sobs subsided. She would then tiptoe to Katy's bedroom and quietly open her door a fraction to check that she was still sleeping soundly. She only settled and returned to her own bedroom when she saw that Suzanna's sobs had not woken her. This became a nightly routine for Sarah that she did not look forward to, but she knew needed to be done.

She snapped out of her trance-like state after this horrific memory and shook her head to clear it. She placed the photo frame carefully back down on her cupboard, wiped a lone tear from her cheek and smiled. She looked up just as Suzanna popped her head into the room.

"Hi, sweetie. Are you joining us?"

"Yeah, I'll be out in a second, Mum," she smiled back.

Sarah, Suzanna and Katy frequently enjoyed cosy picnics in their garden, which still housed Sarah's swing set from all those years ago. The garden stretched far back from the house, and not a bit of it was unkempt. Stan had looked after his garden wonderfully, and it showed even after this lengthy period of time. He had kept all sorts of different foods for his flowers, plants and trees in the huge, wooden shed that he had built for himself at the bottom of the garden. Whenever Sarah had gone inside the shed, it had always reminded her of walking into a hardware shop and garden centre. She had often joked with Stan about him having more stock on his shelves than the stores did. Sarah didn't know the names of half of the gardening tools he kept in there or what he did with them. He had called his garden his 'third child', and he had taken pride in its appearance. He could often be seen talking to the neighbours over the garden fence, mostly giving them tips on watering their grass or when the best time of the year was to plant different types of flowers.

Sarah had loved waking up on sunny days to find Stan in the garden in his oversized hat, which he called Harold, tending to one plant or another whilst whistling merrily to himself. Suzanna was usually passing him the items he needed or coming in and out of the house with cool drinks on a tray. She worried that he would get dehydrated in the sun, so she made him have a drink every twenty minutes! Light chuckles and mutters of, 'such a worrywart' could be heard from Stan as soon as Suzanna's back was turned.

Since he had gone, Suzanna had become head gardener, and she was now just as proud of it as Stan had been. She told Sarah and Katy that being in the garden made her feel closer to their dad, and she wanted to keep it as brilliant and vibrant as he had done himself. Even now, the colours of the flowers, plants and trees seemed so much brighter than in the neighbour's gardens. The leaves on the trees looked like they had been painted a vivid botanical green colour, and the flowers were ablaze with all the colours of the rainbow.

Sarah went outside to join her mum and sister on the frayed red picnic blanket that they had used many times over the years. They had used it on family outings and on numerous occasions like this when they had just wanted a picnic in the garden. Sarah stood in the doorway, watching Suzanna and Katy talking and laughing together for a few minutes. They both looked similar to Sarah, with the same shaped faces and hair colour. The exception was their eye colour which was a chocolate brown. Suzanna looked Sarah's way and spotted her.

"Coo-ee Sarah! Come and sit down!"

Sarah took her place between them and loaded up her paper plate with sandwiches and salad. They were still outside when it started to get dark and chilly, so they packed up the picnic things and went inside, where they continued their conversation on the blanket in the living room. They were discussing the fundraiser that would be taking place at the hospital where Sarah worked as an A&E nurse. It would be a silent auction, and Suzanna was one of the many organisers. She made sure that she was involved every year. She felt she owed it to the hospital for the amazing care they had given to her husband in the final weeks of his life.

Sarah loved her job, and she was very popular with the staff and the patients who she cared for. Her best friend and colleague was a lady called Tina. She had long blonde hair, which reminded Sarah of golden silk, the biggest blue eyes and a warm, kind face. Her smile was contagious, and her joyful attitude seemed to rub off on everybody she met. Tina worked alongside Sarah in the accident and emergency department. They were both passionate about caring for people, and they always tried to make a dire situation better for their patients and their families with a friendly smile and kind words, as well as the first-class care they provided. Sarah and Tina had gone through college and university together, and they were as close as sisters by the time they graduated. They had shared the best and worst times of their lives with each other, including the passing of both of Tina's parents as she had been working her way through her nursing degree in university. Tina never had any siblings, so Sarah, Suzanna and Katy became like a second family to her. They included her in everything they did as a family, such as weddings, birthday parties and even holidays.

When Tina got married, Sarah stood by her side as her bridesmaid and watched as she married Bill, the man who Tina had claimed was "*the man of her dreams*". She was sat by her side less than six months later when Tina, with silent tears streaming down her face, scribbled her signature on her and Bill's divorce papers. It had taken Tina the whole day to finally sign them. Tina slammed her finger onto the word infidelity, and commented to Sarah about how Bill had decided that he preferred to spend time with his boss's daughter instead of her. As soon as she had finished signing the papers, Tina's upset turned to anger.

"Good luck to them," she spat bitterly. "Did you know Bill's boss didn't even know that he was married? None of his colleagues knew either. No wonder nobody from his work turned up to the wedding! Apparently, he never wore his wedding ring at work and never talked about me," she paused. "His boss brought his daughter into his work one day, and Bill obviously liked the look of her, so he set them up!" Tina then started to laugh hysterically, making Sarah worry about her friend.

"I think you should stay at my house tonight, Tina," Sarah

said calmly. "My mum and sister are out for the night at the hospital fundraiser, so we would have the house to ourselves. We could watch films, eat popcorn, have a girly chat? Anything you want."

Tina looked around sadly at the house that she shared with Bill and let out a sigh. She wondered if it was somehow her fault that Bill had done the dirty on her as she looked at her wedding photographs on the wall. Bill was in a smart blue suit, and she was wearing a gorgeous ivory lace gown that made her feel like a princess. In the photographs, they were smiling at each other as if they didn't have a care in the world. Now he had run off with his boss's daughter and left her feeling worthless.

"Thanks for the offer, but I think I am going to stay here and just have some time to myself and think about what I need to do."

"What do you mean by that?" Sarah asked.

"Oh, Bill seems to think that I will be moving out as soon as we are divorced. He thinks I will let him buy me out." Tina seemed amused as she said this. "I have told him to prepare himself for a fight because I am not leaving this house. He thinks he can cheat on me and then move '*the best thing that's ever happened to him*' in here? I don't think so." She walked Sarah to the front door, sniggering.

Sarah got into her car alone after pleading with her friend to go with her, and after a lot of insisting from Tina that she would be fine on her own, she drove home wondering if leaving her was the best idea.

"I'm being silly," Sarah said to herself as she was driving along a winding road. "She's a big girl and she can make her own decisions. If she needs me she will call, and I will be back with her as quick as anything."

This pep talk did not make her feel any better about the

situation, though, so she called Tina as soon as she arrived home.

"Sarah, I'm fine," Tina laughed as she answered the phone on the second ring. "Honestly, I've completely chilled out now. I'm just going to have a nice long relaxing bath with a glass of Bill's very expensive wine, which is calling out to me. There is only enough left in the bottle for one bloody glass, but I am going to thoroughly enjoy it, and then I am going to bed. I'm planning on having a lazy morning, so I will see you at work tomorrow night."

"Okay, if you're really, really sure. I'll see you tomorrow. Love you."

"I love you too, Sar."

Sarah ended the call but held onto her phone. She had a feeling of dread in the pit of her stomach.

"Stop worrying," she said aloud. "She will be fine."

She ran herself a bath, poured a glass of wine and read her favourite book. She left her phone in her bedroom, so hadn't noticed the message that had pinged through while she was in the bath. She got into bed feeling like she had storm clouds above her head and drifted off into an uneasy sleep. She was awoken soon after to her phone ringing, piercing the quietness of her bedroom. She was awake instantly, panicking and wondering who would be calling her at 1:10 a.m. She looked at the caller ID; it was Tina. Her nerves subsided slightly when she saw her name, knowing that Tina would just be needing to hear some comforting words.

"Hi, Tina, are you okay?" Sarah tried to sound as cheerful as she could so Tina wouldn't feel guilty about waking her up, but the person who answered her was not Tina. Sarah's heart suddenly began hammering in her chest at the sound of this unfamiliar male voice. He sounded grave.

"Hello is this Sarah?" said the voice.

"Yes. Who are you, and why do you have Tina's phone?" Sarah said in an accusatory tone.

"This is PC Guthridge from the Middlesbrough police department." Sarah could hear sirens blaring in the background. "I'm so sorry to be calling you at this hour, but I'm afraid I have some bad news regarding Tina Lynch. I believe you knew her?"

"Yes, she's my best… hold on, what do you mean *knew* her? What's happened to her?" Sarah's voice began to rise and tears were now rolling down her cheeks like heavy raindrops.

"I'm really sorry to have to tell you this, but I'm afraid that Tina has been in a car accident and unfortunately she has died due to her injuries." PC Guthridge sounded like he was fighting to hold back his own tears. "You are the emergency contact in her phone, and we need you to go to the hospital so she can be formally identified." Sarah mumbled that she would go right away and hung up the phone.

In a haze of complete shock and disbelief, Sarah headed to the hospital. She called her mother before she left the house and asked her to meet her there. Suzanna agreed at once and hopped in the car with Katy quick on her heels. Torturously, when they arrived at the hospital, they had to walk through the department where Sarah and Tina worked. Sarah pretended she hadn't seen her colleagues looking at her with mournful looks on their faces and tears in their eyes that were threatening to fall at any moment. She kept her eyes on the floor and walked hand in hand with Suzanna to the same room that Sarah had shown grieving families to, time and time again.

It was a small side room, called the 'Relative Room' with two comfortable armchairs, a long red sofa and a circular table inside. The table had two items on top of it, a lonely box of tissues and a telephone. Sarah stared at the phone for a while, knowing only too well about some of the awful conversations that had taken place on it. The walls were plastered with posters about dealing with grief and numbers that you could call if you needed to speak to anybody about it, but this made her feel worse. She knew that the only number she would use if she was struggling with grief would never be answered again. At this point, she broke into tears and hugged her mother tight.

After what seemed like an eternity, two doctors came into the room and asked Sarah and Suzanna to follow them to the room where Tina lay. Katy stood, not knowing what to do with herself, but after a shake of the head from Suzanna, she returned to her seat.

Hesitating at first, Sarah made her way down the corridor whilst holding on to her mother. Her legs felt like unbelievably heavy weights, and it took her all of her strength to keep them moving forward. She could feel the tears coming again as she watched one of the doctors open the door and walk in. He looked at Sarah and Suzanna with a sorry look on his face and pulled back the crisp white sheet just enough so they could see Tina's face. She had a cut on her forehead and her nose was bloody, yet she looked so peaceful. Sarah leaned close to the face she had seen happy and smiling so many times, and she kissed Tina softly on her cheek. She felt her mother's comforting hand rubbing her back as she stood there staring at Tina, realising that this nightmare had really happened and that she would never see her friend smile or hear her voice ever again. Sarah sobbed as she dropped to her knees in grief and despair.

Chapter Two

A few days after Tina's death, Sarah was at home when there was a quiet knock on the door. She opened it and was surprised to see Bill standing there with his eyes puffy and red from crying.

"Bill… what are you doing here?" Sarah hadn't intended to, but she sounded angry.

"Hello, Sarah. I'm so sorry to turn up unannounced like this, and I know I don't deserve your help, but could I please come in? I need your help with Tina's funeral."

Sarah had not anticipated this. She couldn't bring herself to even think about Tina's funeral, and it had only just occurred to her now, standing at her front door, that she could have ended up planning it herself given that Tina had lost her mother and father and that she was the closest person to her. She looked at the fresh tears welling in Bill's eyes and held the door open for him to come inside. They entered the warm living room and were soon joined by Suzanna. She did not seem to be in as much of a forgiving mood as Sarah, so she took herself away into the kitchen to put the kettle on. When Suzanna returned to the living room with a plate of biscuits and a coffee each for Sarah and Bill, she banged Bill's down on the table in front of him, spilling some as she did so. She sat down next to Sarah with her lips pursed.

"So, what brings you here?" Suzanna asked crossly.

"I… I need Sarah's help with Tina's funeral. I can't possibly plan this on my own, and I don't know who else to turn to for help." He wiped his nose on his sleeve. Suzanna tutted and snatched a clean tissue from the box on the coffee table. She handed it to Bill with a disgusted look on her face.

"So you treat your wife like something that you have trodden in, and now you come round to her best friend's house to ask for her help?" Suzanna was getting angrier by the second. Sarah did not want this situation to be any more awkward than it already was, so she patted her mother's knee and gave her a look that said, *please calm down and let me deal with this*.

"Please… I know I don't deserve this, Sarah, but I know that you will give Tina a beautiful send-off. You knew all of the things she liked, the things that made her smile and laugh. I know that I was not the best husband from day one. I wasn't even the best boyfriend from day one." He shrugged his shoulders pathetically. "I should have treated her much better than I did, and I truly am sorry for how it ended between us."

Sarah doubted this very much because not once had he called Tina to ask how she was after he had left her, and Sarah knew for a fact that he hadn't even apologised to Tina. He had left Sarah to pick up the pieces and try to put Tina back together again. She let out a heavy sigh in an attempt to make her anger ebb away, and she let him continue.

"I know we were having a bad time with the house and everything and constantly shouting at each other, but I never thought that anything like this would happen to her. The last thing I said to her… I told her that I would get her out of my house one way or the other." He dissolved into loud sobs and covered his face with his hands.

Sarah's eyes started to fill with tears, but she could not bring herself to comfort Bill. She felt like it would be downright disrespectful to Tina if she did. She felt that if she did comfort him, she would be forgiving him for what he had done to her best friend. Sarah sat and watched him, just letting him cry. Suzanna stood and ran hastily from the room. Sarah strongly suspected that she had gone to her bedroom to let her grief out too. Bill eventually started to calm down and grabbed another tissue from the box. He blew his nose, which sounded like a trumpet and raised his watery eyes to Sarah again.

"I will help you," she croaked in response to Bill's pleading look. "But I will not be inviting you here to sort the details; we will only call or text each other. I don't know if you would have had the cheek to invite your little thing to the funeral, but she will not be coming, do you understand me?"

Bill nodded. "Yes, of course. I won't be inviting her. I would have told her that it wouldn't be the best idea for her to come anyway, even if she had asked."

"Indeed, Bill, because when you attend a person's funeral, you do that to pay your respects, but neither of you had any respect for Tina when you decided to carry on with each other behind her back, did you?"

Bill grimaced. "I deserve that I know, but Gemma didn't know that I was married…"

Sarah cut him off with an icy stare. "You knew you were married," she said quietly.

"Yes, but Gemma didn't know until…"

Bill trailed off. He knew that he had said the wrong thing. He had awoken the beast that had been lying dormant inside Sarah since Tina had died. She immediately got to her feet and sent the biscuits that were still on the coffee table flying across the room.

"UNTIL YOU TOOK HER INTO THE HOUSE THAT YOU SHARED WITH TINA AND SHE SAW YOUR WEDDING PHOTOGRAPHS ON THE WALL! THEN YOU

PROCEEDED TO WALK PAST THEM ON THE WAY UP TO THE BEDROOM WHERE YOU HAD SEX WITH HER IN THE BED THAT, OH YEAH, GUESS WHAT, YOU ALSO SHARED WITH TINA! Yeah, I know all about that! I know because Tina told me that she found some false eyelashes and a couple of nails under the pillows when she was changing the bed covers." Sarah was sobbing now but managed to speak more calmly. "And I know that after finding the evidence that you had cheated on her, she broke down into tears, slid to the floor and cried into your pillow because she knew at that moment that her marriage was over."

Bill said nothing at this. He sat with his hands covering his mouth in shock, tears gushing from his eyes once more. A few minutes passed with both Bill and Sarah sitting in silence, not looking at each other until Bill spoke.

"How could I have been so selfish?"

"I was wondering the same thing. After all the years that you were together, you cheat as soon as you get married. Why?"

"I don't know, Sarah."

"Did you want to marry Tina?"

Sarah never found out the answer to this question because Bill stood up suddenly and announced that he had to leave. Sarah knew that this was an excuse because she didn't think he had wanted to marry Tina. She watched him get into his old red Renault Megane through the living room window and saw him wipe his eyes before driving off down the road. She waited for around an hour and then picked up her phone and tapped out a message to Bill.

Find a church for Tina's funeral. I will organise the rest. Sarah.

Sarah started to organise the funeral the very next day. She made a humongous list of what she would need to arrange so she wouldn't forget anything. She made an appointment with an advisor called Matthew from Harrington and Sons Funeral Care for the following day and called Bill to let him know.

"Bill? It's Sarah." She still sounded sharp with him but she couldn't help it. She didn't know why but she felt that Tina's death would have been prevented if it weren't for him somehow.

"Hi, Sarah. How… how are you?" he stuttered.

"Fine. Have you decided on a church yet because I have somebody coming from a funeral home tomorrow?"

Bill paused and then said softly, "Yes. I decided on the church where we got married. Tina chose it for the wedding, so I would like it to be there."

"Okay, thank you. I will let you know when I have arranged everything. Bye, Bill."

Sarah didn't give him the opportunity to say anything else before she hung up the phone. She spent the rest of the day on the phone and computer trying to find prices for everything, such as flowers and a venue for the wake after the funeral. She put together a list of Tina's favourite songs and then scribbled some out as she decided that most would not be appropriate to be played at her funeral. After many hours, she had a list that she was happy with and wrote notes next to the songs specifying at which point they should be played. Sarah printed the last photograph she had taken of Tina to give to the funeral director for the order of service. It was one that Sarah had taken when she surprised Tina with a meal and drinks in a fancy restaurant in an attempt to cheer her up after she had found out about Bill and Gemma.

At eleven a.m. the following morning, Matthew from Harrington and Sons arrived at Suzanna's house dressed in a smart black suit and tie. He looked the part but Sarah did not get a good vibe from him. Suzanna had set up the dining room table with a teapot and cups, muffins that she had baked to keep herself busy and a pen and paper for Sarah just in case she needed to write any information down. Matthew sat down at the table and pulled an impressive leather folder that was as thick as two yellow pages phone books from his briefcase. It had the company name brandished on it in thick silver lettering. It looked really heavy, and Matthew had to pick it up using both of his hands.

"So, Sarah. As you can see, I have a lot of information here but don't worry, we don't need to go through this page by page," he said, tapping the folder annoyingly. "We would be arranging our own funerals by the time we had finished if we did that."

Sarah did not find Matthew's joke funny at all, but he laughed hysterically, letting out huge snorts every now and then. He stopped chortling at once when he noticed the look Sarah was giving him across the table. She wondered if this was how he got through his days working as a funeral director; she suspected that you wouldn't laugh a lot in that sort of job. Matthew carried on talking, looking slightly awkward but thankfully more serious now. Sarah knew she wouldn't be able to put up with any more of Matthew's stupid jokes.

"You said on the phone that Tina was your best friend; I wonder were you thinking of writing a eulogy for her at all?"

"Er, I hadn't really thought about it, to be honest, but it would be nice to do that. Yes, I will write a eulogy for her."

He retrieved a form from his fancy folder and wrote Tina's name across the top. Next to where it said 'eulogy', he wrote, 'Yes – Sarah Bailey (best friend).

“Okay, that’s great. Any thoughts on which church you would like Tina’s funeral to be held in?” he asked.

“Yes, it will be the one on Miller Road, All Saints Church. Tina was married there.” Sarah answered.

“Okay, thank you,” he murmured as he jotted the name of the church down on his form. “And how many cars will you be needing to get family and friends to the church and to your venue afterwards?”

“Er, the one that Tina will be arriving in and another one.”

Sarah inhaled at the icy look that was being shot in her direction from her mother’s eyes. She had purposely not told Suzanna that they would be sharing a car with Bill and his mother, Sheila. Tina only had Bill and Sheila as relatives because her parents had no siblings either, so she didn’t have any aunts, uncles, nieces or nephews around. Sarah hadn’t seen the need to take up two cars when there would only be five people who needed it. Sarah was not looking forward to the conversation she would be having with her mother when Matthew left.

He had been sitting at Suzanna’s dining room table for nearly an hour when he asked Sarah for a photograph of Tina and the music that was to be played in the church. Sarah handed them over along with an obituary for Tina that would be shown in the local paper. Matthew promised to be in touch with her with a date for Tina’s funeral, then shook Sarah and Suzanna’s hands and left. Sarah quickly ran to her bedroom before Suzanna could ask any questions about the cars.

The following day, Matthew called Sarah to let her know that Tina’s funeral was going to be happening the following week, on Friday afternoon at one p.m. Now that she had the date, Sarah hopped into her car and drove into town to see if she could make arrangements with Tina’s favourite florist, Betty. Tina had insisted that Betty be the lady from who she bought wedding flowers, so in Sarah's mind, there was no other person who she would trust to provide the flowers for Tina's funeral. Sarah parked her car in a bay outside Betty's shop and went inside. The bell tinkled merrily as Sarah pushed open the door.

"Good morning, Betty," Sarah said cheerfully.

Sarah guessed that Betty had to be nearly seventy years old. She had previously told Sarah that the thought of retiring and leaving her shop was a *complete no-no*. She had short curly grey hair and chubby cheeks. She always wore a cardigan and a floaty skirt and hung her glasses from a chain around her neck, reminding Sarah of one of her school teachers.

"Hi… I recognise your face, but I'm so sorry I can't remember your name. I'm terrible with names. My grandchildren joke that they are going to wear name tags when they come to visit me, the little tinkers," she giggled, lifting her glasses to her face.

"That's okay. I'm Sarah; I came in here with my friend six months ago for wedding flowers."

"Oh yes, I remember now." Betty flapped her hands and shuffled over to a wall that was filled with photographs of people who had bought flowers from her. She tapped a photo that Sarah recognised instantly. "Here they are, Tina and Bill," said Betty, reading the names beneath the photograph. It was one of Tina's favourites, Sarah in her violet bridesmaid dress standing next to Tina and Bill on their wedding day. "Such a lovely, sweet girl. She bought me this photo a few weeks after her wedding day with a thank you note and a box of chocolates. How is she?"

Sarah knew that Tina's name would be mentioned sooner rather than later, and she had prepared herself for the conversation.

"Unfortunately, she had a car accident, and she didn't make it."

Betty put her hand over her mouth in shock. "Oh! I'm so sorry, Sarah, that's a real shame. How is poor Bill handling this? So sad, having just gotten married."

"Well, he's not great, as expected. They had just started divorce proceedings." There was silence from Betty. Sarah continued. "I'm here to place an order with you for the flowers for her funeral if you are able to? It's next Friday, the 9th of March?"

Betty snapped out of her trance and placed her hand on her heart. "Goodness, that poor girl. Of course I can fit you in, don't you worry about that."

Sarah left the shop forty-five minutes later with a receipt for the funeral flowers and a gargantuan bunch of lilies from Betty, free of charge. *Think of your friend when you look at them*, she had told Sarah.

The next task on her to-do list was to find a venue for the wake after Tina's funeral. She had a place in mind which was a short distance from the church. It was a pretty little pub where Sarah and Tina had been for countless meals together on many different occasions, whether it be a birthday celebration, a meal to make them feel better or, more often than not, just a normal Saturday night. It had a very friendly atmosphere; Sarah knew the owners and a lot of the regular customers by name, which is why she wasn't surprised at all when she was pulled into a gigantic bear hug as soon as she set foot inside. Fred and Maureen, the owners, were already aware of Tina's death, and they told Sarah that they had made sure to be keeping availability just in case Sarah had wanted their cosy pub to be the venue for Tina's wake.

Maureen and Sarah walked around the restaurant area together, with Maureen pointing out where the buffet would be and where a projector screen and Sarah's computer could be set up. This was so important to Sarah because she wanted to include lots of photographs of Tina on the day, which would play on the projector screen in the background. Maureen offered Sarah a cup of tea which she gladly accepted, and they sat together in two snuggly armchairs reminiscing about Tina and the many lives she had touched through her love and kindness.

Fred came over to join them a little while later and told Sarah that not only would they be closing the pub on the morning of Tina's funeral so he and Maureen could attend to pay their respects, but also that they would not be charging Sarah for use of the venue or the food.

When Sarah got up to leave after finishing a second cup of tea, she told Fred and Maureen that she was so happy that they would be coming to the funeral, and she thanked them both profusely for their hospitality and for their very generous offer.

Sarah felt drained when she arrived home later that day. She carefully picked up her gift of lilies that Betty the florist had given to her and carried them inside the house. She searched through the kitchen cupboards for her favourite fuchsia pink vase and placed the lilies inside it one by one. She carried the vase into her bedroom and over to the set of drawers where she kept some of her sentimental items – her gorgeous love heart necklace that her father had given to her on her prom night, a photograph of Suzanna and Stan on their wedding day and a bottle of Stan's favourite cologne, which she sometimes sprayed a little amount of onto herself when she felt she needed to be close to him. She made a space for the vase and carefully placed it down. She stood for a second admiring the lilies, then sat down on her bed with her laptop so she could choose the photographs of Tina that she wanted to display at Fred and Maureen's place.

Three days later, Katy hurried into the living room with a newspaper tucked under her arm. She sat down at Sarah's side and shoved the paper under her nose, which was open on the death notices page. There she saw a smaller version of the photograph of Tina that she had given to Matthew and the obituary that they had written together:

> 'LYNCH Tina, aged twenty-eight, died on 25th February 2018. The dearly loved friend of Sarah, Suzanna and Katy, wife of Bill and daughter-in-law to Sheila. Treasured daughter of the late Robert and the late Iris. Funeral to be held at All Saints Church, Miller Road, on Friday, 9th March 2018. Please wear something sparkly
> and any donations to be given to Middlesbrough Hospital where Tina worked as a much-loved nurse.'

The day that Sarah was dreading soon came round and she, Suzanna and Katy were waiting anxiously and tearfully outside Tina's house dressed in three of her sparkly tops. Tina had always told Sarah that she would want sparkles and glitter even at her funeral, so Sarah felt that it was the right thing to do, to adhere to Tina's wishes. They were standing hand in hand when the hearse carrying Tina appeared a little way further down the road, followed by the car that she would be getting into with Bill and his mother. Sarah's heart started to pound at this sight, and tears instantly started to fall from her eyes. She had her arms around Suzanna and Katy when she heard anguished cries just behind her. She turned and found Bill standing on the threshold of his house, wailing and clinging onto the door frame as if his life depended on it. Sheila patted his back as she dabbed her cheeks with her handkerchief.

The journey to the church was silent apart from Sarah and Bill's sniffling. When the driver of their car rounded the final corner and pulled into the car park of the church, they were gobsmacked by the number of people they saw. Sarah recognised nearly all of them as they were patients that had been treated by Tina and herself, but there were a couple of faces that she didn't know. Maybe they were people from Bill's side of the family, she wondered. Sarah looked over at Bill to see if he showed any signs of recognition, but he had buried his face into his handkerchief. Even though her heart was breaking again, she was glad to see that most of the people gathered here had included glitter somewhere in their outfit for Tina.

The church was beautiful. It was a tan coloured brick building with tiling on the roof and immaculate stained glass windows. The ivy which made its way up and across the front of the church gave it a fairy tale look. Sarah looked up at the bells which had rung out for her friend just six months ago on her wedding day. A soft twinkling melody rang out from inside the church and grew steadily louder as Father Green opened the huge wooden doors. He invited the mourners inside and greeted them all with a handshake as they entered.

The service started and Sarah, Suzanna and Katy were sitting at the front of the church with Tina's oak coffin, covered in sweet-smelling roses, just in front of them. Bill was seated next to his mother in the pews on the opposite side of the aisle. He had his head on her shoulder, tears coming thick and fast down his cheeks. Anybody who didn't know what had happened between Tina and Bill would never have guessed, given his reaction to having his ex-wife's coffin in front of him. He was absolutely devastated, and Sarah didn't expect to, but she felt sorry for him.

The time had come for Sarah to stand behind the podium. She got to her feet and willed her legs to move forward. She faced the congregation and read.

"Tina was much more than my best friend. Being around her was like being around another sister. We got up to all sorts of mischief together, especially during our time at university. She was such a strong person, and she was always the one that people came to for advice, a shoulder to cry on, and if you wanted to have the best night out in your life!"

She heard light chuckling and started to laugh through her tears, but she kept her eyes firmly on her piece of paper. She had to continue, and she knew she would not be able to if she looked up.

"I remember after our graduation ceremony, we were at my house celebrating. We had the house to ourselves while my mum went to visit my grandparents to show my graduation photos off. Tina and I had planned to order some food in and watch a film while we were eating – basically just to have a quiet night. I had bought a bottle of champagne, not realising that Tina had done the same. We thought it was best to open just one of them and save the other for another time. Well, that plan went out of the window. The further down the first bottle we got, the more sense it made to open the second. We got really, really drunk and ended up feeling quite ill. When my mum came in later that night, we tried to pass it off as '*dodgy food served at the graduation*'. Then we realised that my mum had gone to the fridge to get a glass of her favourite wine and we panicked. We knew that she wasn't going to find it because I had hidden the empty bottle under my bed!"

There was raucous laughter now, and Sarah sneaked a peek at her mum, who had the same glint in her eye as she had when Sarah had been naughty as a child, but she was laughing too. Everybody settled down and Sarah continued:

"I had some awesome times with her, and I am sure lots of you sitting here today would say the same. I just want to end by saying that she changed a lot of lives just by bringing pure joy to people, and she saved countless lives by being the greatest nurse possible, and I am so proud of her. I love you, Teeny."

Sarah's eulogy brought the funeral to a close, and she stood by Tina's coffin allowing everybody else to leave the church before her. She thanked Father Green for the lovely service and made her way back to the car that would take her to the site where Tina was to be laid to rest.

Chapter Three

After the horrendous time that Sarah had endured with losing her best friend in such a cruel and very sudden way, she realised that Tina had been right all along when she had told her that life really was too short. Funnily enough, Sarah had never thought like this, even though she was a nurse. Tina had told Sarah to never miss out on anything that she really wanted to do, be happy and to go with her heart. So with Tina's words in mind, she grabbed her laptop and searched for what she was looking for.

She had found out that her favourite singer was coming over to England as part of his concert tour. He would be performing in London. She had always wanted to see Nick Taylor live in person and she had always wanted to visit London, so she bought a ticket for the concert and a week-long stay in a small but cosy hotel near to the venue. She couldn't believe her luck!

A month later she packed her suitcase, and after having kissed and hugged her mother and sister, she was finally on her way to London. She was really looking forward to having some time to herself. She rarely had time off from work because she loved to be there, and more often than not, she put in extra shifts. But just lately, the endless conversations she had with staff and her colleagues about Tina and how close they were had started to affect her because she missed her immensely. She thought a short break away would be great for her and take her mind off the terrible situation for a while.

She was enjoying the train journey from Middlesbrough to London, and she had paid extra for a first-class ticket, so she felt like her holiday had started before she had even arrived at her destination. The first-class compartment was huge. Just the space in front of her seat made Sarah smile ridiculously. It had an ample amount of leg room; it was so spacious, in fact, that she could stretch her legs out all the way and still have more room. She was seated next to the window, and she stared out of it for a lot of the time that she was on the train. The views were fantastic, lots of countryside, cows and sheep with their calves and lambs and all different kinds of beautiful trees. The leaves on the trees were swaying softly in the light breeze. Sarah followed the movement with her eyes, feeling her anxiety ebb with each second that passed. She even saw a lake with swans and ducks swimming in it and a child playing with his remote control boat. She guessed it was the father of the boy who was standing behind him desperately trying to steer the boat away from the family of gliding swans. The boy's mother had her face in her hands, too nervous to watch what was happening. Sarah turned away from the window just as the father had succeeded in wrestling the controller from his son's hands and guided the boat back towards the edge of the lake.

There was a young family sitting across from her on the other side of the train, and she found herself watching them, hoping that one day she would have her own family. The two boys, who she guessed were around six and eight years old, seemed to be having a wonderful time with their parents, playing games and colouring in lots of pictures that the train staff had handed out. The family had just started a game of who can make the best animal noises, which made Sarah laugh out loud when the waitress appeared with refreshments on a trolley. She bought herself a cheese and onion sandwich, a packet of smoky bacon crisps and a bottle of fresh orange juice. She was ravenous so she opened them without hesitation. The two boys looked over at Sarah's tray to see what she was eating, and they smiled at her as they tucked into their own lunch.

Just over four hours after she departed the train station in Middlesbrough, she was checking into the Hanvia Rose Hotel in London. Sarah was so excited to start exploring that she just dumped her suitcase in her room without opening it, then hurried back down the stairs to start sightseeing. The weather was glorious on that Friday afternoon, and she was having a fabulous time treating herself to the scrumptious food and drinks that the cafes had to offer. As she was walking around humming to herself, she came across a cosy shop which sold souvenirs. She went inside and greeted the cheerful man behind the counter with a hearty "Good afternoon!" She walked around his shop looking at all of the items on the shelves and felt spoilt for choice because of the sheer amount of objects he had for sale. He had fridge magnets, ornaments, mugs, snow globes, teddy bears, different items of clothing that said 'I Love London', and so much more. She had been wandering around the shop for nearly twenty minutes before she decided to buy a fridge magnet for Suzanna and a cuddly pink teddy bear for Katy. Sarah thought it would fit in well with the rest of Katy's teddy bear collection.

When she arrived back at her hotel with her purchases later on that day she opened her suitcase. She had placed a framed photograph of Tina and herself at their graduation ceremony on top of everything else in there. She pulled it out, kissed her friend in the photograph and put it on the bedside cabinet so it would be the last thing she saw before she went to sleep and the first thing she saw when she woke up. She had done this at home ever since that horrific night when Sarah felt as though her world had ended. She listened to Nick Taylor's music on her mobile phone as she unpacked the rest of her suitcase. When she had finished, she had a long soak in the bath then ordered room service. It was something she had never done before so the idea of it was really exciting. She pored over the menu for half an hour before she finally settled on two juicy and tender chicken breasts smothered in a creamy herb sauce with potatoes and vegetables for her main meal and a sumptuous sticky toffee pudding for dessert. The smell that hit her when she lifted the metal dome that covered her plate was divine, and it was cooked to perfection. It was one of the tastiest meals she had ever eaten and she devoured the lot. Shortly after her meal, Sarah fell into bed and into the most peaceful sleep she'd had in months.

Sarah woke the next morning feeling completely rejuvenated and refreshed. She showered, dressed, put on her make-up and gave herself a little smile and a wink in the mirror. She strolled down to the hotel restaurant, the smells getting more and more amazing the closer she got. She joined the back of the breakfast queue and grabbed a plate. As the queue moved further up she spotted the delicious food on offer. There were fat juicy sausages, endless rashers of bacon and a selection of different types of egg for people to choose from. There was a gigantic bowl of beans that looked like it was never-ending, golden hash browns which were her favourite, stacks of bread, brown and white, cooked tomatoes and button mushrooms. She licked her lips and piled her plate full, which was so unlike her as she normally opted for porridge or fresh fruit with yoghurt for breakfast. She poured herself a cup of coffee on the way to her table and helped herself to two portions of butter for her toast.

After breakfast, she walked back up to her room and thought

about her day ahead. She decided she would go for another walk around London and maybe have a ride on the London Eye before coming back to get herself ready for Nick's concert. She remembered that there was a little bakery that she liked the look of that she had seen the previous day. It had the most spectacular cakes in the window. She headed out with her phone and a little bit of spending money and made straight for the London Eye. She was astounded by how far she could see when she was sitting at the very top, and she snapped away with the camera on her phone so she could show her mother and Katy when she arrived home. Next, she found the bakery with the yummy cakes inside and bought herself the biggest and gooiest chocolate muffin she had ever seen and a tangy lemon tart with a mountain of soft marshmallowy meringue on top.

She set the sat nav on her phone to Buckingham Palace and ate her chocolate muffin on the way. She had only just finished it when she arrived nearly half an hour later. She stood by the gates of the Palace and snapped a selfie with it behind her giving her camera a cheesy grin and a thumbs up. She strolled back to the Hanvia Rose shortly after so she could finally start getting ready for Nick Taylor's concert.

She showered again, then applied her make-up, and after choosing what to wear, she styled her hair into elegant waves and clipped it up at the sides with two shiny silver hair grips. She had chosen her pink glittery top, which had thin straps over the shoulders and a sweetheart neckline. She matched her top with light blue jeans with a sparkly belt, and comfortable silver shoes. She made sure she packed flat ones because she knew she would be dancing at the concert. Sarah checked herself in the mirror and was happy with what she saw. She looked like she was glowing from the inside out. She picked up her bag and phone and made the short walk to the stadium where the concert was being held.

She arrived really early and was glad she had because she managed to get a place standing right in front of the stage, directly in line with Nick's microphone stand. She couldn't believe she was here.

As the lights in the stadium went down at seven p.m. on the dot and the stage lit up with hundreds of lights, Sarah could not contain her excitement any longer. She threw her arms in the air, and the scream that she had been desperate to let out all day suddenly escaped her. She could not hear anything apart from all of the other tumultuous screams that had come from the fans around her. Nick Taylor appeared on the stage looking as gorgeous as ever. He had short brown hair that he had styled perfectly. He was wearing a fitted dark blue shirt underneath a leather jacket, and an impressive belt was threaded through the loops on his matching leather trousers. His piercing blue eyes looked out at the crowd, and his mouth turned up at the corners into a handsome grin. The sex appeal oozed out of every pore of his body.

The band started to play and Nick immediately began to dance across the stage, moving his body to the beat of the drums. He was in his element. Sarah was enjoying every single second of dancing and singing along with him, and she didn't even mind that her feet had never ached so much in her life. Halfway through the concert, Nick was performing what Sarah privately referred to as his 'sexy song' when he made her stop dancing and stand completely still with her eyes popping out of her head. He was snaking his hips from side to side in a salsa move, and he was running his hands up and down his microphone stand. Before this night, Sarah would have found it laughable if anybody had ever told her she would one day be jealous of a microphone stand.

But here and now, watching Nick caress it like that, she felt insanely jealous, so much so she wanted to snap it in two! She shrugged off the ridiculous thought and glued her eyes to him once more. He was mesmerising to watch.

For nearly two hours, Nick danced and sang his heart out perfectly, giving his all to his audience. When the concert started coming to a close, Sarah was glad that most of the songs she loved had been performed. She would never forget tonight for as long as she lived; it had been an amazing show. Through all of the excitement and exhilaration that she felt, a small portion of disappointment niggled away at her. He had not performed 'All My Love'. She had been hoping that her favourite would have made an appearance, but with a look around, she realised how lucky she was to even be here. Then, the lights at the top of the stage flashed in time to the opening chords of 'All My Love'. Sarah resumed her energetic dancing, and in her elation, she hugged the person next to her. When Nick started to sing the chorus, a tall security guard with a friendly face walked over to the barrier that Sarah was standing behind.

"Hi," he said, leaning over the barrier. "Would you like to go up onstage to meet Nick?" He pointed towards the stage.

Sarah, in shock, stood there for a second, looking like a fish with her mouth gaped open and her eyes wide, but then, without saying a word, proceeded to climb over the barrier holding onto the security guard for support. She ran to the stage, almost falling over in her haste to get there. Before she climbed the steps to the stage, she patted her hair to get rid of the windswept look and smoothed down her glittery pink top. At the top of the steps, she started to feel very nervous. Nick spotted her, and the audience went wild, their cheers were deafening. He sauntered towards her in time with the music and gently tugged on her hand until they were in the centre of the stage. Still holding onto her hand, he sang the words that were so familiar to her. She felt like she was dreaming, and she would be woken up at any second because things like this did not happen to her. In the middle of the song, the crowd cheered again when Nick twirled Sarah around. She burst into overwhelmed tears after he did this as he was facing the audience. He turned back to her and noticed that she was crying. He jumped back to her in a flash, wiping away her tears, still crooning away to her. At the end of the song, Nick wrapped his arms around Sarah and spoke softly in her ear.

"Please, would you come backstage with me?" Sarah nearly melted at the sound of his voice and his breath on her neck. She nodded and allowed him to lead her off the stage. Nick looked over his shoulder and waved at the audience to more thunderous cheers. She was too shocked to speak at first but soon snapped out of it when Nick held out his hand for her to shake.

"Hi, what's your name," he asked her.

"Er, I'm Sarah," she replied nervously, shaking his hand.

"Have you enjoyed the show so far?"

"Yes, I have, it's fantastic. Thank you for inviting me onto the stage."

"Oh, that's no problem. It's great to meet you, and thank you for coming. I appreciate my fans more than anything. I love seeing all of you singing and dancing along with me. It makes my job so much easier because if I get tired of singing, I just hold my microphone out towards the audience, and you carry on. I'm kidding!" He caught her with his winning smile, and she felt her cheeks flush. "I have two more songs left to sing, but would you like to come back here again after the show so we can talk a bit more?"

Sarah could not believe what she was hearing but gladly

accepted. She thanked Nick and returned to her place in front of the stage, where she and the rest of the audience were enchanted by him once again. When the concert finished, Nick wished a goodnight to the crowd and disappeared through the curtain which led backstage. Sarah stayed where she was, wondering if she had to wait for Nick behind the barrier or try to hop over it and hope she wouldn't make a complete fool of herself by falling, when the security guard with the friendly face came over to her again. He removed the barrier in front of her. She had been able to control herself this time, so she walked in step with the security guard instead of darting to the stage. Her stomach was doing somersaults, and she hoped that Nick would not be able to see her heart beating through her pink top. The security guard cleared his throat and announced her arrival.

"Hi, Sarah!" Nick greeted her politely and embraced her.

"Hi, Nick. That was the best show I have ever seen."

He looked at her while sipping his water. She felt braver than she did the first time she had come backstage.

"Would you mind if we had a picture taken together, please?" she asked him, hoping he would say yes.

"No, I don't mind at all. I would be more than happy to have a picture with you."

Nick watched her take her phone out of her bag and hand it to Tim, the friendly security guard. She had not expected him to do what he did next. He handed his own phone to his manager and asked him to take one on his phone too. Nick put his arm around Sarah, and they both smiled for the cameras. When they faced each other again, Nick noticed that she had bought a tour programme.

"Would you like me to sign that for you?" he asked, pointing to the programme.

Sarah frantically started to search in her bag for her pen and then suddenly remembered that Katy had asked her if she could borrow it. Her darling sister had not returned it. Sarah made a promise to herself that she would go back to the souvenir shop tomorrow and buy Katy a pack of her very own pens. She looked up at Nick to tell him that she didn't have a pen with her and saw that he was leaning casually against a table, which had about a hundred bottles of water on it, holding up several pens in different colours. He chuckled as she handed him her programme.

"Well, at least you have come prepared," she laughed, feeling more comfortable now.

"Don't worry about it." He winked at her, and she felt a jelly-like feeling in her legs. "Do you live around here?" He asked when he passed her programme back to her.

"No, I don't; I live in Middlesbrough. I'm here until next Saturday. I came down here for your show and to have some time away from work and the stresses of everyday life, you know." She suddenly felt a bit hot, and she hoped that she hadn't said all of that too quickly.

"Yeah, sure, I'm here until Saturday too. There are a couple of events that I have been asked to attend while I am here in London." A gleeful but nervous look appeared on his face. "Would you er, maybe like to meet up with me this week while we are both staying here. I mean, it's fine if not, if you have plans, I wouldn't expect you to change them just because I asked if you would like to meet up with me again and…" He stopped talking when Sarah put her hand on his arm.

"Yes. I would." He exhaled and looked at Sarah with a relieved look on his face. "I'll give you my number so you can reach me," Sarah said.

Nick's manager, who was still holding his phone, handed it to Sarah so she could input her number into it. She saved it and handed the phone to Nick. She retrieved her own phone from Tim and thanked Nick again for inviting her onto the stage, for the photos and for signing her programme. He hugged her and told her that he would call her in a few days. With a spring in her step and a huge grin on her face, she left the stadium and skipped back to her hotel.

Sarah arrived back inside her hotel room a surprisingly short time later and flicked on the kettle. She felt she needed a strong cup of tea to calm her nerves after the unexpected twist the night had taken. She sat down at the desk while she waited for it to boil and opened the photo gallery on her phone. And there he was again. Nick Taylor looking beautiful, standing next to her with a megawatt smile on his face. After staring at the photo for several minutes, she swiped through her gallery expecting to see the photographs she had taken earlier that day when she saw another photo of herself and Nick and then another one after that! The security guard had snapped away with her camera twice more, once when Nick was signing her programme and then again when they had looked at each other when she had put her hand on his arm, without them even noticing. Sarah was still staring at the photos when a new message popped up on her phone. It was from 'unknown number'. The message read:

Thank you for coming tonight. NT xx

She froze when she saw who had sent it. Nick Taylor had messaged her. She forgot all about her cup of tea and fell onto her bed fully clothed. She laughed at the madness of it all. She lay down thinking about the night's events and then eventually dozed off, still holding tightly onto her phone.

Chapter Four

Nick smiled to himself after he had sent the message to Sarah. He felt bad that he had to hide his phone number from her, but his manager, Greg, had insisted that he had the block in place.

You don't know this girl Nick, how do you know that you can trust her? Greg had said to him.

Nick couldn't explain it, but there was just something about her. He didn't know what it was, but it had felt so right when she was on stage with him. He had insisted to Tim that she was the one he was to allow onto the stage. He wanted to be able to speak to Sarah properly, just the two of them with nobody else around, so he immediately started to make plans with Elizabeth, his hotel's manager, to see if she could arrange a private dinner for two. He looked at the photographs of himself and Sarah that Greg had taken for around the tenth time that evening and planned to call her in the morning.

Sarah awoke on Sunday morning, not realising she had even fallen to sleep. She checked her phone, the time told her it was eight fifteen, and she quickly checked her messages and her photo gallery to make sure she had not been dreaming. She hadn't, and her excitement flooded her once more when she re-read Nick's text and stared at his photos some more. She jumped into the shower that morning, singing a cheerful tune very loudly. When she got out, she hoped that she had not woken the people in the room next door. She was just making herself a cup of coffee and getting dressed when her phone started to ring. She picked it up thinking that it would be Katy asking about the concert, but it wasn't. When she looked at it she saw that it read 'unknown number'. She squealed, knowing who it would be on the other end of the phone. Sarah calmed herself and cleared her throat before she answered it.

"Hello," she said, hoping she sounded casual instead of a giddy schoolgirl.

"Good morning, Sarah. It's Nick Taylor."

Sarah started to fan herself with her hand. The same warm feeling that had engulfed her the previous night, when Nick had breathed softly on her neck, had returned in full force just from the sound of him uttering those six words.

"Nick, hi. I thought you would be having a lie-in after all that dancing you did last night". *Why have I just said that?* she thought, embarrassed and annoyed at herself. *Why couldn't I have just said hi how are you?*

He laughed. "No, I think my body is used to all of the dancing I do by now, and I can't sleep in, I'm an early bird. Er, I'm calling to ask you if you are free tomorrow night for dinner and a drink?"

Sarah hadn't realised that she was holding her breath and exhaled before she answered him. "Yes, I am free; I would love to meet with you. Do you have an idea of where?"

"I hope you don't mind, but my manager has insisted that it be at my hotel because of me getting recognised when I go out. Would that be okay?"

"Yes, that sounds great, and I understand that you are limited to where you can go."

"Okay, thank you. I'll ask my security guard to come and collect you at seven thirty p.m.?"

"Seven thirty will be fine; I'm at the Hanvia Rose hotel." She was trying her hardest not to squeal down the phone.

"Okay, I'll let him know where you are, and I'll see you tomorrow, Sarah."

"Bye, Nick."

She froze and just stared at her phone in disbelief. Seven thirty tomorrow night could not come quickly enough.

Finally, it did. Sarah was so excited to be meeting Nick again. She flew down the stairs and into the hotel lobby dressed in a burgundy lace knee-length dress with a V-shaped neckline and long sleeves. It was one of her favourite dresses, and she was extremely happy that she had packed it in her suitcase.

Upon entering the lobby, she recognised the security guard at once. He walked over to her and shook her hand.

"Hi Sarah, I'm Tim. It's nice to see you again."

"Hi Tim, it's lovely to see you too. Thank you for collecting me." Sarah was glad that he had told her what his name was so she could stop thinking of him as 'the friendly security guard'.

Tim led her out of the doors and towards a midnight blue Range Rover with tinted windows. He held the back door on the passenger side open for her, and she hopped in. The leather interior gave it a 'new car' sort of smell. It was very spacious inside, and she felt like she had sat on a pile of cushions as she made herself comfortable on the seat. She buckled up and off they went. She wished the butterflies in her stomach would stop flapping, but she had a feeling they were only going to get worse as soon as she saw Nick.

They arrived at his hotel around fifteen minutes later, and Sarah couldn't believe her eyes. She had to lift her chin as far as it would go to see the top of the hotel! It was twenty storeys high, and the name, The Grand Star, was lit up in lights in the middle of the building. All of the windows and the door to the entrance had gold frames around them. The bushes that sat neatly underneath the ground floor windows were lit up from inside them and had delicate pink and red flowers dotted throughout them. Sarah was gobsmacked when she walked inside with Tim, the hotel lobby was enormous; she couldn't appreciate quite how big it actually was from outside the building. The white marble flooring was spotless, and six crystal chandeliers glittered in the light. She stared at them for a while, enchanted by their beauty. Behind the reception desk sat a pretty lady, very smartly dressed in the hotel uniform. Her badge told Sarah her name was Eve. Instead of a wall behind Eve, there was a gigantic fish tank that had the most colourful and graceful tropical fish inside. Sarah had always wanted a tropical fish tank but certainly not one as big as this because it would take up most of her living room! There were two sweeping staircases on each side of the reception desk that curved round and upwards to the floors above. Each step was made of the same marble as the floor in the lobby, with soft lighting trickling from underneath each one.

Sarah sat down on one of the stone-grey sofas that fitted in so well with the surrounding decor as she waited for Tim, who was speaking with the receptionist. When he came back to her, he gestured towards the double doors to her left and held one of them open for her. She got up from her seat and walked into a vast dining room.

It was just as grand as the lobby but it was twice the size. It was filled with around fifty tables covered with pristine white tablecloths. The tables were set so neatly but Sarah wondered why one person needed so many forks. Each place setting had its own brown leather-bound menu laid out in between the many items of cutlery. The centrepieces on each of the tables consisted of fresh flowers in tall, thin glass vases. Sarah had never seen such a pretty-looking dining room before. She looked around wanting to take it all in, when it occurred to her that the dining room was empty. She scanned the room in search of Tim. He was talking to a man behind the bar who was dressed in the same smart uniform as Eve, the receptionist. He pointed Tim in the direction of a curtained-off area at the back of the room.

"Come on, Sarah," said Tim. "Your date is awaiting your presence."

Together, they walked past the bar that ran along the wall and into the private curtained area. The butterflies had flown straight up from her stomach and seemed to be fluttering somewhere near her heart when she clapped eyes on Nick. His face lit up with joy as soon as he saw Sarah, and he stood to greet her. He was wearing a crisp white shirt and black trousers, and he looked incredible. His hair was styled just as perfectly as it was at his concert, and when he leaned over to peck her on her cheek, Sarah could smell his cologne. It was heavenly.

Tim smiled at them both then made himself scarce. Nick held Sarah's chair out for her and pushed it smoothly up to the table when she had sat down. He returned to his own seat opposite her and found himself gazing into Sarah's eyes. She blushed, lost her nerve and looked away from him. He chuckled and handed her a menu.

"You look beautiful," he stared at her a moment longer. "Would you like some wine?"

"Thank you, and yes, wine sounds good." She sounded nervous. "It's lovely here. Do you always stay in this hotel when you come to London?"

"Yes, I do. I love it here, it's got everything I need and the service the hotel provides is flawless. I always try to get the same room if I can."

Sarah smiled, looked down at her menu and almost fell out of her chair. These prices were astonishing. Her eyes glanced over to the main meals and she had to do a double-take. The surprise on her face must have shown.

"Sarah, please order anything you want. It's okay, really." Nick showed her his gorgeous smile again.

"Okay, thank you." She looked down at the food this time instead of the prices and chose the smoked salmon salad. Nick put his hand in the air, and almost immediately a waiter appeared at their table. He pulled out a fancy-looking device and tapped away on it as Nick reeled off their order, then disappeared off into the kitchen. Sarah and Nick chatted comfortably as if they had known each other forever while they waited for their food to arrive.

"Tell me something about you," Nick said to Sarah as he sipped his wine.

"Okay. I am a nurse in the accident and emergency department in my local hospital. I am twenty-eight years old and I live with my mum Suzanna and my younger sister Katy. I just couldn't bring myself to move out." They both laughed and she continued. "I went to college and university where I met my best friend Tina, and it was really great and quite astonishing really that we both managed to get a job in the same department of the same hospital."

She paused. She didn't want to say anything else to Nick about Tina. It was too soon. She brushed over her pause and instead decided to tell him about Katy.

"Katy is twenty-one years old, and she is the best little sister ever. She's so clever and she really knows what she wants to do with her life. She's in university at the moment studying to be a vet; she says it's tough but she's enjoying it." She smiled as Katy's face appeared in her mind. "I am so proud of her. Tell me something about you."

Sarah thought she knew a lot about him already because she had seen nearly every interview he had given on all sorts of different television and chat shows and had watched countless videos of him performing, but she was sure there was a lot more to him than just interviews and performances.

"Sure. My full name is Nicholas Andrew Taylor. I am thirty years old and the youngest of four siblings. I have older twin brothers called Chad and Cole, and they used to tease me constantly about wanting to become a singer. They told me that I would never succeed in being a singer/songwriter. Now, naturally, I remind them of that all the time." He winked. "My sister is called Rachel, she is the eldest one which according to her makes her the boss, and she sings too. She isn't very well known, though, because she is more comfortable doing small gigs for private parties, weddings and things like that, and that's exactly how she likes it. I love writing songs in my garden because it's so peaceful and calm. In fact, most of my songs were written in my garden. What do you do in your spare time?"

"Um, I don't really get a lot of spare time due to working at the hospital, but when I do, I go to dance classes at a school not far from where I live. I find it helps me to blow off steam and get rid of the stresses that come with being a nurse. I'm sure you get even less spare time than me, but is there anything apart from writing songs that helps you to unwind?"

"Yeah, I like cooking, but I will admit, I'm not very good at it, though. I spend more time wafting my towel under my smoke detectors than doing any actual cooking. I usually get rescued by my housekeeper, she carries on with the cooking while I carry on wafting." He made a wafting movement with his arms which made Sarah giggle.

They were chatting about their childhoods when their food arrived at the table. Sarah had not realised how hungry she was until their meals had been placed on the table in front of them. Nick thanked the waiter, who bowed his head and hurried off back into the kitchen behind the bar, then he raised his wine glass. Sarah did the same and waited for him to speak.

"To us and hopefully some great times ahead," he said. They clinked their glasses together and had small sips of their wine. "Now, let's tuck in," he added with a laugh.

Sarah's salad was delicious, and judging by how fast Nick's cheese bruschetta had disappeared from his plate, his starter was too. They moved on to the main meals, which were chicken pie, vegetables and potatoes for Sarah and the biggest piece of steak that she had ever seen for Nick.

"Where are you going to put all that?" she asked him, shocked. He smiled in response and started to eat.

Sarah found it so easy to be in Nick's company, the conversation flowed freely, and he captivated her with every word he uttered. Before she had left her hotel that evening, she feared there would be awkward silences and wondered what they would possibly find to talk about given that their lifestyles were so different, but being around him was like being with family. He gave off an incredibly calming vibe that made Sarah feel so at ease. They skipped dessert, opting to talk to each other over drinks instead. Sarah preferred this because if she had dessert, she would need to keep looking away from Nick.

Later on that night, Sarah glanced down at her watch. It was nearly one o'clock in the morning. She gasped and told Nick the time just as Tim came trotting up to their table.

“Sorry to disturb you, Nick, but I have had a call from Greg, and he has asked me to remind you about your early outing tomorrow.” Nick rolled his eyes. Sarah melted.

“That’s okay, Tim, not to worry. Please could you wait for us by the bar and we will come over to you shortly?”

“Of course.” Tim smiled at the two of them and scooted off back to the bar.

Nick stood and walked round to Sarah’s side of the table. He held out his hand to Sarah, which she gladly accepted. They stood face to face, not taking their eyes off each other. Sarah placed her hand on Nick’s chest, she could feel his heart beating. *Is he going to kiss me?* she wondered. Just then, Nick jumped and pulled his phone out of his pocket. He turned the screen to her and rolled his eyes again. Greg’s name was flashing up on the screen. Nick huffed and answered his phone.

“Hi, Greg… Yes, I know what time it is… I am fully aware of my visit to the performing arts school tomorrow, thank you… Yes, Tim has been over already… Bye, Greg.” Nick pulled the phone away from his ear with Greg still yapping and ended the call.

“Anybody would think he was my babysitter,” he said, huffing. He threw his phone onto the table and embraced Sarah warmly. *Nice one Greg*, she thought sarcastically, *totally ruined the moment!*

“So, as you know from Greg, I am busy tomorrow but please, could I see you again before I leave?” he asked.

“Yes, I would like that very much,” she said.

He kissed her on her cheek and squeezed her hand.

“I’ll call you. Bye, Sarah.”

“Bye, Nick.”

Tim appeared as if by magic. He and Sarah walked back

through the dining room and into the lobby. Sarah turned and glanced back at Nick before the doors closed.

Nick wished he could have driven Sarah back to her hotel himself, but he didn't want to risk any paparazzi seeing him with her. He didn't want her to get the same hounding that he had to endure nearly every time he ventured out anywhere. He sat back down at the table and picked his phone up. He opened up the photo gallery and gazed at the three photos that had very quickly become his favourites. He messaged Sarah.

Goodnight and sweet dreams. I'll speak to you soon xxx

Chapter Five

Nick called Sarah late the following night at eleven p.m. He had only just arrived back at his hotel after spending the whole day at a school for students who were studying performing arts and music. He'd had a special meet and greet with the students where he told them all about how his first taste of being onstage came through dancing in competitions before he started singing. He gave the students a tremendous amount of inspiration by telling them about all he had achieved and about the awards he had won. He kept them captivated when he described the places he had seen on tour. The meet and greet had run way over the time that Greg had specified to the school, but Nick knew it had been amazing and so worthwhile for those students who would give anything to be where he was.

"Hello you, it's Nick," he said.

"Hi, how are you? Have you had a good day?"

"Yeah, it was fun. The talent that those kids have is mind-blowing. There are going to be a lot of stars coming from that school, believe me." He yawned loudly. Sarah giggled.

"Wow, you sound like you need your bed!"

"I definitely do, but I wanted to call you to hear your voice and to invite you to a party on Friday night if you would like to come? It's at a private venue away from the cameras and prying eyes. My friend Pete has organised it for his wife's birthday, and he's performing for her too. He's a really good guy who I met in a recording studio a few years back. We started chatting about our love of music and we have been firm friends ever since. It will be a really fun night."

"That sounds brilliant, yeah. What time is the party?"

Nick punched the air silently in delight. He composed himself before continuing with the conversation.

"It starts at six thirty p.m. so Tim will come to your hotel at six p.m. I'll wait for you at the bar so we can go in together." Sarah could tell that Nick was smiling down the phone.

"Okay, great! I'll see you soon and goodnight."

"Goodnight, beautiful."

Sarah had been panicking since their phone call on Tuesday night because the only dress she had packed in her suitcase was her burgundy lace one that she had worn for her date with Nick. He had messaged her to say that it was formal wear to the party, so she wanted something long and elegant. She spent the next two days and nearly all of Friday searching in numerous shops for the perfect dress. She hadn't found anything she liked so far so she started to get worried. There were only four hours left until she would be meeting Nick at the party. Then, in the last dress shop she went to, she finally found the one. It was a long, navy blue dress with short sleeves that covered her shoulders and a belt around her waist embellished with lace and sequins. She tried it on and it fit her like a glove, as if it had been made specially for her. She found a pair of navy blue stilettos with a bow detail on the front to match. She paid for her outfit and rushed back to her hotel.

She couldn't wait for the party tonight and she had no idea what to expect. Nick had told her there were going to be a few famous faces there, but she knew the only one she would be interested in was his. She had just finished putting her earrings in when the receptionist of her hotel called her at six p.m. to inform her that Tim was waiting in reception. They chatted all the way from the Hanvia Rose up until the point where Sarah laid eyes on Nick.

"Oh my goodness!" Sarah exclaimed when she saw him standing at the bar. He looked dapper in his suit and tie, absolutely gorgeous. He was laughing along with Greg and had not noticed her walk through the doors. She sidled up to him and gently touched his back.

"Wow!" he cried when he turned and saw her. "Sarah, you look amazing!"

"Thank you. You don't look so bad yourself." She looked so confident on the outside but on the inside, she was a jangling bag of nerves. Nick softly stroked her back and showed her to their table in the hall where all of the guests were gathering.

The hall was impressive. The ceilings were sky high and the chandeliers were sparkling. There were lots of round tables decorated in silver tablecloths with royal blue runners and matching seat covers. Sarah sat down and noticed her place card, which read 'Guest of Nick Taylor'. She chuckled and looked up at the stage where a band was setting up ready for Pete's performance. The waiters were lined up on each side of the room, patiently waiting for everybody to find their names on the table plan before they sprang into action, offering wine and water to each guest. Gentle music was playing in the background giving the room a friendly atmosphere. When the last few guests had been served their drinks, the doors to the hall closed and Pete appeared on stage with his wife who looked very nervous.

"Friends!" Pete shouted down his microphone. "Thank you for coming tonight. I have organised this party in honour of my very beautiful wife Gail's fortieth birthday party!"

The crowd gave whoops and cheers. Pete laughed and pulled Gail closer to him.

"We are going to start with a delicious meal; you will all find your menus full of mouth-watering dishes underneath your napkins," he said, winking. "So these very fine-looking waiters will now make their way round to each table and take your orders. Enjoy everybody!"

The guests applauded Pete and reached for their menus. Sarah was pleasantly surprised when she opened hers. She had expected to see dishes that she had never heard of before or food with names that she didn't even know how to pronounce. Instead, she saw burgers, onion rings, garlic bread, pizza and her personal favourite, spaghetti Bolognese. She ordered her favourite with a stack of garlic bread and washed it down with a glass of sparkling fruity wine.

"Are you enjoying yourself?" Nick asked when he had finished his last mouthful of a meat feast pizza.

"Yes, I am. I was taken aback by the menu."

"Really? What were you expecting?" He had a cheeky look in his eyes as if he knew what she was going to say.

"Well, this place is rather fancy so I thought I wasn't going to be able to pronounce any of the names of the food and that I would be having to ask you what everything was," she laughed.

The waiters appeared once again, refilling glasses, collecting plates and taking orders for dessert. Sarah couldn't wait to try her warm gooey chocolate fudge cake with lots of whipped cream. Nick had chosen the same. After this, Sarah only just managed to squeeze in her after-dinner mint.

After the meal, the guests stayed seated at their tables for a while, drinking and talking. Sarah suspected that many of them were struggling to move thanks to the gargantuan feast they had all enjoyed. Nick stood eventually and made the guests on their table very happy when he graciously offered to buy them all a drink. Greg accompanied him to the bar. Sarah's eyes followed Nick across the room, and she found herself gazing at him. She couldn't take her eyes off him. Nick and Greg turned and caught her staring, so she quickly pretended she was searching for something in her bag, wishing that she could have climbed in!

"That girl has the hots for you, Nicholas!" Greg teased.

"The feeling is definitely mutual, Gregory," Nick replied.

Pete graced the stage again. He placed his microphone in the stand in front of him and picked up his guitar. The lights in the room faded and twinkling lights on the ceiling looked like stars in the night sky. Everybody stood and cheered for Pete and his band. It was a spectacular scene. Gail walked onto the dance floor where the guests had gathered. You could tell from the adoring looks on the guests' faces that Pete was highly respected by every single one of them in the room.

"The song I am about to sing is Gail's favourite song of all time. It is obviously one of mine." He straightened his tie and winked at his wife. "Although, as much as I hate to do this, I have to give *some* credit to Nick Taylor. He just helped with a tiny bit of it." He gestured towards Nick and laughed. Nick shook his head but chuckled along with him.

"Cheeky thing he is," Nick murmured to Sarah. "I wrote the lyrics! I'll get him back but not tonight. Look how great he and Gail are together."

Sarah saw how lovingly Pete and Gail looked at each other as Pete strummed his guitar along with the rhythm. He sang to her as if they were the only people in the room. The song was slow, and the couples on the dancefloor were looking extremely close. Nick held his hand out to Sarah and asked if she would like to dance. Sarah agreed and took his hand. He twirled her around effortlessly and placed his left hand on the small of her back and took her right hand in his. They spun around and stepped in time to the slow rhythm of the music. Sarah was surprised at how in sync they were with each other. She was so grateful to her dance teacher at this moment for teaching her moves like this. Nick drew her in closer to him, and the look in his eyes changed. It was so intense but she couldn't break the contact, she didn't want to. He leaned close to her ear and whispered.

"Come with me."

He led her off the dance floor at high speed, heading for the double doors that led to a seating area. Still standing, Nick pulled Sarah close to him once more.

"I really like you, Sarah," he told her.

He moved his face down towards hers as she tilted her head up and closed her eyes. He placed his hands on each side of her face and brushed his lips against hers so gently. She put her hands on his waist and kissed him back. He lingered on her lips for a few seconds then pulled away.

"I have been wanting to do that since I met you." Nick laughed and Sarah felt his body relax.

"Really? I've been wanting you to do that since you met me too!" Nick looked relieved and wrapped his arms around Sarah's waist.

"Will you come back to my hotel with me later? I want to talk to you about something."

"Yes, I will."

He kissed her on her forehead and held her hand as they went to re-join the party.

Later on that night, they travelled to Nick's hotel together with Tim in the drivers' seat and Greg alongside him in the passenger seat. Nick and Sarah held each other's hands in the back of the car and chatted about the party. Some people would definitely have sore heads in the morning, Nick told her.

Tim pulled up outside the front doors of the hotel. Nick jumped out first and held his hand out for Sarah to take as she climbed out of the car. Sarah felt like she was walking on air as she entered the glorious lobby for the second time that week. They waited inside for Tim and Greg so they could get the elevator up to Nick's room together. It was located on the top floor of the hotel, so it felt like it had taken them an age to get there.

"Gosh!" Sarah exclaimed when she entered. Nick's room was huge. It was, in fact, an apartment. It was decorated in white and grey shades just like the lobby downstairs. Many of the items in the room, such as the coffee table in the living area and the chess set that sat on top of it, were made of glass. Sarah couldn't help but notice the television, which looked more like a cinema screen fixed to the wall. It faced a grey cushioned sofa large enough to easily provide seating for six people. Her eyes wandered over to the kitchen area, which housed a bar that was fully stocked with all sorts of wines, beers, spirits and gins.

Nick took Sarah's hand and led her over to the doors of the balcony. She stepped outside and was greeted by a cool breeze which was refreshing on her face. Nick appeared beside her and pointed out the landmarks of London that they could see. She would never be able to make out her hotel from up here, next to this, hers looked like a shoebox.

"Is this view the reason you always try to get this room when you stay here?" she asked him.

"One of the reasons, yeah. The other one is because this is the biggest suite in the hotel. I usually have meetings and interviews going on when I'm on tour, so I need a big room for the number of people that are usually in here with me, and it's nice to have the space to relax after my shows." He stared off into the distance. "Can I talk to you in the bedroom, please? I don't want Tim and Greg to eavesdrop; they are so nosey." He whispered the last part to her.

"Yes, of course," she whispered back.

He put his finger to his lips and sneaked back towards the balcony doors. He popped his head around the curtain, and sure enough, he found Tim and Greg standing on the other side of the doors with their ears pressed up against them. He walked back into the room and asked Sarah to follow him. Tim and Greg were now trying to act nonchalant by looking at everything around the room bar Nick and Sarah.

With an unsurprised look on his face, Nick pointed at Tim and Greg. "And these two are the other reasons why I like the big rooms…" he told Sarah, "... so I can escape from them! Shall we?" Taking her hand, he strolled to the bedroom. He looked back and caught Tim and Greg silently celebrating and giving each other high fives.

The bedroom was just as stunning as the living and kitchen areas. Nick flicked a light switch when he came into the room behind Sarah, and a lamp and the white fairy lights that ran all along the edge of the ceiling came to life, showering the room in a warm glow. The soft red and orange decor worked amazingly well together here, and it made the room feel so homely and cosy. Sarah liked that it wasn't the same white and grey as the rest of the apartment or the lobby. In the middle of the room sat a luxurious four-poster king-size bed with sheets of red silk attached at the top and around all four posts. Nick invited Sarah to have a seat on the small terracotta sofa at the end of the bed. He sat down next to her and draped his arm across the top of the sofa.

"I invited you back here tonight because I have something that I would like to ask you and to see what your thoughts are."

Sarah had a baffled look on her face wondering what this could possibly be. "All right, I'm listening," she smiled.

"Okay, here goes. I would really like it if we kept in touch with each other because I want to get to know you better. How would you feel about that?" His body language showed that he was very nervous.

"I would love to keep in touch with you, Nick. Shall I give you my email address?"

"I was thinking about maybe having your home address so we can write letters to each other. I know it sounds a bit old-fashioned, but I find that you can write so much more in a letter than a text message, and it is more personal than an email. I mean, I will take your email address too, of course I will; it's just that I am more of a letter type of guy." He looked at her curiously, trying to figure out how she would react to this.

"I've never thought of letter writing in that way before, but I am game for that. Yes, you can have my address."

They wrote their addresses down, email and home, and handed them to one another.

"I've lifted the block on my phone that hides my number from you, so now you will be able to see my number and you can call or text me whenever you want to. Greg makes me have it on '*for my own safety*'," he imitated Greg as he said this. "I felt bad that I wasn't allowed to give you my number backstage at my concert, but he doesn't want my number to fall into the wrong hands." He was really apologetic.

"That's understandable. It's a sensible thing to do."

There was a knock on the door.

"Speaking of Greg… Yes, Greg?" Nick shouted at the door, looking irritable.

The door opened slowly and Greg popped his head round it sheepishly. "So sorry to interrupt, Nick," he said.

"Yeah, I'm sure you are."

Greg laughed nervously. "I am sorry but we really need to start packing."

"Yes, I know, please leave us alone, Greg. We will be out in a second." Nick rolled his eyes and turned back to Sarah. He loved how understanding she was about everything. *She really is a special lady*, he thought.

"I had better get going, I haven't packed yet either, and I have an early train tomorrow," Sarah said, suddenly.

Neither of them wanted the night to end now, but they both knew that Nick was very limited on his time, plus he was constantly being watched and interrupted by nosey Greg. Nick placed a soft kiss on Sarah's lips before she left his room and hoped more than anything that it would not be too long before he saw her again.

Chapter Six

Saturday morning arrived, and Sarah was sad that she was going home but happy that she would be seeing her mum and sister soon. She had really missed them; she had never been away from home on her own before. She felt like she had been in a bubble with Nick all week and she couldn't wait to tell them all about him, though she wanted to keep the kiss private. She opened the back of the frame that had the photograph of herself and Tina in, placed Nick's phone number and address inside and closed it again. She was looking forward to writing letters to Nick even if she did think it was a teeny bit old-fashioned. The downside to this, she thought, would be waiting for his response to her letters. She packed her suitcase, made sure she had everything she needed for her train journey home to hand and checked that she had not forgotten anything. She took one last look at her room and closed the door. She had a feeling that her life may just be about to change.

As she was waiting for her taxi to come that she had arranged that morning, she felt her phone vibrate in her pocket. It was a message from Nick:

Thank you for everything this week. I had a phenomenal time with you. Have a safe journey home. Nick xxx

She replied:

Thank you too. I loved every second. Sarah xox

She napped for a while on the train on the journey home. She had been unable to sleep for most of the night thinking about Nick and what had happened between them. There were so many questions buzzing around in her head. *Are his feelings for me real? Is he really going to write to me? Should I have let him kiss me?* A feeling of guilt crept in because she didn't want to think of him in a bad way. He seemed so genuine, he had given her his address and phone number. *Surely that should say something about how he feels about you? He trusted you enough to give you his number*, she thought to herself. She didn't want to overthink the situation with Nick, so she put on her music but avoided any of his in an attempt to get out of the Nick bubble for a little bit and try to clear her head. She rested her head against her seat and closed her eyes, letting the music wash over her. She opened them again when the smell of strong coffee wafted up her nose. She looked up to find a man serving a young couple in the seats in front of her. *Just what I need*, she thought as she ordered a very generous-sized cup of coffee and an enormous chocolate cake. She settled back into her seat when the man had trundled off with his trolley and listened to her music until the train came to a stop at her station.

She put any thoughts of Nick to the back of her mind as soon as she saw Suzanna and Katy rushing up to her, smiling as if they hadn't seen her for months. Sarah couldn't wait until they got home to give them their presents, so she reached into her bag and grabbed Suzanna's fridge magnet and Katy's teddy bear. Nick was at the forefront of her mind once again when she handed over the pens she had bought for Katy while she had been out dress shopping. *The way he looked at her while he signed her programme, him leaning against the table with a sexy smile on his face, the smell of his cologne, the photos of them together, their kiss...*

"Ooooo, two presents for me? Thanks, sis!" Katy's shout brought Sarah out of her amazing daydream and back to reality. Sarah couldn't remember handing the pens over, but she must have done so because Katy was examining the 'I Love London!' image on the back of the pen box.

"Errr, you pinched my pen out of my bag, so I thought I had better buy you your own, so you don't do it again!" she told Katy.

"Whoops, I'm sorry. Surely you didn't need a pen that badly though, did you?"

"You just don't know when you will need a pen." She went on quickly, avoiding the question, not willing to share any information about the 'pen situation' at Nick's concert. "Shall we go home then? I've been dying for one of Mum's coffees all week."

Sarah had decided whilst she was on the train not to tell them anything about Nick until he gave her some definite indication that he would really want to see her again. That day came sooner rather than later when she received a handwritten letter from him.

Dear Sarah,
Thank you for agreeing to write to me. Like I said before, I know it's a little old-fashioned, especially these days when we can video call.

I just think you can put your heart into a letter when you're writing it.

I certainly wouldn't mind seeing your beautiful face on a video call, though! ;-) I know I have already told you this, but I had an amazing time with you. I have never been so lucky as to meet somebody as special as you before, and I want you to know that even though we are thousands of miles apart, I would love to see you again. I was thinking of nothing but you all the way

home. I'm so happy that you came to my show. I just knew from the moment I saw you singing and dancing along with me that I had to speak to you. I must have looked at the photos that Greg took of us backstage a thousand times by now, and I didn't know that he had taken more than one. He took three!
Love,
Nick xxx

Sarah read his letter twice, then grabbed her paper and pen and wrote her response.

Dear Nick,
Thank you for your letter, it has made my day! It's so great to hear from you. I had the best time with you. I just wish it hadn't had gone so fast. Greg and Tim must have been talking to each other when those photos were taken because I have three too, and I've been looking at them non-stop! I think Greg and Tim are both lovely guys, by the way (although not as lovely as you!). I loved our long chat on our date, finding out about each other and our families. I could have listened to you talk all night. Hopefully, we will be able to arrange to see each other soon because I would love that too. I don't expect you to come here to see me; I will be more than happy to fly out to you.
Love Sarah xoxox

She sealed the letter and left it in her bedroom next to her car keys so she wouldn't forget to take it with her and send it to Nick when she went to work later on. She skipped over to the kettle to make a cup of coffee for herself and her mother, then decided that this was the time when she would divulge what had happened with Nick in London. She placed the coffee on the table and sat down next to her mother.

"I have something to tell you," she said quietly. She felt nervous; she didn't know how Suzanna would take this. She was quite glad that Katy was not at home as she only felt brave enough to tell one person at once. Suzanna switched the TV off and turned to face Sarah.

"Okay… is something wrong?"

"Oh no, no no, something feels very right actually," she stammered. "So, when I was in London, you know I went to Nick Taylor's concert."

"Yes," Suzanna said, looking baffled. She had never seen Sarah like this before, so fidgety and on edge.

"Well, I sort of got invited onto the stage by Nick, and then he asked me to go backstage where I had a few photos taken with him, and he signed my programme." Sarah fiddled with a loose thread on one of the cushions.

"Okay, so did something happen backstage?" Suzanna asked curiously.

"Obviously nothing dodgy because his staff were there." Suzanna raised her eyebrows and reached slowly for her coffee, not taking her eyes off Sarah. "I mean, not that anything dodgy would have happened even if his staff weren't there because you know I'm not like that, don't you?" Sarah was talking fast.

"Sarah, will you slow down and tell me what's going on?"

"Okay, yeah, sure… Nick asked me if I would like to meet up with him again while we were both still in London, and I said yes, so I gave him my number. He asked me out on a date which had to be at his hotel because obviously he is mega-famous, so he can't really go out anywhere without getting mobbed. Anyway, we had a really nice chat that night and the day after he invited me to a party which we went to the night before I came home. It was mint! I went back to his hotel room after the party with him and two other guys where he asked me if we could write to each other, so I said yes and I have just received a letter from him and he has asked me if we can see each other again!" Sarah was breathless. She had not slowed down; she had sped up!

Suzanna's face seemed to be frozen. "I have a few questions, Sarah."

"Okay, shoot."

"First of all, what did you mean exactly when you said you went back to Nick's hotel room with him and 'two other guys'?"

"Oh, his manager and his security guard. I've just got what that sounded like, but it was nothing like what you are probably thinking. I meant we just travelled there together." Sarah smiled at her mother.

"Okay, next one. Has anything other than letter writing happened between you two?"

"No, of course not." She looked away so her mother wouldn't see her blushing. She looked back, and Suzanna was staring at her with a typical mum look on her face which said, '*I'm not stupid*'. "Okay yeah, just a little peck at the party, a lingering peck, I would say."

"I didn't need a description but thank you." Suzanna was laughing now, and Sarah relaxed. "Honestly, darling, if you are happy with him then I think that's great. He's obviously made an impression on you; I've never seen you act like this before, but why didn't you say anything when you came back?"

"I wanted to see if his feelings were real, so I waited until he wrote to me because I thought that he wouldn't write if he wasn't interested in me. I felt a bit bad though for questioning his feelings. I suppose I have just been in disbelief that he would go for me?" She shrugged.

“That was a smart thing to do if you felt a little uneasy, to wait. But how could he not be interested in you? You are beautiful, and you are a lovely, warm, kind and generous person. All traits you get from me, obviously. Seriously though, Sarah, write back and see where these letters take you.”

They hugged, and Sarah wondered why she was ever nervous about telling her mum at all. *She is so cool*, she thought.

Chapter Seven

Two months after Sarah had met Nick, she received a short email from him. They had been writing mostly via letter, Nick's preferred way, with the odd video call between them, so it was strange for him to be emailing her. She opened it up eagerly.

Dear Sarah,
I am doing a performance in a club here in Los Angeles next month on July 7th, and I have two weeks off after, so I wondered if you would come to see me and spend the two weeks with me? You are more than welcome to bring somebody with you.

Please respond to me as soon as you can when you get this so I can make arrangements if you decide to come over. Please say yes.
Love Nick xxx

Sarah did respond to him immediately, tapping out an email back to Nick in seconds.

Dear Nick,
Of course I will come over to see you. I will bring my mother with me because she would love to meet you. Let me know the details of where we need to go, and we will be there on 7th July. See you very soon.
Love Sarah xoxox

“Mum!” Sarah shouted, not being able to contain herself. Suzanna rushed into Sarah’s bedroom in a panic.

“Sarah, what’s wrong?”

“Oh nothing,” she said casually. “Just wondered if you could maybe take some time off work for two weeks from the 6th of July so you can, I don’t know, come to America with me and meet Nick!”

Suzanna screamed. “Really? He has invited us over? That’s great, of course I’ll come with you. Katy will be jealous, but she is off on a trip with her uni pals in July.”

“I bet she will, but we will tell her all about it when we get home.”

Finally, the 6th of July arrived, and Sarah and Suzanna were travelling to Manchester Airport for their flight out to Los Angeles. Sarah had all sorts of feelings jumping around inside of her, nervousness, excitement, happiness. She couldn’t wait to see Nick, it felt much longer than nearly three months since she had last seen him and she had really missed him.

It was ten thirty p.m. when Sarah looked out of the taxi's window that was taking them to the airport. They were not far away when she saw a plane that must have taken off a few minutes before. She started to feel very anxious at the thought of being on an aeroplane for eleven hours. She was petrified of flying. She squeezed Suzanna’s hand and told herself that she would be fine. She repeated this to herself over and over again before she took her seat on the plane. She heard the engines start to whirr, and the panic gripped her again. She closed her eyes and tried her best to concentrate on the comforting words that her mother was muttering in her ear in her soothing voice. They held hands as the plane picked up speed on the runway, and then before they knew it, they were up in the air. Sarah exhaled and opened her eyes to her mother's smiling face. It made her smile too. She was so pleased that Suzanna was here with her and that she still held her hand just like she had done when she was a child.

The flight was long but very comfortable. Sarah and Suzanna slept most of the way there, so by the time they touched down in Los Angeles, they both felt extremely well-rested. They collected their luggage and walked through the airport to the main doors, where they found Tim holding up a sign with 'Sarah Bailey' written on it. His face lit up when he saw her.

"Sarah, it's lovely to see you again. How are you, and who is this beautiful lady you have brought with you?"

"Hi, Tim, this is my mum, Suzanna, and we are great, thank you. Really excited to be here finally. How's Nick?"

Tim shook hands with Suzanna and kissed the back of her hand. Sarah was surprised to see her mother blush. She had never seen that happen before.

"Nick is fantastic, and he can't wait to see you. He wanted to come to fetch you himself, but he couldn't for obvious reasons. He's asked me to apologise to you because he won't be able to see you before his performance. He's setting up ready for it, and he has a few interviews to do first thing this morning." Sarah checked her watch, baffled, she was still on UK time, so to her, it was three in the afternoon. "He's booked a luxury hotel for you to stay and relax in, so I'll take you there now, and then we will go to the club later on this evening."

Sarah couldn't believe what she was seeing when Tim pulled up in front of the hotel that Nick had booked. It looked like a palace! Remembering her and Nick's conversation back in London about top floor rooms, she wondered if their room would be right at the top of the hotel. It was. It was one of only two on this floor. Tim unlocked the door with a shiny key card and wheeled Sarah and Suzanna's luggage inside. Sarah wondered why there were only two rooms on this floor given the size of the hotel, but when she entered, she soon found out. They would only be able to fit two of these rooms on one floor because of the sheer size of them. She assumed the one next door was very similar. It reminded her of the room that Nick had stayed in at the Grand Star in London. It had a gigantic living space, and its own kitchen, with a separate bedroom at the back, closed off with double doors. The room looked like it was fit for royalty decorated in red and gold throughout. It was immaculate, so much care had been taken to keep the room looking this way. Even the covers on the bed were perfect; there was not a thread out of place.

Suzanna gaped around the room whilst Sarah's eyes fell onto the magnificent bunch of flowers on the desk. She could see a note peeking through the top and snatched it up.

Sarah,

I can't wait to see you.

Love, Nick xxx

She tapped out a text message.

The flowers are beautiful, thank you. I can't wait to see you either xoxox

Nick had been checking his phone for hours, wondering if Sarah had landed or if she had arrived at the hotel yet. He was just about to do a sound check in the club when he felt his phone vibrate in his pocket. He read the text from Sarah and felt his mood lift considerably. He jumped onto the stage feeling lighter than air.

Sarah checked her watch, it was nearly two p.m., and her tummy was rumbling with hunger. She and Suzanna had plenty of time before Nick's performance, so they had lunch in the restaurant downstairs. There was a stage in here, which Sarah thought was strange but then figured that this was where the entertainment for the hotel guests took place.

"This place is wonderful, Sarah. I can't believe Nick has booked us in here for two weeks. It must have cost him a fortune!" Suzanna exclaimed.

"I know. He's very generous."

"So, who is Tim? He looks very smart in his suit." Suzanna seemed to be scanning the room for a glimpse of him. Sarah raised her eyebrows at her mother.

"Tim is one of Nick's security guards, but they seem more like best friends. He's the one who asked me if I would like to go on stage to meet Nick. You seem very interested."

Suzanna started to flap. It was humorous to Sarah. "No, no darling, I'm not interested. Well, I am, but not in *that* way. I wondered who he was because I was expecting to see Nick at the airport." Suzanna seemed to have become transfixed by the tablecloth; red blushes were emerging on her cheeks. She seized her glass of wine and sloshed some down her front.

"Mum, Nick would have been mobbed if he came to the airport. It's even worse for him over here than in London, and are you sure you aren't interested in Tim in '*that way*'?"

"Don't talk such nonsense and eat your food." Suzanna pointed her fork at Sarah and tried but failed to look angry.

Six p.m. was fast approaching, and Sarah's excitement was apparent as Tim drove them towards the club. The street outside of the club was crammed with people waiting to get in. Other artists' photos who were performing were plastered on the wall next to Nick's, but most of the waiting crowd were showing their love for Nick. A lot of girls were wearing T-shirts with his face printed all over them. Sarah and Suzanna scurried past them all, keeping close to Tim. He ushered them into the club after having had a quiet word with the guard on the door. He showed them where to stand and headed off backstage to let Nick know that they were in the audience. The club soon filled up with people all around them, and it was becoming increasingly difficult for Sarah to hear what her mother was saying to her, so they watched Nick's band start to set up on stage. He was performing first.

The music started up, and it was one of Nick's rocky numbers. He came out on stage wearing a silver shirt and black leather trousers. He looked delicious. He spotted Sarah in the crowd and kept his eyes on her as he started to sing. He danced his way across the stage interacting with his dancers and band members, his eyes occasionally drifting back to Sarah. While he was performing, he was thinking about their kiss at the party and wondered if she thought about it as often as he did. As much as he was enjoying himself on stage, he couldn't wait to finish so he could get his hands on her again. The music ended, and he stood drinking in the applause and cheers of his fans.

Sarah and Suzanna stood behind the barrier, just like Sarah had done at Nick's concert, waiting for Tim to come out. He appeared with his typical Tim smile and escorted them backstage. Nick was in mid-conversation with Greg but stopped immediately when Sarah walked into his dressing room. He scooped her up into a huge bear hug, and she felt her feet leave the floor for a moment.

"Hi, that was fantastic; thank you for inviting us." She turned to Suzanna. "This is my mum Suzanna. Mum, this is Nick." They shook hands politely.

"Hi, it's a pleasure to meet you, Suzanna, and I'm so glad you are both here. I hope you will have a lot of fun and enjoy your time here. I have a confession to make." Sarah looked baffled. "I have one more performance to do before I can have some time off, but I wanted you to be here for it. It's at the hotel where you are staying, and it's tonight at eight p.m. I've arranged for you and your mother to have dinner before it starts and please order anything you want." They both giggled as they remembered Sarah's reaction to the prices of the meals in London when Sarah had met with Nick at his hotel. "I've reserved a table for you close to the stage."

"Wow, great, thank you, I can't wait. I would love to see you perform again," she told him.

"We just need to pack everything up here, and I need to get refreshed, so I'll see you there at eight." He held his hands out to her and pulled her towards him. They hugged, and she inhaled the intoxicating scent of him.

"I've missed you," he whispered in her ear and pecked her on the cheek.

"I've missed you too," Sarah whispered back.

They looked into each other's eyes and paused, wondering if one was going to kiss the other when Greg interrupted them again. *He's really becoming a pain in the ass!* Sarah thought.

Chapter Eight

At the hotel, Sarah changed into a floaty, cream dress with sparkly sequins and diamante detail on the bodice. The high-heeled cream strappy shoes she had bought while she was in London set the outfit off tremendously. Suzanna's eyes welled up with tears when Sarah walked back into the living area of their room.

"Oh my goodness, Sarah!" she exclaimed. "You look wonderful!"

"Thanks, Mum," she said, checking her reflection in the mirror. "So, shall we go eat?"

The restaurant was packed when they entered. Sarah was grateful that Nick had reserved a table for them, and she was extremely pleased that it was at the front so she would not have anything obscuring her view of Nick. They finished their dessert and were pouring themselves a second glass of wine when Suzanna's eyes flitted past Sarah to something behind her. Sarah turned and just managed to spot Tim's back retreating behind a curtain next to the stage. Luckily for Suzanna, it was eight p.m., the lights faded in the restaurant, and bright lights lit up the stage. Sarah would not question her about Tim now but promised herself that they would definitely have this very interesting conversation later.

Nick's silhouette could be seen in the centre of the stage, and he strolled up to his microphone stand when the music started. It was a song that Sarah had never heard. He sang in a falsetto voice which gave her goosebumps on her arms. "*The first night we met, I knew I had to get to know you…*" he sang. Sarah had never heard him sing like this before, and she completely lost herself in the song. She was transfixed. As he started to sing the second verse, he walked to the steps at the side of the stage. Sarah came out of her trance as she watched him walk towards her table. *What is he doing?* she thought. Her breathing quickened when he knelt down in front of her, singing to her so sweetly. She stroked his face, eyes on nothing else but him. She felt like they were the only people in the room. It was silent except for the enchanting music and Nick's gorgeous voice ringing out around the room. "*You mesmerise me, baby…*"

Nick walked slowly back to the stage but didn't climb the stairs. Instead, as if he had changed his mind, he made his way back to Sarah and held his hand out to her. She took it without hesitation. Nick twirled her around straight into his arms, and they danced together, bodies closer together than they had been even when they had kissed. He sang a few of the lyrics to her while they were dancing. "*I think I'm falling for you so deep…*" He twirled her around once more and led her back to her table, where Suzanna was sitting with tears in her eyes again. He ambled back to the stage, and this time he did climb the stairs. He sang the last few lines and saw Sarah and Suzanna clasp hands across their table and smile gleefully at each other. It made him feel so happy. He was eager to speak with Sarah as soon he could and share the last surprise he had for her.

After the performance, Greg sauntered over to Sarah and Suzanna's table, looking important. "Ah, Sarah, how are you?" he asked her.

"Well, I'm a lot warmer than I was a few minutes ago but

very good, thank you."

"Splendid, splendid, and you are Sarah's mother?" he asked, holding out his hand to Suzanna. He shook then kissed the back of her hand as she nodded. She was too taken aback to say anything.

"Nick has asked me to come out here first to apologise to you, he said he didn't mean to embarrass you like that in front of all these people and second, to ask if you wouldn't mind going back to your room, really, if you don't mind," he insisted. "He doesn't want you getting any unwanted attention." Greg looked around the room suspiciously; eyes narrowed as if everybody was suddenly about to run up to Sarah with dictaphones and notebooks in their hands. "He wants to know if he can speak with you in his room when he's finished up backstage?"

"Yes, I will speak with him, and we don't mind going back to our room; we were going to do that anyway," she answered, looking over her shoulder. Greg had put her on edge.

"Marvellous, thank you. Myself or Tim will give you a knock when he's ready." Greg turned to go, but Sarah stopped him.

"Can you please tell him that I loved that performance?"

Greg smiled, "I will."

Sarah power walked to her room with Suzanna trailing behind, struggling to keep up. She held the door open for her mother and nearly slammed it when she was inside. All that she was feeling came flooding out of her. She paced the room, unable to sit down.

"What has just happened, Mother? How has this whole thing happened? Just over two months ago, I was a fan at Nick Taylor's concert. Now he has invited us to America for two weeks so we can spend time with him, and he has just knelt down and sang to me in front of all those people?"

"Well... he definitely likes you, and I *know* you like him." Suzanna paused. "Come on, Sarah, it's obvious why he's done all of this. He likes you a lot more than you think he does. You wanted to know if his feelings were genuine; what does this tell you?"

"I know, I know. I guess I just can't believe that this is happening to me. He could have anybody." Sarah sat down slowly next to Suzanna.

"He's a very lucky man," Suzanna told her daughter.

"Nothing has really happened between us, Mum, so how can you say that?"

"Just wait, darling, you'll see."

Sarah was just starting to calm down when there was a knock on the door. Suzanna answered it and found herself face to face with Tim. Sarah chuckled as Suzanna patted her dress, and Tim straightened his tie.

"Hi erm... Nick would like a word with Sarah if that's okay?" Tim stuttered.

"Sure. Sarah? Nick is ready for you," Suzanna called to her.

Sarah told Tim she would be out in a minute and clicked the door closed quietly. She turned to face Suzanna.

"Don't think you're going to get away with not speaking to me about who *you* like." Sarah pointed at the door that Tim was waiting behind and lowered her voice so he wouldn't hear her. "You can see what's going to happen between myself and Nick, but you can't see what's right in front of you?"

"What do you mean?" Suzanna asked as if she had no idea what Sarah was talking about.

"Seriously, Mother? I think you should talk to Tim and see if that takes *you* anywhere. I know you still miss Dad, but he has been gone for years now and I know he would want you to be happy. You put your life on hold when he died because of me and Katy, but we are adults now. It's time you concentrated on yourself again. Talk to Tim when you feel that the time is right and see what happens. It could be great for you." Suzanna took in Sarah's words and hugged her.

"Go on now, Sarah. Your Prince Charming is waiting."

Sarah followed Tim to Nick's room, which was the other gigantic one on the same floor, next door to hers. There were so many people in here, Greg, Tim, Nick's dancers, his band, his backup singers and others that were wandering around the room. Lots of faces looked at Sarah as she walked in nervously behind Tim. She wondered where Nick was when a couple of people moved around the room, and she saw him leaning against the door frame of the bedroom. He winked and flicked his head, silently asking her to join him. Head down so she could avoid the staring eyes, Sarah walked briskly over to Nick. She saw him make a shooing motion with his hand; she guessed this was to Greg before he closed the door. She sat down on the bed and waited for him to speak.

"Okay, first off, I wanted to apologise for my actions when I was performing downstairs. I didn't mean to come off the stage and embarrass you in front of all those people and..."

Sarah interrupted him.

"Woah, woah, woah! You think you embarrassed me? I'm more than happy you did that. I thoroughly enjoyed it! That song is the most beautiful song I've ever heard," she smiled at him and he visibly relaxed.

"Oh, good. I really get into my performances, as you know, and when I saw you sitting there looking so lovely as usual, I thought back to when I was writing the song, and I just couldn't help myself. I was so desperate for you to come over here for this performance because I didn't want you to miss it. See, I wrote it when I came back from London after meeting you." He smiled, then looked away shyly.

"So you mean you wrote that song with me in mind?" she asked, shocked.

He nodded. "I wanted to tell you how I felt about you properly face to face. I express myself through songs, and I did write it about you, which is why I wanted you here so I could perform it to you. The lyrics flowed from inside so easily. I wanted to tell you that I liked you more than I was making out after the party in London, but I used up all my courage when I kissed you!" They were both laughing loudly now. They settled down and heard shushing outside the door.

"Get lost, Greg!" Nick shouted.

"Sorry, Nick," a muffled voice muttered back.

"That man really annoys me," Nick told Sarah matter of factly.

"Honestly, I can see why," she laughed.

"Now, where were we? Ah yes, I wanted to ask you something. It's another little surprise for you, and you can, of course, say no," he rambled. "Would you and your mother like to come and stay at my house with me while you're here?"

"Really? Yes, we would love to. I thought we would be staying here. I was just about to unpack!"

"Oh, that's great. I hoped you would. I have a beautiful guest house within the grounds that you can both stay in." Nick held out his arms and squeezed her tight when she threw herself into them.

In his happiness, he nearly sprinted over to the bedroom door and walked through the living area with her, arm around her waist. The many pairs of eyes were staring again.

"Will you let your mother know before she does unpack, and I'll knock on your door when Tim and I are ready to leave so we can go together?"

"Yeah, I will. We'll see you soon."

They pecked each other on the cheek, and Sarah went back to her room to share the news with Suzanna. She was standing in front of her hotel room door when she looked back towards Nick's. She jumped when she saw that he was standing with his head hanging out of the doorway, watching her go. She giggled, opened her door and went inside.

My god, she is an angel, Nick thought as he closed his door. He straightened up, turned and found Greg staring at him, smiling with his eyebrows raised and his arms folded.

"What?" Nick laughed and sauntered off back to his bedroom to change.

Chapter Nine

When they arrived at Nick's house an hour later, Sarah was awestruck. This was not a house; it was a mansion. Nick had still managed to make it look cosy outside even though it was massive, with lots of trees and flowers sitting neatly around it. The trees had lights draped through them, which gave off a magical atmosphere. She and Suzanna were still looking all around them, gawping at his house and his land, when Sarah felt Nick's hand on her back.

"What do you think," he asked them, grinning widely.

"My goodness, it's beautiful, Nick," Suzanna answered.

"Thank you," he replied.

"It is," Sarah agreed. "I just have one problem, though." Nick looked concerned. "You told me you lived in a house!" They all chuckled as Tim came over with Sarah and Suzanna's suitcases.

"Thanks, Tim." He turned to Sarah and Suzanna. "We'll take you down to the guest house so we can drop your bags off, then I'll give you a tour. Tim, lead the way, my friend." Nick held Sarah's hand as they walked down to the guest house. Tim held his arm out to Suzanna, and Sarah felt so happy inside when she saw Suzanna link him. *My mum deserves this*, she thought. Nick had noticed too.

"I think your mom and Tim are getting quite friendly with each other, Sarah," he whispered.

"I know, I think it's great. She's trying to convince me that she doesn't have feelings for him, but I know, *and she knows*, that she does. I haven't told you but my dad died when I was seventeen years old, and I think she just feels so guilty about liking Tim. She's worried about feeling like she would be cheating on my dad if anything happened between them. I've told her that she deserves this after putting her life on hold for my sister and me. Our house is full of photos of my dad; he's on nearly every wall. I understand this was her way of coping, but I just hope that being away from our house and all those photographs for a while will make her see that she is not just a mum or a widow, but a woman who is allowed to be happy."

She hadn't realised that she and Nick had stopped walking. He was hanging on her every word. Nick hugged her and whispered, "I'm so glad I met you; you have a beautiful soul."

"Thank you," she answered.

"Well, we had better carry on, or else your mother will wonder where we've got to, and she will hunt me down."

They approached the guest house a couple of minutes later. It was a cute little cottage that had square windows with shutters on the outside and an archway of peonies and dahlias around the front door. The lights were on inside, and the door stood ajar.

"Wow!" Sarah breathed. "How pretty!"

"Thank you. My mom decorated this cottage. To be honest, it was built for my mom. She comes to stay with me sometimes, usually when I come back from a tour because she likes to make sure I eat enough and look after myself while I am on tour. I thought she would want her own space while she was here, so I surprised her one day when she came over. She's always loved cottages, and she instantly fell in love with it. Shall we go inside?"

Nick and Sarah walked through the pretty door and found

Tim and Suzanna chatting away like old friends in the kitchen. They left them to talk whilst Nick showed Sarah around the cottage. There were large wooden beams on the ceiling just like they have in old cottages and a large living space with a comfortable sofa and a huge TV. The fireplace was surrounded by house bricks which gave it an older feel. Sarah guessed that the fireplace was more for decorative purposes than warmth here in LA. They proceeded up the wooden staircase where there were two double bedrooms. Sarah's suitcase had been placed on the double bed in the slightly smaller of the two rooms. She peered out of the window and could see Nick's house. She was happy that his house was the first thing she would see each morning. Suzanna's bedroom window had a view of a pretty pond and a wooden gazebo that was built into the ground. The gazebo housed a grey half moon sofa big enough for eight people and had two matching chairs on either side. There was a table in the middle of the gazebo with candles and flowers on it. A chandelier and twinkling lights dangled from the ceiling. *How romantic,* Sarah thought.

"Do you sit out there often, Nick?" Sarah asked, pointing to the gazebo.

"I sit out there nearly every day when I'm home because it's such a calming space. I've written most of my songs whilst sitting there. In fact, the one I wrote for you was written there." They stared at each other for a moment.

"Nick! The carts are here!" Tim called from downstairs.

Sarah heard her mother laugh and exclaim, "We're going in these? How fun!"

Nick took Sarah by the hand. They walked downstairs and back through the front door of the cottage. There sat two gleaming white golf carts with red cushioned seats. Tim and

Suzanna had already settled themselves into the one at the front by the time Sarah had walked to the other.

"Go easy, Tim. I'm not racing with two beautiful ladies in our presence." He chuckled and jumped into the driver's seat next to Sarah.

"You race these?" Sarah asked incredulously.

"No, I'm kidding." He had such a naughty look on his face, Sarah didn't know whether to believe him or not. "Let's go on a tour then."

They set off behind Tim and Suzanna. As they drove all around the grounds, Nick pointed out where fun times had happened with his family and where he had once set up a marquee for his brothers' birthday party. They could see Tim pointing around the grounds, too, and they wondered what he could be telling Suzanna because she quite often threw her head back and laughed. Nick and Tim drove the carts past the pond where they could see goldfish, koi carp and golden orfes swimming smoothly through the peaceful water. Sarah could see the carp so clearly from the bridge that Nick had driven on to. He stopped and let her look at them for a while. She leaned sideways out of her seat, she was fascinated.

"You like them?" he asked her.

"Yes, I love to watch fish glide through the water so effortlessly. Your place is fantastic, Nick. You are so lucky to live here."

"Thank you, that's very kind of you to say. Would you like to head back to the house? My housekeeper has put together a few nibbles and drinks for us, and I have something that I would like to show you."

"Yes, that sounds lovely, thanks."

He picked up a walkie-talkie from a console inside the cart

and lifted it to his mouth.

"Tim, head back to the house when you're ready."

It crackled into life.

"Will do, boss," Tim replied.

They pulled in behind Tim and Suzanna's cart five minutes later. Tim and Suzanna were still seated inside it, laughing and chatting. Suzanna was glowing. Tim was having a real effect on her, and it was amazing to see. They hadn't noticed Nick and Sarah pull up behind them, and they both jumped when Nick suddenly landed on the back seat of their cart.

"Come on, you two, we have drinks and nibbles to get through," he told them.

They all walked inside Nick's house together. Sarah and Suzanna gasped with shock after only stepping one foot inside the door. Just the size of the foyer was unbelievable. It reminded Sarah of the lobby of Nick's hotel back in London. He, too, had sweeping staircases leading up to the floor above. In between the two staircases sat a grand piano with a sheet of music on the stand written in pencil. Sarah wondered if this was the song he had performed especially for her that evening. She followed Nick into his living room and did a double-take. His coffee table, which was nearly the same size as Suzanna's dining table, was laden with food. *Nick's housekeeper must have been preparing this all day*, Sarah thought. There were enough sandwiches for ten each as well as mountains of crisps, sausage rolls and pork pies. The housekeeper had also laid out some pretty cupcakes which looked like they had come from a professional baker, lots of different fruits placed in patterns on the plate and the biggest bowl of trifle she had ever seen!

"I hope you're hungry… dig in," Nick told them all, rubbing his hands together. He disappeared off to his kitchen and came back with a bottle of very expensive champagne and four champagne flutes. He filled them up and passed them round to Sarah, Suzanna and Tim. Nick wondered where Miranda, the housekeeper, had got to but assumed she had purposely made herself scarce after putting the food out. He raised his glass. "I would like to say how happy I am that you were both able to join us for the next two weeks, and I really hope you enjoy your time here. To us!" he shouted.

He took a gulp of his drink and grabbed a plate which he piled high with food. Sarah sat down with her own plate and had a good look around the room. The flooring was a dark coloured wood, and a patterned rug was placed in front of the cosy fireplace and a comfortable seating area. The television, which was enormous, was on the wall in front of them where they were sitting on two leather recliner sofas, Nick and Sarah on one and Tim and Suzanna on the other. Nick had many photographs displayed on the wall. Sarah assumed that the happy older lady he had his arm around in one of them was his mother. He had her nose and friendly smile. Another one she was drawn to showed Nick standing in the middle of his twin brothers.

An hour passed with them all talking happily away to one another, finding out more about each other's lives. Lots of stories involved Sarah as a child, thanks to Suzanna, and most of them were very embarrassing. Nick, who could see that Sarah's cheeks were flushed with colour, stroked her leg to comfort her. They caught each other's eyes and could feel the electricity between them. Sarah's eyes were glued to his; she couldn't stop staring at him. All humour had gone from his face, and there was a fire in his eyes. *He is so sexy*, Sarah thought.

Just then, a loud yawn came from her mother's direction. Stretching, Suzanna announced that she was exhausted and was going to bed. Tim stood up immediately to escort her to the guest house. The look on Suzanna's face made it very clear that she was more than happy for him to do this.

"Goodnight, you two. Have a lovely night. I'll see you in the morning, darling," she added quietly to Sarah.

"No, Mum, you will see me in a few hours," Sarah insisted, whispering back.

Suzanna winked at Sarah and stroked her cheek. Sarah shook her head and laughed at the way Suzanna sashayed out of the room, holding onto Tim's arm just like she had when they'd arrived. Sarah leaned over to the coffee table and grabbed another handful of crisps from the bowl.

"These are yummy, your housekeeper has excellent taste in food!" she laughed.

"I know, Miranda is great. It's like having my mom around when she's here. She always tells me off when I put my feet up on my coffee table or when I go outside with no shoes on. Once, she even made me sit down so she could take my temperature because I took my jumper off outside when it was raining." He laughed to himself. "It's nice, though, that feeling of having somebody care about you like that." He paused for a minute. "So, what brought you to my concert, Sarah?" he asked her, sitting back and getting comfortable.

Sarah sat silent for a moment, not really knowing where to start. She opened her mouth, but no words came out, and her eyes started to well up with tears. Nick looked worried.

"Sarah, are you okay? You don't have to tell me. It's okay."

"Yes, I'm fine, just give me a second." She fought back her tears and exhaled. "Okay, I'm ready now. I'm sorry for the tears, it's just that it's a very sad story, but I want you to know about it, so here goes. My best friend Tina, that I mentioned to you when we had dinner in your hotel, was like my family. She and her husband Bill were getting divorced because he had cheated on her with his boss's daughter. She was devastated. They had been together for years, and it came completely out of the blue. I was with her when she signed her divorce papers, and she was an absolute mess. I asked her to come over to my house so she wasn't on her own that night, but she refused. She said she would be fine." Sarah went into a trance-like state as fresh tears pricked her eyes. Nick stroked her hand, but he didn't say a word. "I got a phone call in the early hours from a policeman. Tina had… she'd passed away in a car accident." The tears trickled down her cheeks. "I was in a panic. I can't remember the journey to the hospital, and because of the state I was in, I hadn't noticed that Tina had sent me a text message not long after I left her." Sarah rummaged in her bag for her phone and found the message. She showed it to Nick.

Sar! I've decided that you are right yet again – I do need you! I'm setting out for your house in five minutes, so get the kettle on, babe! I'll see you very soon. Love you xx

Sarah dissolved into sobs. Nick wrapped his arms around her whilst fighting back his own tears. He held her until she settled down.

"Oh Sarah, I'm so sorry," he wiped the tears from her cheeks. "You don't need to tell me any more; really, it's okay."

"No, I'm fine. I guess I just felt guilty because I kept telling myself that if I had seen that message, I would have asked her if she wanted me to go to her and then if she had said yes, the accident wouldn't have happened."

"You can't think like that. This is your head's way of trying to make sense of it all and trying to figure out if there was a way it could have been prevented. Is she likely to have asked you to go to her, or did she want to get out of her house? You have nothing to feel guilty about, Sarah. You are not to blame." He rubbed her shoulders and pulled her into his arms again. She stopped crying and wiped her eyes.

"I know I shouldn't. I was just having a really hard time getting my head around her death because for years, it was me and her everywhere we went. People used to say you would never see one without the other." She was smiling and laughing now, remembering some of their best times. "She used to tell me to make the most out of life and do what makes me happy, so that's why I bought a ticket to come and see you. I had wanted to see you for ages, so I decided to just do it, and I am so glad that I did." Sarah winked playfully at Nick, and she grabbed his hand and held on tight.

"I never expected that, and I am sorry that I made you think about it all again," he said.

"Oh, don't worry, it was a normal question to ask and obviously you couldn't have known. I would have told you about Tina at some point while I was here, but I'm relieved that you know now."

"Thank you for sharing that with me; I know it wasn't easy." He picked up his glass, looked up and said, "To Tina."

"To Tina," Sarah echoed.

They talked non-stop for a couple of hours after Nick had finally stopped apologising for upsetting Sarah. Miranda had appeared out of nowhere with a bottle of wine in her hand. She placed it on the table in front of them as she bade them goodnight. Nick offered some to Sarah and re-filled her glass as she told him lots of happy stories about herself and Tina and showed him some photos of the two of them together on her phone. He, in turn, told her more about his parents and his siblings, waving his hand towards the photos on his wall. He suddenly jumped up as if somebody had pinched him.

"I almost forgot," he told her. "I have something that I would really like you to see."

He had a huge grin on his face, and he was bouncing on the balls of his feet in excitement. He hurried over to a floor-to-ceiling bookcase and selected a white DVD case from it. He held it up to show Sarah, but there was no writing on the front of it, and Nick did not tell her what it was. She was intrigued as he slotted a disc into the side of the television. As she watched, a familiar song reached her ears, and she recognised the stage that was on the screen.

"Oh my gosh, is this the concert I came to?" she asked, amazed.

"Yes, it was filmed for a tour DVD. Greg sent this footage to me. He thought we both might like to see it. As you can probably tell, I've already seen it. I couldn't help myself." He had a sexy smirk on his face.

Sarah watched herself at the top of the stage steps as Nick sidled over to her, microphone in hand. She sat glued to the TV and put her hand to her mouth as she saw herself cry.

"I never asked you why you got upset there." Nick pointed at the screen and looked across at her.

With her eyes still fixed on the screen, she answered him. "It was so surreal to me to be standing on stage with you singing to me like that. I felt like the luckiest person in the world, so I couldn't have been happier, but at the same time, I felt sad. I thought I was only going to have a couple of minutes with you, and that would be it. You made me feel so special, and I just didn't want to leave you."

She looked at him. Nick moved closer and leaned in to kiss her. This was what she had been waiting for. His kiss was urgent and passionate; she could taste wine on his tongue as he massaged hers with his own. Sarah ran her fingers through his soft hair as his hands travelled from her face all the way down her body. Nick wanted this just as much as she did. When they pulled apart, Nick stood and gently tugged on Sarah's hands so she would stand too. They didn't need to say anything; they both knew what was about to happen.

He led her to his bedroom and leaned into her again as he unzipped her dress and placed spine-tingling kisses on her neck, then worked his way down towards her breasts. She threw her head back in ecstasy and let her dress fall to the floor. He caressed her back, running his fingers up and down her spine as she unbuttoned his silky shirt. The smell of it was enticing, and the desperation for him that she felt right now was immense. She kissed his chest as she fumbled with the last two buttons of his shirt in her haste to remove it from his fantastic body.

"You are gorgeous," he whispered, his hand moving south.

He teased her with his fingers over and over again, making her knees go weak, then he slid his hands round to her bum and picked her up effortlessly. With Sarah's legs wrapped around his waist, still kissing her, Nick walked over to his king-sized bed and placed her down carefully. He stood, unzipped his trousers and discarded them and his boxer shorts on the floor as he gazed down at Sarah's naked body, wanting her more and more with each second that passed. He opened the drawer in his bedside cabinet and pulled a condom out. Sarah watched as he ripped the wrapper open, rolled it down his erection and gave her a smouldering look. He spread her legs, climbed on top of her and eased himself inside. She moaned at the full feeling and gazed into his eyes. They moved together as one, sweat building up on their bodies. Sarah felt herself building up, and she dug her fingernails into Nick's back as her orgasm ripped through her body. Nick threw his head back and closed his eyes as he gave in to his own orgasm.

He leant towards her and kissed her softly. They lay next to each other, staring and studying each other's faces, both feeling a sense of complete bliss.

"Will you stay here with me tonight?" he asked.

"Yes," she answered, kissing his forehead and cuddling into him. Sarah thanked her lucky stars that she had met Nick and that he felt the same way she did. Everything felt so right with him, and she had started to feel a lot more for him than she thought.

Chapter Ten

The next morning, Sarah woke up to Nick putting a strong cup of coffee on his bedside table for her.

"Good morning, beautiful," he sang.

"Hello, handsome. How did you sleep?" she asked, smiling broadly at him.

"Absolutely marvellous," he shouted. "And you?"

"Lovely, thank you. You are really comfortable." She sat up in bed so she could grab her coffee, and the smell of cooking bacon hit her. "Oh my gosh! That bacon smells gorgeous!"

"Yeah, I know. Miranda is cooking breakfast for us, your mom and Tim. It wouldn't smell like that if I was cooking it, believe me. She won't even let me in the kitchen in case I accidentally burn anything!"

Sarah giggled. "Okay, I'll drink up and have a walk down to fetch my mum."

She enjoyed her walk down to the cottage. She could hear lots of birds in the trees singing their merry tunes to each other. She looked up and saw a mother bird with a twig in its mouth, adding it to her nest. The door to the cottage was unlocked when she arrived. She opened it and heard the familiar laughter that she had heard the night before. Tim was sitting on the sofa next to Suzanna in a pair of sunshine yellow shorts and a bright blue T-shirt. They seemed surprised when she entered the living room. Sarah saw her mother's eyes look her up and down, and Tim excused himself and got up from the sofa. He left the cottage, winking at Suzanna and headed in the direction of Nick's house.

"Good morning, Mum. How was your night? I'm sorry I didn't come back here last night," she said as she sat down in the spot that Tim had just vacated.

"Are you sorry?" she asked her. "I told you I would see you in the morning, didn't I? To answer your question, I had a fantastic night, darling and to be honest, I'm glad you stayed with Nick!"

"Oh, thanks, Mum!" she said, pretending to be mad. "I'm assuming that means you had a chance to talk to Tim?"

"Well, yes, as a matter of fact, I did, and we did just that, by the way, before you start thinking anything." Suzanna held her hands up as if to put a stop to any thoughts that Sarah may have started to have. "It was really late when he got up to leave, so I asked him if he would like to stay the night. He slept on the sofa just in case you decided to come back. I knew that was never going to happen, and by the look of the smile on your face, I know you will be spending the rest of our time here snuggled up next to Nick. His shirt suits you, by the way."

Sarah looked down and saw that she had walked down here in the shirt that Nick was wearing the previous night and a pair of his shorts.

"Yes, well, my suitcase was here, wasn't it, and I didn't want to come down here in the middle of the night for my pyjamas, so I just grabbed the first thing I saw that was on the floor this morning and put it on." Suzanna raised her eyebrows at her daughter.

Oops, Sarah thought. *I think I just told my mother I was naked with Nick; that's just bloody great!*

"So anyway," she carried on quickly. "Did you tell Tim that

you like him?"

Suzanna smiled at the mention of his name. "He said it first, and then I told him how I felt too. He said he would like to spend some time with me while we are here and get to know me better."

"Aww, Mum, that's really great. I'm so happy for you." She slid over to her mum and cuddled her. "Shall we go up to Nick's house? Miranda is cooking breakfast for us, and it smells delicious!"

"Sure. Are you going back up wearing his clothes?" Suzanna teased.

"No, obviously not. I'll just go and find something in my suitcase."

Sarah hurried up the stairs and found a summery maxi dress and sandals. She put them on along with a large spritz of perfume and ran back downstairs to where Suzanna was waiting for her.

The next two weeks passed in a blur. Nick had taken Sarah, Suzanna and Tim to a zoo which they had to themselves. Nick and Sarah walked round hand in hand, with Nick giving her lots of fascinating facts about the animals they were looking at. It was clear to Sarah how much he loved animals. He had studied them. In fact, most of the books that Sarah had seen in his living room were about animals. Sarah startled Nick when she suddenly bolted towards the otters. Otters were her favourite animal, and she started speaking to them in a gentle voice. They seemed drawn to her, immediately running up to the wall that Sarah was peeking over. She giggled as one of them slid underneath the water and popped its head back up at once. It floated through the water on its back, grooming itself as it went. Nick and Sarah carried on walking along the path, not noticing that the otters had run through their enclosure alongside them so they could still see

Sarah.

After spending the day at the zoo, they had arrived back at Nick's house, arms laden with candy floss and plenty of sweet treats. Nick had bought a cuddly otter toy for Sarah, who she had called Oscar Otter. She sat him on the table under the gazebo in Nick's garden, where she sat with Suzanna, watching Nick and Tim load up the barbecue.

Another day Nick had arranged a meal out for them all in a swanky restaurant not far from his house. As they waited for dessert, Nick took out his phone and started snapping away with the camera.

"This one's going in a frame!" he announced as he looked at the selfie he had just taken of the four of them.

Sarah cuddled into Nick as he flicked through the photos he had just taken. They were admiring one he had taken of himself and Sarah when they heard a kissing noise from across the table. Sarah looked up slowly and found her mother's cheeks were ablaze with colour, even though she had the biggest grin on her face. Tim looked like the cat that had got the cream. Nick and Sarah did not want to ruin this moment for them, so they peered back down at Nick's phone, pretending that they hadn't noticed.

By the end of the two weeks, Sarah had still not forgiven Nick for taking her on the highest and fastest rollercoaster she had ever seen in the theme park that he had wanted to go to. He had insisted it wasn't that fast and that she would enjoy it… he looked sheepish as he held her hair back as she vomited at the exit gate! Most of her time after that incident was spent watching Nick and Tim on the rides while she waited for her head to stop spinning. He apologised non-stop, and she had to admit that she was glad she made him happy when she agreed to join him, Suzanna and Tim on the log flume at the end of the day.

She had much preferred the chilled evenings they had all shared together in his garden, talking, sipping wine and eating lots of pizza. This was how they spent their last night together. Tim and Suzanna had gone for a wander through the garden in the cool night air. Nick and Sarah danced together to the slow rhythm of the music that was playing through the sound system that was hooked up outside. *I never want to let him go*, Sarah thought as he kissed her softly.

On their last morning together, Nick and Sarah ate breakfast under the gazebo. It was a beautiful atmosphere, the sun was shining, and everything was so still and quiet. Sarah stared at Nick as he ate his last few mouthfuls. She was astonished that she had fallen for him like this in such a short time. He had been quiet since they had woken up that morning, and he didn't say anything as he looked back at her.

"What's the matter, Nick?" she asked nervously.

He sighed and tilted his head in a way that made her want to pounce on him. "Well, the matter is that I am not ready for you to go home yet."

"Me neither," she said, her voice shaking. Nick reached for her hands across the table and squeezed them.

"I want you to stay here with me," he said matter of factly. "I've been thinking about it while you've been here, and it's made more and more sense to me with each day that's passed. I need you, Sarah, and I can tell that you don't want to leave. I hope you don't think it's too soon for me to say this, but I love you, and I want us to be together." Sarah's mouth fell open at his words, and tears trickled quickly down her cheeks.

"I love you too!" she sobbed.

Nick flew off his chair and threw himself at Sarah. He kissed her as if his life depended on it. They could feel the tension leaving both of their bodies and felt as light as air when Nick returned to his seat. Hands clasped tightly in each other's again, Sarah spoke.

"I didn't expect you to say that," she laughed as she dabbed her eyes with her napkin. "I want us to be together too, but how will this work?"

"I've been thinking about that too. I would love for you to come and live here with me, but I am more than happy to come over to England to look for a place of our own there so you can stay close to your mom and sister." Sarah couldn't believe the lengths Nick would go to so they could be together. It took her a millisecond to decide what she wanted to do.

"I've made up my mind."

"Already? Don't you want to think about it for a while first? I've told you now so you can have some time away from me, so it's easier for you to think about it without me around."

"No, I don't need to think about it. The thought of leaving you fills me with dread, and I know that I do not want to be without you ever… so I would love to come and live here with you!"

Nick left his seat once more, did a running jump, clicked his heels in mid-air and spun Sarah around with one arm. She laughed jovially, even though the spin had made her feel rather dizzy. Nick put her down gently and held her chair out for her so she could take her seat again.

"Woo!" Nick cheered as he sat down. "Now we need to tell your mom!"

Sarah had not seen her mother since that morning when she and Tim had walked past the gazebo hand in hand. Now she was sitting nervously in Nick's living room awaiting her arrival, the anxiety of telling her mother she would be moving to America, written all over her face. She jumped up from her chair when she heard the front door open and her mother's laughter ring out. Suzanna waltzed into the room with Tim, who had Suzanna's lipstick all over his lips, and stopped abruptly when she saw Sarah's facial expression. She was by her side in seconds.

"Sarah, what's wrong, sweetheart?" she asked, concerned.

"Mum, please sit down. I need to tell you something."

Nick and Tim left the room together, walking quickly to the kitchen whispering to each other. Suzanna sat down on the sofa, and Sarah perched on the coffee table.

"Okay, this won't be easy, but I can do this," she said more to herself than Suzanna. "Mum, I have been talking to Nick about what will happen between myself and him when we have to go home." She paused so she could prepare herself to tell Suzanna the next bit of the conversation. "I have fallen completely in love with him, and I know that this has happened really fast, but he feels the same way about me. So here's the difficult part. I will be moving in here with Nick because we are together now. It makes a lot more sense for me to move here than for him to move to England and find a place there." Suzanna did not speak, so Sarah continued. "As much as I would want to, I cannot live with you forever, and I will miss you and Katy more than anything, but this feels so right. Please say something, Mum."

Suzanna's eyes welled with tears. "I'm so happy for you, darling!" Suzanna reached out her arms to hug her daughter. She squeezed her harder than she ever had done before.

Nick appeared in the kitchen doorway, one hand on his chest, the other holding onto Tim for support. He was relieved and was just starting to breathe normally again, not realising he had been holding his breath. He decided to stay where he was so Sarah and Suzanna could talk to each other properly about this.

"I'm so happy you've just said that!" said Sarah, laughing.

"Let me tell you something. You are a wonderful daughter," said Suzanna. "You make me so proud and you deserve all of the happiness in the world. Nick is a fantastic person and I can tell that he absolutely adores you. He's unleashed all of this joy that you have within you, and it's made you glow from the inside out. You have always been the one who was there for everybody else, always the one to make everybody else smile. Now it's time for you to start smiling for a change. I've watched how close you two have become since we got here, and this is definitely the right thing for you to do. You were made for each other and I am so glad that you found each other. Now," she raised her voice. "Where is my daughter's boyfriend?"

Nick appeared instantly through the kitchen door, it looked like he had been pushed from the other side. He straightened up, ran his fingers through his hair and walked calmly towards Suzanna.

"Sorry about that. Tim's excited." Tim appeared seconds later with a bottle of champagne and four glasses. He set them down on the coffee table and hugged Sarah. Suzanna turned her attention back to Nick.

"Thank you," she said simply.

"For what?" Nick asked, baffled.

"You are responsible for putting that smile back on my daughter's face where it belongs. I can tell that you love her, and although I am going to miss her more than you could ever imagine, I will be so happy knowing that she is here with you and that you will be by her side." Nick grabbed Suzanna by the hand.

"Suzanna, I love Sarah more than anything. I can't wait for

her to be here with me permanently. I promise I will treat her the way she deserves to be treated, and I will protect her at all costs. You will be welcome here anytime you want. Just let me know and I will book the first flight available for you and Katy."

"You are very generous, Nick. Now let's go celebrate."

Chapter Eleven

Sarah and Suzanna dumped their suitcases in the living room and collapsed onto their sofas when they arrived home. Nick and Tim had driven them to the airport, and after very tearful goodbyes all round, Sarah and Suzanna had finally gotten onto the plane. Neither of them had managed to sleep a wink on the flight, and they hardly spoke. Sarah had tears spilling from her eyes most of the way home, and Suzanna looked like the life had been sucked out of her.

They were still lying where they had landed on the sofas when Katy ran into the living room hours later, breathless but so excitable.

"Hi!" she screamed, then stopped when she saw the looks on their faces. "Erm, did you have a bad flight?"

Suzanna got up first and embraced her youngest daughter. "No, no, the flight was okay. We just didn't expect our trip to turn out the way it did. How are you, darling?"

"I'm great, Mum, I'm glad you're back, but you two don't seem to be. Did something bad happen over there?" she asked curiously.

Sarah appeared just behind Suzanna, arms outstretched as she reached Katy. "We are glad to be back, sis, but we just wish two very special things could have come back with us."

"What things?" Nobody answered her. "Will somebody please explain what these two things are and why you two look so miserable?" Katy stamped her feet as she said the last few words.

Sarah took Katy by the shoulders and sat her down between herself and Suzanna on one of the sofas, and started to talk. She told her about Nick's performances, his house, everywhere he had taken them and then finally that she was now in a relationship with him. Suzanna told her all about Tim but was still trying to act as though it was not a big deal. When they had finished, Katy was gobsmacked.

"You didn't give much away in your text messages, did you? You went to America as a single lady and came back looking like a lovesick puppy because you had to leave your megastar boyfriend behind! Okay then, not what I expected you to say when you came back, but yes, fine." She held her hands up to Sarah and then faced her mother. "And you, Mother. I'm sure Sarah has already told you this, but it's okay to fall in love with someone else after Dad, you know. I've never met Tim, but I can tell he's made you so happy already." She raised her eyebrows, daring Suzanna to deny it.

"Sweetheart, that's nice of you to say, but I'm not in love with Tim."

"Er, yeah you are." Sarah and Katy answered in unison.

Monday morning arrived. Sarah pulled into her usual car parking space at the hospital and glanced at the huge building that held so many good and bad memories for her. Before she got out of her car, she checked her handbag for about the tenth time, making sure her resignation letter was tucked safely inside. She had enjoyed working at the hospital so much, so she was dreading telling her boss, Anita, that she would be leaving. Sarah could not fault her boss at all, and she had been a great friend to her as well as her boss. Anita was the one to put up a memorial plaque for

Tina on the wall behind the reception desk in their department, so she would never be forgotten. Sarah stopped and stared at it for a few moments as she came into the A&E department, and felt a huge lump in her throat when she thought about Tina and how much she was going to miss all of her colleagues and friends here. They had all shown her lots of love and compassion after Tina's death. In a weird way, the hospital was where she felt closest to Tina; she could almost feel her spirit around her as she worked, like an angel on her shoulder. Sarah could never have imagined leaving the hospital, but this was what needed to happen now so she could finally allow herself to be happy, move on as best she could and start the next chapter of her life with Nick.

She let out a nervous breath and walked into the staff room, where she found Anita stirring a hot cup of coffee and singing to herself. Sarah put her bags down on one of the comfy chairs and joined Anita by the kettle.

"Good morning, Sarah, how are you? Did you have a nice holiday?" Anita asked cheerfully.

"I'm good thanks, Anita, and yes, it was fantastic." *Just get this over with*, she told herself. "Anita, can we go to your office, please? I really need to speak to you about something important?" The nervousness was starting to show on her face.

"Yes, of course. After you." Anita held her hand out to allow Sarah to go ahead of her. They walked in silence down the corridor to Anita's office.

Sarah could feel teeth marks in her bottom lip when she walked into the office, from biting down too hard in her anxiety to get her news off her chest. *Focus on something else*, she thought. Images of Nick's gorgeous eyes and playful smile flashed through her mind, and she suddenly felt a lot happier. She took a seat opposite Anita.

"Okay, what's on your mind, Sarah?" Sarah snapped back into life when she heard her name. She was still thinking about Nick, but now she had images in her head that she did not want to share with Anita or anybody else!

"Oh sorry, I was miles away then," she said smiling. She felt her cheeks redden. "I want to thank you for everything you have done for me and taught me over the years; you have been an amazing mentor. And I'd like to thank you for how great you treated me when we lost Tina. I could never have gotten through my days here without you after that night. You really are a wonderful person and a great friend."

"Well, thank you, that's really kind of you to say." As much as Anita appreciated this, she knew that this was not the reason Sarah was in her office now.

"Now the next thing I need to tell you is that I do really love it here, but… I need to give you my resignation letter." Sarah slid the paper across the desk. Anita stared at it, then looked up with a dumbfounded expression on her face. "Let me explain. I have met somebody who lives in America, and I will be moving in with him, so I'm leaving so I can be with him. That's where I went on my holiday." She didn't want to tell Anita who she had fallen for because of who he was, and she didn't know what else to say, so she sat in silence. Anita suddenly got up from her chair, hurried round to Sarah's side of the desk and engulfed her in a hug.

"I'm so happy for you," Anita told her. She returned to her chair when she had finished squeezing Sarah. "You need to do what makes you happy, Sarah. You have been through your fair share of heartache over the years, so this is the time for you. You can breathe now," she laughed. "I could tell you were nervous as soon as you came to me in the staff room. I know you so well. You are feeling guilty right now about leaving." Sarah nodded. "But please don't worry about anything here. Just focus on your mystery man," Anita winked, "and packing your suitcases. For how often you and Tina went clothes shopping, it's going to take you all month to pack them!" They laughed again, and with that, Sarah's mind was put completely at ease. She drank her coffee, and after another big cuddle, she left the office and started her day with a spring in her step and the biggest smile on her face.

Later on that day, when Sarah's break time came, she sent a text message to Nick.

I've done it – I've handed in my resignation letter :-) Xoxoxoxox

Nick typed back.

That's fantastic. This is the start of us being able to be together forever. How did your boss take it? Xxxxxxx

Sarah replied.

She was really great about it. She gave me a cuddle and told me to do what makes me happy and focus on my mystery man :-) I want to come back to you now I've done it. This is going to be the LONGEST month ever! I love you xoxoxoxoxox

Another message pinged through from Nick.

I know it will, babe, but once you are back here, we will never have to be apart again. I can't wait to see you, and I love you too xxxxxxxxxxxx

Sarah smiled at her phone and put it back into her locker. She was now officially on countdown. There were only a few patients in A&E that afternoon, so she used the free time to write down what she needed to start organising when she arrived home that evening, right down to what she would need to do a few days before she left. She had loads to do and she would definitely need to draft in her mother and sister for help.

She started sorting her things out as soon as she arrived home that evening, she couldn't see her bed for the amount of clothes she had piled onto it. By the time Suzanna announced that she had made a massive bowlful of stew for Sarah, she had divided her clothes into three piles. One pile for the clothes that she was taking with her, one for the charity shop and the last one for Katy. This one consisted of the clothes she hardly wore any more, thanks to Katy taking them from her wardrobe and wearing them every chance she got. She wiped a stray tear from her face as she thought about the good times she'd spent with her sister.

Sarah loaded the clothes she was taking with her into the ginormous box that would be getting shipped across to Nick a couple of days before she left. She would be living in her work uniform, pyjamas and the clothes for the charity shop until then. When she wasn't working, she was busy packing, organising or visiting family members to tell them she was leaving.

The week before her flight, Sarah was looking at websites for car garages on her phone to see where she could sell her car when it started to ring. It was an American phone number, but it wasn't Nick's. Instantly the fear that she felt when Tina died gripped her again. With trembling hands, she answered the call.

"Hello."

"Hi Sarah, this is Nick's sister Rachel." She was whispering but sounded very happy, so Sarah relaxed a bit. "I'm sorry to be calling you when we haven't even met yet, but I just had to speak to you. I had to tell my brother a little white lie so I could get your number from his phone. I hope you don't mind?"

"No, I don't mind. Is everything okay with Nick?" Sarah

asked, praying the answer was going to be yes.

"Well, he's a little sad because he is missing you like crazy, but other than that, he is great!" Rachel exclaimed.

"Oh, phew!" Sarah breathed a sigh of relief, and now she felt as happy as Rachel sounded. "I'm sorry, I must have come across as really rude. I was worried something had happened to him because I didn't know your number."

"Oh, that's okay, honey. Now listen, I wondered if you would like to be part of my plan to surprise my brother?"

"Yes, I would love to." Sarah was curious and listened intently as Rachel spoke.

"Fab! Now I know you are coming over on the 26th August, but how would you feel if I changed your flight to Saturday 25th and we didn't mention it to Nick?" Rachel giggled.

"That would make me tremendously happy," Sarah laughed.

"Ooo goody, I'm getting excited already. Okay, here's what we need to do. I will change your flight and send you the details via email – I've pinched your email address and your original flight information from Nick's phone as well; sorry about that. I will be waiting for you at the airport when you land, and then I will drive us to a venue where I am performing for charity that night in LA. You can freshen up and change your clothes in my dressing room. Nick will be in the building because he's performing too, and he's agreed to sing back up for me, so I may have to hide you, but we can worry about that later." She chuckled and quickly carried on. "I'll fill you in on the rest when you get here and when we are in the privacy of my dressing room because I'm hidden away in Nick's bathroom at the moment, so I can't talk long."

"Okay, why are you hiding in Nick's bathroom?" Sarah asked.

"I couldn't wait until I got home to call you, and I wanted to be somewhere I wouldn't be overheard, but they will be wondering where I've got to, so I'd better go," she said, apologetically.

Sarah laughed. "Okay, thank you so much, Rachel, I'll look out for your email and I look forward to meeting you."

"Yeah, you too. It's been lovely talking to you. I'll see you very soon, honey."

"Bye." The phone clicked off, and Sarah stared at it as if she didn't know what it was. Then she jumped off her bed.

"Mum!" she screamed as she dived through her bedroom door into the living room where Suzanna was relaxing with a bowl of strawberry ice cream and the latest novel from her favourite author. She sat up rigidly at the sound of Sarah's screams, dropped a huge dollop of ice cream on the lush material of her sofa, then breathed a sigh of relief when she saw Sarah's smile.

"Bloody hell, Sarah, I've just nearly swallowed my spoon! What's happened?"

"Mum, it's the best thing ever! Nick's sister has just called me and asked me to go over there a day earlier so we can surprise Nick! Isn't that great?"

"It is, darling. I'm so happy for you," she sighed.

"Then why do you look so sad?" Sarah asked.

"Well, it's just a day less that I'm going to have both of my babies with me."

"Oh, I'm sorry, Mum, I didn't think about it like that. I promise we will have the best last night together before I go." She hugged her mother.

"I know we will, and I don't mean to act like a soppy old goat. It's just that I'm going to miss you so much."

“I’m going to miss you too, but we will make sure that we can see each other as often as we can and don’t forget, Tim will be desperate to see you too, so he won’t want you to stay away for long.” She winked and headed back to her bedroom.

Chapter Twelve

The next morning, Sarah tried to keep herself busy, but her eyes kept wandering over to her computer. She was eager to open her emails, but she knew if she did that, she would sit staring at the screen, willing an email to come through from Rachel. She gave up on packing the rest of her things away and lay on her bed, put her earphones in and listened to her boyfriend's smooth, silky voice singing the songs she knew so well. She felt relaxed when her favourite album of his had finished, so she decided to go out and buy presents for Suzanna and Katy to open on their last night together.

The walk around the town was refreshing, and Sarah enjoyed the time on her own. The first shop she went into was a perfume shop that Suzanna always insisted on going into whenever they came into town. Sarah bought her mother a bottle of her favourite perfume called 'Starlights', which was a tiny bottle with a hefty price tag. Sarah could hear her father's voice in her mind as the cashier handed her the receipt, '*use it sparingly, Suzanna!*' Her next stop was to the sweet shop for Katy. Katy loved the old sweets that shops used to sell and always came home with a bag full of them. Sarah went inside and spent nearly as much on the sweets as she had on her mother's perfume. *Katy will still be eating these at Christmas!* Sarah thought as she wedged the sweets into her handbag so none of them would fall out. After walking around town for a few more hours, only stopping briefly to indulge in a slice of carrot cake and the creamiest hot chocolate she had ever tasted in a nearby cafe, she started to head back to her car with her bags.

On her way, she peeked into a shop she had been into a few times with Tina. The shop was called 'Seductive'. It had floor-to-ceiling windows at the front with mannequins standing elegantly inside them. They were either wearing sexy lingerie or were draped in silk. The logo above the shop's doors stood out among the rest on this row. The red lettering and lipstick mark seemed to jump off the black background, highlighting it perfectly.

Sarah had never dared to go in on her own before because some of the other items they sold made her blush. Since meeting Nick, she had gained a lot more confidence, so she nodded to herself and walked in.

A shop assistant wearing a red silk blouse strutted up to Sarah with a twinkle in her eye. "Good morning lovely, my name is Davina. Is there anything I can help you with today?" Davina seemed to be able to read Sarah's thoughts. "Hmmm, you want to be daring, but you are worried about looking silly? What else? Ahhh, yes, you want something to excite your special man?" She winked, picked up a basket and rested the handle on one of her arms.

She linked Sarah with the other and started to lead her around the shop, saying things like, "red would suit you," and "step out of your comfort zone a little." They stopped at the lingerie section. Davina picked up an almost see-through red dress. It had thin spaghetti straps and a single button in the middle. *The skirt may as well not even be there for how short it is!* Sarah thought to herself. She looked at Davina with raised eyebrows.

"Oh, come on, darling, how long will this stay on anyway?"

She winked again. "If you want to excite your man with this before anything… happens, you could always wear a bra and panties underneath." Davina put the see-through dress in Sarah's basket and sashayed over to the bra and panty section. Sarah followed slowly, gulping. She was starting to wish she had carried on walking and not come into the shop.

"Now, personally, I think black underwear looks great underneath red sheer," Davina stated matter-of-factly. She looked at Sarah's body for a few seconds then rifled through the different sizes of underwear. Sarah was amazed when she saw that Davina had picked up her exact size. Davina laughed at the look of astonishment on Sarah's face. "Don't look so surprised. I'm the best at what I do." Davina threw the panties in Sarah's basket and held the bra up to Sarah's chest. The amount of padding inside made Sarah a little concerned at how close her boobs would be to her chin! Davina nodded and threw the bra into the basket along with the panties.

The next part of the shop that Davina led her to was the food and naughty games section. Davina put several different flavours of sauces into the basket, as well as candy underwear and a pack of game cards that had very naughty dares on them. Sarah wondered how Nick would feel about all this stuff in her basket.

"Let's see how brave you really are!" Davina said excitedly as she walked up to a pair of thick velvet curtains. She pulled one aside so Sarah could go inside the hidden room. Sarah took one step inside and immediately flew straight back out!

"No, no, no! No way! I am definitely not brave enough for those!" She could feel her face glowing. Davina giggled and linked Sarah's arm again, guiding her back into the room. "See, I told you red would suit you," she said, pointing to Sarah's cheeks. "Just have a look around and see if anything tickles your fancy. You want to be adventurous and daring, don't you?" Davina teased.

"Okay, I'll look, but don't go throwing anything into my basket because that…" Sarah insisted, pointing to a whip, "is a very firm no!"

"Very firm? Hmm, I know what you have on the brain!" Sarah laughed along with Davina at the irony of her words. "Fine, no whips, but how do you feel about our stock of buzzing friends?"

"Okay, I think," she answered slowly. "I've never tried one before, but I suppose I'm up for that."

"Fantastic! Just remember, you can enjoy it together!" Davina winked once more.

Still chuckling as she left the shop, Sarah walked back to her car with her purchases. She tried to hide the bag, which had her new little friend inside, behind the others. She blushed profusely if anybody looked her way. She scolded herself. *Stop being silly. None of these people have x-ray vision; they can't see through your bag!* Still, she upped her pace and hastily threw her bags into her car.

Sarah arrived back home and unzipped the suitcase she would be taking with her. Then a thought occurred to her… *Will they see this through my suitcase at the airport?* She froze and wondered. Sarah didn't want to ask her sister, and she certainly did not want to have this conversation with her mother! It was silly times like this when she needed her best friend. Tina would have laughed hysterically at this situation, especially since she had always told Sarah that she was a 'prude'. Sarah could feel tears sting the back of her eyes at the thought of Tina, and she lay on her bed while she composed herself. The ping of a new email brought Sarah back to reality, and she suddenly remembered the conversation that she'd had with Rachel the previous night. Heart pounding, she sat up and pulled her laptop towards her. Rachel's name popped up at the top of her email inbox. Sarah opened the email.

Hey Sarah, Rachel here. I'm so excited I got to speak to you.

I cannot wait to meet you in person, Nick has not stopped talking about you.

I hope asking you to come early hasn't messed up any of your plans with your mother and sister? Nick tells me you are incredibly close to them both so I wouldn't have wanted to ruin anything.

I've booked a new flight for you. It leaves Manchester Airport at ten a.m.

It's a direct flight so you should arrive here at around nine p.m. (your time).

I'll be there to pick you up, don't worry, you will know who I am :-)

I'll see you very soon!

Rachel xxx

Sarah hastily tapped out a reply.

Hi Rachel,

Thank you so much for sorting this out for me. I cannot wait to meet you either!

I have missed Nick so much. I'm almost packed and ready to go!

See you soon, Sarah xoxox

Excitement flooded through Sarah. She re-read Rachel's email over and over again. It made it feel more real that she was going to live in America with Nick. She pulled herself together and had a look around her room. Her eyes fell on the bags she had gotten from town. She decided she would put her little friend in the boxes she would be shipping over to Nick a couple of days before she left. *Hopefully, he won't try to be helpful and unpack anything for me*, she thought to herself.

August 25th arrived, and Suzanna woke first, at three a.m. She peeked into Sarah's bedroom and almost burst into tears when she saw both of her daughters cuddled up together in Sarah's bed just like they used to do when they were children. Suzanna felt overjoyed that Sarah had found somebody who loved her more than anything and made her so happy, but she was also sad that she wouldn't be able to see her every day.

Suzanna thought back to the previous night when it was just her, Sarah and Katy snuggled up on the sofa together, having a girl's night in, watching movies, chatting and eating way too much junk food. The night had turned very teary when Sarah had given them the presents she had bought for them. It had become real for Suzanna at that moment that her eldest daughter was moving thousands of miles away from her.

"Good morning, Mum," Sarah said softly. Suzanna jumped.

"Oh, good morning, sweetie. You made me jump."

"I know. You seemed lost in your own world then. What are you doing up so early?" Suzanna checked her watch. It was now three thirty. She hadn't realised that she had been sitting thinking about everything for half an hour. She took a swig of her now freezing cold coffee then screwed up her face.

"Oh, nothing. I was just thinking about things." She shrugged.

"You didn't have a very good sleep either, then?" asked Sarah.

"No, not really. You seemed really cosy cuddled up with Katy."

"Yeah. She's the reason I got to sleep in the first place. She sneaked into my room thinking I was asleep, so I gave her quite the fright when I spoke to her." They both laughed.

"She's going to miss you so much," Suzanna said.

The next couple of hours flew by. Sarah had written what felt like a hundred emails to work colleagues and family members to say goodbye to them one more time. She checked her car one final time to make sure that she had taken everything out of it, ready for Suzanna to drop off at the car dealership the following day. She helped Katy fill her wardrobe with the new additions that she had given to her. By the time Sarah had finished, she was ready for a nice hot bath and a cup of coffee, but time only allowed her a very quick shower and a glass of water.

The early morning weather turned from cloudy but dry to a downpour just as Sarah, Suzanna and Katy were loading Suzanna's car with Sarah's suitcases and hand luggage. Suzanna flicked on the radio and the very cheerful presenter announced that it was six a.m. on the dot. *Right on time!* Sarah thought. As they drove down the street, Sarah looked back at the house she had grown up in, wondering when she would be back. She looked down at her phone at the smiling faces of herself and Nick from the first time they met backstage at Nick's show. She was so desperate to call or message him to tell him she was on her way, but she couldn't ruin the surprise. Instead, she messaged Rachel.

'Hi, Rachel. I'm on my way to the airport! I'll see you at one p.m. your time :-) Sarah xoxox PS. I think I'm getting better with the different time zones!'

They arrived at the airport and waited in the long queue to check-in. The balding man behind the check-in desk raised his eyebrows when he saw the amount of luggage that Sarah was dragging behind her as she approached him.

"Er, where are you going to, the moon?" he asked in a bored tone.

"No," she said firmly. "I'm moving to Los Angeles."

"Hmm," was all he said in reply. The bored man stickered up her suitcases without saying another word and sent her on her way.

The sun was just coming out from behind the clouds when they arrived at the departure lounge. Suzanna and Katy weren't allowed to go inside.

"So this is it, Mum. I'm finally moving out!" Sarah laughed, although she had tears running down her face.

"I thought I would look forward to this day back when you were a child, but I couldn't be more wrong, sweetheart!" Sarah knew that her mother was trying to make her feel better. Suzanna stroked her cheek.

"Come on, Sarah, you shouldn't be crying!" Katy said, nudging her. "We all know you would have lived with Mum forever if you had the chance, but it will be so worth it when you see Nick again. Now dry your eyes, give us cuddles, get on your flight and send me loads of photos when you get there!"

Sarah straightened up and saluted Katy. "Okay, boss, I will. I'm going to miss you both so much. I love you!"

They huddled together in a group hug, and when Sarah finally let go of her mum and sister, she had a huge smile on her face. She was about to push the door to the departure lounge open when Katy called to her.

"Sarah! By the way, don't leave it too long before you bring Nick home to meet me so I can see if I approve or not," she winked. "Also, make sure Mum's fancy man comes along too!"

Sarah laughed when Suzanna playfully poked Katy. She blew them both a kiss, then walked into the lounge and found herself a seat.

This is it, she thought. *Another step closer to Nick!*

Chapter Thirteen

For once, Sarah sat on the plane with no fear. She couldn't be more excited to be going back to Nick, and she was really looking forward to meeting Rachel and the rest of his family. She felt a little gutted for Suzanna, she could tell that she really wanted to see Tim again, and Sarah expected him to be sporting the same glum expression when she saw him again.

Suzanna and Tim had written letters to each other since they had returned to England. Sarah knew immediately when a letter had arrived for Suzanna, the giddiness that she herself had felt whenever a letter from Nick had landed on the doormat was mirrored in her mother. Sarah had never asked Suzanna what she and Tim wrote to each other in the letters, that was their business, of course, but she couldn't help but wonder if they were making plans to see each other again or if something more could happen between them one day. She hoped so, and from the many late-night conversations she'd had with Katy, she clearly thought so too.

The plane started to descend a short time after the pilot had spoken on the intercom asking the passengers to fasten their seatbelts. The butterflies Sarah had felt when she was on stage with Nick the first time she met him returned with a vengeance. She felt so many emotions at the thought of seeing him later that day, and she was so happy that she would be seeing him perform again. Her heart was pounding, and tears welled in her eyes as the landing gear on the plane touched down on the runway.

Seconds after the plane had come to a stop, the passengers around her stood up with looks of determination written all over their faces. Some launched themselves into the aisles, pushing and shoving other passengers and crew trying their best to be the first ones off the plane. Sarah stayed seated during the commotion, allowing the unruly bunch on the left side of the plane to leave way ahead of her.

When the plane had nearly emptied, Sarah took a few deep breaths, checked around her seat to make sure nothing had fallen from her hand luggage and walked down the aisle herself to the open door and into the warm and welcoming Los Angeles air. She smiled when she saw the airport, knowing that Rachel was within those walls somewhere, and she knew just from speaking with her that she would be waiting with a huge grin and open arms.

As soon as she could, once she was inside the airport, Sarah switched on her mobile phone and messaged Suzanna.

I'm here Mummy and I miss you both already! I'm going to fetch my suitcases from baggage claim and then see if I can find Rachel. The flight was nice and comfortable, and my meals were great! I'll send Katy a photo now and tell her I expect lots in return! I'll call you when I can. I love you xoxox

Sarah felt like she was waiting forever for her suitcases to come round the belt to her. She was eager to get going now that she was here. While she was waiting, she took a selfie with the plane that she had just left in view behind her on the tarmac and sent it to Katy.

Her suitcases finally appeared, and she yanked them off with strength she never knew she had. Dragging her suitcases behind her, she moved away from the conveyor belt and walked towards a group of people holding up signs with different people's names on them. She didn't need to scan around the room for long before she spotted Rachel. She was holding a massive bright pink card in front of her with Sarah's name on it and a little love heart drawn in the corner. Sure enough, she did have a huge smile and outstretched arms, and she couldn't have looked happier to see Sarah.

She was a very pretty lady, and the resemblance to Nick was remarkable. She had a mass of curly brown hair, which was the same shade as Nick's. The vibe that she gave off was very calming and friendly, much like the one Sarah had felt when she met Tina for the first time. Sarah instantly felt that Rachel was a woman that she could trust with anything. She was impeccably dressed and looked like she had come to the airport from a glossy magazine photoshoot in her floaty, tanned skirt and brown leather boots. Her pearly white silk shirt looked as if it was brand new and the oversized pair of sunglasses on the top of her head kept her shiny hair off her face. She embraced Sarah as if they were best friends.

"Hi, Sarah, I'm so glad to finally meet you! Nick has not shut up about you; it's so cute!" She squeezed Sarah and rocked her from side to side.

"Hi, it's great to meet you too. I can't believe I'm finally here at last!"

Rachel inhaled sharply when she checked her watch. "It's 1.20 p.m. Come on, honey; we've gotta dash!"

She grabbed the handle of one of Sarah's suitcases and ran towards the exit. Sarah couldn't help chuckling at the sight of Rachel tearing through the airport in heels whilst dragging a heavy suitcase behind her. Once or twice, Rachel nearly lost control of it and had to swerve to stop it from hitting a group of pensioners. She looked back, giggling and slowed her pace so Sarah could catch up, but she was soon off again just as fast as before when she spotted the exit doors.

They made it to Rachel's beautiful Jaguar XF without bashing into anybody or anything. The sapphire blue metallic colour had caught Sarah's attention immediately. It reminded her of the colour of the sexy fitted shirt that Nick had been wearing at his concert.

"Wow! We really did dash!" Rachel exclaimed. "Now, we have lots to do before the performances tonight. Jump in quickly. We need to get to the Diamond!"

Sarah did as she was told and got into the perfectly polished car.

"What's the Diamond?"

"Oh, it's the venue we are performing in. Its full name is The Diamond Lily Hall. It's the most stunning place you'll ever see. The gardens and statues surrounding it are breathtaking. It's such a lovely place to be. I'm so excited for tonight; let's get going!"

Sarah and Rachel talked the whole way to The Diamond Lily Hall. Rachel told Sarah all about the building's history and about the many charitable functions it had hosted. She had performed at many of them and helped raise money as well as donated her own.

Rachel parked her car right beside the backstage door and looked around in all directions as if she was on a mission. Then she relaxed and giggled at Sarah's baffled face.

"I had to check that Nick wasn't here already. He has a habit of turning up way too early to his performances. Let's go before we run into anybody."

Rachel swung her car door open, climbed out and had opened Sarah's door before she was even able to pick up her handbag. She grabbed Sarah's suitcase, which she would be needing for tonight, from the back of the car. She wheeled it to

Sarah, nearly losing control of it in the process. She was practically bouncing on the spot and yanked Sarah by the arm into the building. Rachel clasped Sarah's hand and began power walking through the backstage area. Sarah felt like she was training for a marathon behind her. They finally stopped when they arrived at a door with Rachel's name on it. She unlocked the door, pulled Sarah and the suitcase through it and locked it behind them within seconds.

"Phew, sorry about that, honey, I couldn't risk you being seen by anybody! People will be asking Nick who I'm with if they see me with you, and that would completely ruin the whole plan because he's very nosey and would come knocking." She moved a few stray hairs out of her face, placed her sunglasses back on her head and turned around to look at Sarah. "Are you okay?" she asked, concerned at Sarah's red, puffy face.

"I'll be fine when I've got my breath back," Sarah smiled. Rachel handed her a towel to wipe the sweat from her face and poured her a glass of water. "You can walk really fast without even breaking a sweat!" Sarah laughed.

"You have to when you have an extremely famous brother; you have no choice! He's pushed and pulled me in all directions before now, and trust me; he's nowhere near as gentle as I was with you. Here's a tip for you, Sarah, run fast, so Nick doesn't accidentally pull your arm out of the socket!"

Sarah was having a wonderful time with Rachel. She reminded her a bit of Tina. The warmth oozed out of her just like it had done with her best friend. Sarah's instinct told her that Rachel was indeed a trustworthy person, so she told her all about Tina, including her death. She mentioned the hatred that she had felt for Bill because of what he and Gemma had put Tina through, and she told her how she owed everything that had happened with Nick to Tina.

"She was the reason I bought the ticket to Nick's concert,"

she said. "She always told me to live like each day was my last and to do what feels right. Seize the day! I used to think she was a bit silly for saying that because some of the situations we found ourselves in because of her were extremely stupid and some quite dangerous! After she died, it was like she had embedded her words into my brain. Almost like she was nudging me along to do something I had never done before. That's when I saw that Nick was coming to London, so I booked a ticket to his show and a week in a hotel."

Rachel was in floods of tears by the time Sarah had finished telling her everything. They cuddled and cried together, then Rachel wandered to the refreshments tray to get a glass of wine for each of them so they could toast Tina, just like Sarah and Nick had done. She jumped and nearly dropped the wine when the door handle rattled. Somebody had pushed it down trying to get in.

"Woah, that scared me!" Rachel exclaimed. "Probably just a cleaner checking to see if the dressing rooms are empty or not." She shrugged and carried on with the task at hand.

"So what time are you on stage, Rach?" Sarah asked her.

"I'm on at five thirty and Nick is on before me, so he will be right where we need him to be."

Rachel raised her glass and Sarah clinked her own against it.

"Cheers!" They both chorused.

With ten minutes to go before Nick's performance, Sarah was dressed and ready to go. She had put on the pale pink chiffon dress that she had bought especially for tonight. She had just come out of the bathroom to ask Rachel what she thought when they heard light tapping on the door and Nick's voice coming from the other side. Rachel's eyebrows nearly hit the ceiling and Sarah was frozen to the spot. He knocked again.

"Rach?"

"Hang on, Nick, I'll be right there," she said, as calmly as she could. Despite the fact that the door was locked, Rachel, panicking, held onto the handle just in case Nick tried to open it. She pointed manically to the bathroom, silently urging Sarah to hide in there. Sarah darted towards the bathroom door, trying not to bang into anything as she went. She shut the door behind her as quietly as she could. Rachel waited a few seconds then opened the dressing room door to a very confused-looking Nick.

"Hi, brother, what's going on?" Rachel asked, hoping she sounded casual.

"Are you… okay, Rach?"

"Yeah, fine, why wouldn't I be?"

She didn't dare let him into the room just in case anything of Sarah's was on show, so she stood in the doorway, blocking the way.

"Ah, a few people have said they haven't seen you all day, which is unusual for you. I've been by here a few times myself and tried the handle, but the door was locked."

"That was you!" Rachel exclaimed, not thinking. "I mean, er, I noticed somebody trying my handle while I was just out stretching my legs, but I was too far away to shout, and I couldn't tell it was you from where I was…."

He raised his eyebrows. "Are you sure you're okay, you seem really nervous?"

"Oh yeah, I am a bit, but I'll be fine when I'm on stage." She smiled sweetly at him. In her head she was begging him to go away. To her relief, he did just that.

"I'll see you out there." He kissed her on the cheek and carried on towards the stage.

She locked the door before telling Sarah to come out. Sarah emerged from the bathroom with tears in her eyes and mascara down her face. She was trying to mop it up by dabbing at it with a tissue.

"I'm sorry, I couldn't help it when I heard his voice!"

"Awww, that's okay, honey. Come on, sit down and let me fix that makeup, then we can put the rest of our plan into action and make you and my brother the happiest people ever!"

A few minutes after Nick had gone, they heard music. Rachel snatched up a television remote from the dressing table where Sarah was sitting. She must have pressed ten different buttons before Sarah saw him on the screen.

Nick!

There he was, dressed in a glittery shirt that lit up his face when the stage lights hit the crystals that were on it. She had missed watching him perform. The way he sang, the way he danced and the way the audiences' faces changed from normal expressions to full-on excitement the second he appeared on stage.

But this time, he didn't look like he normally did. He looked happy to be on stage, but at the same time, he wasn't throwing himself into his performance like he always did so effortlessly. He seemed so drained, like he didn't have the energy for it.

"Rach, what's the matter with him?" Sarah asked sadly.

"Oh, nothing that won't be sorted in, hmmm, around fifteen minutes' time." She grinned as she checked her watch and Sarah whipped round to look at her. "He's missing you, you silly goose! But like I said, he will be fine very, very soon. I think I'd better tell you the final part of the plan."

Chapter Fourteen

"Okay, you ready?" Rachel asked.

"Yeah, let's go!"

They walked slowly towards the stage together, hand in hand, trying not to draw attention to themselves. Rachel had given Sarah a subtle fascinator with a net that covered her face slightly. Rachel popped her head into the hall, where she would put the rest of the plan into action. It was in semi-darkness. The lights around the room had been dimmed, and the stage lights had been turned off and were being reset for Rachel's performance. Nick was still on stage, but he was being kept busy.

"Good, he's distracted. He's helping to set the stage for me," she told Sarah. "On three, run to that support post and hide behind it!"

Sarah did as she was told and ran into the hall to the safety of the enormous stone support post. It stretched from floor to ceiling and was so wide that even if Nick did happen to turn towards them, he would not be able to see that either of them were hidden behind it. It was painted white and had a golden leaf pattern and tiny lights snaking all the way up and around it. It was one of six matching supports placed throughout the hall, and it was the closest one to the stage on the right side of the room.

Sarah felt like she was a child again playing tag, and this was her safe place or her base. Her fingers dug into the stone in anticipation of what she was about to do. She could hardly contain herself, seeing how close Nick was, but she had to. She longed to touch him, but she wasn't about to bring the plan crashing down around them when they were this close. It would be so worth the wait when she could finally show him that she was there.

Rachel snapped her fingers in Sarah's face. "Come back to me, Sarah," she laughed. "You look like you are away with the fairies! Now you know what to do. Stay hidden here until I give you the signal. Then take your fascinator off and walk onto the dance floor just in front of the stage. I'll walk over to Nick while you're getting into position and point to you, so he sees you."

"Okay, then what do I do?"

"You will be swept up into my brother's arms where you belong." Rachel bit on her fist to stop the scream of excitement from escaping her. "And… calm! Right, I'd better go the long way round so it looks like I've come from backstage. I'll see you out there!"

Rachel hugged Sarah tightly then ran back through the way they had come into the hall. Sarah's nerves really kicked in now that Rachel had left her here alone. She was tempted to sneak a peek at Nick but didn't dare just in case she gave the game away. She didn't want him to suddenly spot her head poking out from behind the support post, so she stayed as still as she could behind her colossal hiding place.

A few minutes passed and the stage lit up once again. Rachel's sensational singing voice filled the hall. It only occurred to Sarah now that she had never heard Rachel sing before. Her voice was so beautiful and fluttery. *It matches her personality perfectly*, Sarah thought.

The room around her was still in darkness, and the stage lights were so bright there would be no way that Nick would see her now. She started to get worried about whether Nick would be able to see her at all when she walked out onto the floor, whether Rachel pointed her out or not. Remembering the plan, Sarah turned around so the front of her body was against the support post. That way, Rachel had told her, it would be much easier to keep an eye out for her signal.

Then there it was, towards the end of the song, the thumbs-up signal from Rachel. Sarah exhaled and threw off the fascinator. She walked with a purpose onto the floor and stopped in front of the stage. As she did, a spotlight shone down from above and lit her up, making her look like an angel bathed in the light.

Just as Rachel had said, she skipped over to Nick and pointed at Sarah. His face broadened into a huge smile when he saw her standing there. The crowd parted as Nick cleared the stage steps in one jump and ran at Sarah at full speed. He picked her up and swung her around with one arm whilst still singing the last of his lyrics perfectly. Rachel was still on stage finishing the song, but the whole audience had turned and were now transfixed on Nick and Sarah, who were hugging, smiling, laughing and crying all at the same time.

The audience nearly took the roof off when Nick planted the biggest kiss on Sarah's lips. He didn't care who saw; all he could see was Sarah. She was here; he couldn't believe it! He didn't want to stop touching her. He needed to touch her, to feel her beneath his hands, to know that this was actually real and not a dream that he was about to wake up from. She was back in his arms and he never wanted her to leave them again. He looked over his shoulder at his sneaky sister on the stage. He had about a hundred questions for her later. She winked and laughed but, Nick noticed, she was crying too. He winked back at her and then turned his attention back to Sarah.

"Hi!" Sarah said to Nick. She didn't know what else to say. She was still in disbelief that she was finally back with him.

"Hi. I take it you've met my sister?" Nick laughed.

"Mmm hmm!" Sarah replied.

"I've missed you so much, and your timing couldn't have been better!"

"Why?" Confusion crossed Sarah's face.

Then she heard it.

"All My Love!" Sarah exclaimed. The song that Nick had been singing when she had joined him on the stage at his concert.

He put his microphone in the back pocket of his trousers and lifted Sarah straight off her feet and up into the air. He kissed her as he lowered his arms and smiled at the feel of her body against his. The crowd had formed a circle around them, watching as they danced and swayed together to Nick's song. Even though the room was packed with people, it felt to them both that this was their private moment. Nick started to sing the words that Sarah knew so well and that she had sung herself so many times before. His soft, sexy voice made her feel like she was sinking into a hot bath. He ran his hands down her body as he sang, getting as close to her as he possibly could. Even this wasn't close enough for Sarah, and she felt breathless when he pulled away from her slowly and strolled back onto the stage, happiness radiating from inside him. He had come alive since he had seen Sarah and it showed in his performance.

All eyes were back on Nick, although Sarah did have the occasional stares coming her way. It unnerved her a bit, but she had expected that once Rachel had told her what they would be doing here. She would very soon be having a taste of what Nick had to deal with, the unwelcome attention and god knows how many photographs with people speculating about who she was and how they had met. Sarah looked away from somebody's staring eyes and saw that Tim had placed himself a lot closer to

Sarah than Nick. She felt that there had been some unspoken conversation between Nick and Tim as soon as they had seen that she was there. That he was to protect Sarah first.

It made her nervous to be amongst all of these people who were now very interested in her, and it must have shown on her face. Nick had already danced back towards the stage steps and gestured, telling her to come onto the stage with him. Tim had followed right behind her and stood on the bottom step of the stage with his arms by his sides.

It sounded crazy, but she felt safe up here even though all eyes were on her, because she was in Nick's arms again. When she was with him, she didn't have a care in the world. But without him, she felt lost.

After Nick's performance, they all went back to Rachel's dressing room. Nick was giddy. He still had not got his head around Sarah being here, appearing out of nowhere right in front of him.

"How did this happen?" Nick burst out as soon as they had walked through the door.

Sarah let Rachel explain.

"I saw how miserable you were, and I wanted you to be happy, so I had been thinking for ages about what I could do. I heard you telling Tim how much you were missing Sarah, which gave me the idea to try to get her over here early to surprise you. I got her phone number and email address out of your phone and called her while I was in the bathroom at your place." Nick was silent, listening intently. "So anyway," Rachel continued. "Of course Sarah agreed to come a day earlier than planned, so I arranged a new flight for her, picked her up from the airport this afternoon and then I hid her in here until my performance. Oh yeah, that was why my door was locked. It's a good thing it was too, or else you would have waltzed in and ruined everything!"

He was gobsmacked. "So nobody else knew?"

"No. Just me and Sarah," she grinned. "I couldn't tell anybody else. I couldn't risk you finding out, could I?"

"I'm still in shock." Nick turned to Sarah and softly stroked her face. "Every day without you was torture. I was counting down the hours! I've missed you from the moment we had to say goodbye at the airport, and I hadn't felt like myself again until I saw you." They kissed.

"All right, who wants to celebrate?" Rachel shouted.

After a jovial few hours in Rachel's dressing room, Nick, Sarah and Tim drove back to Nick's house. Sarah sighed contentedly as Tim turned onto the tree-lined driveway.

"Home," she whispered.

"Forever," Nick smiled. "Go inside and make yourself comfortable while we unload the car. Miranda has been looking forward to seeing you again." Sarah smiled at the thought of Miranda, Nick's housekeeper. She was a lovely, jolly lady with the friendliest smile Sarah had ever seen.

Sarah climbed out of the car after Nick and made her way inside her new home. Miranda was waiting in the foyer with two glasses of champagne on a tray.

"Miranda, hi! It's great to see you again!" Sarah exclaimed, hugging her carefully so she didn't knock the tray.

"You too, Sarah. Welcome back! Actually, I should say welcome home!" Miranda said excitedly. "Would you like some champagne?"

"Oooo yes, please." Sarah lifted both glasses from the tray and handed one to Miranda. "Come on, let's go and have a chat while the boys are busy."

Chapter Fifteen

The time had flown by. Sarah had been living with Nick for two months and Nick had proudly shown her off to every member of his family. She had been particularly nervous about meeting his mother Gloria, his father Andrew and his twin brothers. Chad and Cole were definitely a cheeky pair of chaps and teased her from the get-go. Very early on, Sarah learnt that Nick was usually the butt of their jokes, but he always came back with either a quick retort or a rude hand gesture, the latter being only if his mother wasn't around!

Gloria and Andrew were a very sweet couple, and Sarah could tell they were amazing parents. Even though their children were all in their thirties, Gloria still fussed over them whenever she was around them, and she called them nearly every day. She was a very stylish lady who wore flowing skirts and blouses most of the time, and she always piled her curly blonde hair on the top of her head with a single clip.

Andrew, on the other hand, could usually be found in a T-shirt covered with dry paint, grey jogging bottoms and old, battered-looking trainers. Nick had explained to Sarah that his dad liked to potter about in his garden and shed all the time, so he constantly wore his 'ruined clothes', as Andrew would call them. Sarah felt her heart tug at the thought of her own father pottering about in his garden. She felt sad that Stan and Andrew had never got to meet; they would have been the best of friends, swapping gardening tips and tools.

Nick's schedule had taken some getting used to. Sarah didn't realise that he would be out of the house for fifteen hours a day on some days. She missed him when he was out all day, but she kept herself busy. She had signed up for an online photography course and was loving it. She had always had a keen interest in photography. In her teenage years, Sarah used to pretend that she was a photographer at a fashion show and Katy was her model, walking just like the professional models did on the catwalk.

Finding out what Nick had to do each day was always exciting for Sarah. It still seemed a bit unreal to her at times. Sometimes he took her to the sets of his music videos, where she would watch him in astonishment, still feeling the excitement of a fan seeing their favourite artist up close and performing. Another time he had taken her to the recording studio to lay down the background vocals for a new song that he had been working on. He was so at ease behind the microphone. It was like he could feel the music in his veins flowing throughout his body.

One evening he told her that he had an early start on the set of his new music video the following day. He had already left by the time Sarah awoke the next morning. She decided she would take the opportunity while he was out all day to do some exploring of the house. Nick had already shown her every room in the house, of course, but there was one room that she was dying to look at properly. The dance studio.

Sarah gasped when she set foot in the massive space. It was incredible! There were beautiful arches that ran around the back and left side of the room, with an area behind them that you could walk into. Nick had used these spaces for a seating area. There were elaborately carved wooden benches underneath the arches that looked as though they had never been touched. They probably hadn't because Sarah imagined that Nick didn't sit down much when he was in here.

She flicked one of the many switches on the wall, and lights around and under each archway lit up. She smiled at the sight then switched them off again. The next one she flicked was the spotlight switch, which lit up different areas of the floor. The final one she pressed, she left on. Soft lighting lit up all around the edge of the ceiling, which gave the studio a cosy feeling. Sarah thought that would have been impossible given the size of the room. The flooring was a hardwood-based sprung floor. She felt like she was bouncing as she walked across it; it was perfect for dancing.

Wow! Sarah whispered when she noticed the stage. It was a similar setup to how it had been at Nick's concert, except there were no band members behind the instruments and the lights were switched off. She guessed Nick used this stage when he planned his concerts. She stood for a moment and imagined him swaying to his songs behind the microphone stand. Then, something tucked under the archway to the right of the stage caught her eye. She went to investigate and found a large trophy cabinet that was full of dancing trophies and medals. She laughed when she saw a photograph of a very young-looking Nick with his hair slicked back with copious amounts of hair gel. He was standing shyly in front of an older boy who had his hands resting on Nick's shoulders and a shiny medal around his neck. Nick was shaking hands with the lady who was smiling broadly on the left-hand side of him, handing him the trophy that this photograph was leaning against. Sarah read the engraving: *Nick Taylor – Street dance champion – Los Angeles – 1999.* She perused the trophy cabinet a little longer before making her way to the grand stage.

She climbed the steps to the stage and saw a sound system

with lots of different buttons on it. She ran her fingers gently over them before deciding that she didn't dare press any other than the play button. She figured she would leave it running and hope there was something on here that she could dance to. She had been longing to get her dancing shoes on, blast some music and dance her heart out in here since the moment she saw it, but she wanted to be alone when she did for the first time. She saw her opportunity when Nick was out of the house, filming his new video.

Sarah was a decent dancer herself, but she felt nervous at the thought of dancing in front of anybody other than her former dance teacher and classmates, especially Nick. He was such a fantastic dancer, and she knew she would instantly go to pieces if he watched her.

The music started. It was an upbeat song that she had never heard before, and she broke into the warm-up routine that had been embedded into her brain by her dance teacher. She giggled at herself in the mirror, which stretched all the way along the right side of the studio. At this moment, she felt completely carefree. She had not danced properly since Tina died, and she had forgotten how much she loved it. It took her back to the days when she was performing on stage alongside her classmates, the thrill she had felt then and what she was feeling now was electric. She had missed this. She had been in the studio for hours when she started to get giddy. She was ecstatic when she began performing routines she thought she had forgotten. She was enjoying herself so much that she completely lost track of time and didn't notice when the door to the studio creaked open.

Nick sneaked into the dance studio and hid himself behind one of the archways so Sarah wouldn't see him. He peeked around the wall and was instantly enthralled by her. The way she moved her body in time to the music was exquisite. He watched as she got into a familiar position and perfectly pulled off one of his own dance moves that he often performed on stage. He giggled and smirked as he slowly and very quietly walked past each archway, making his way around the room unnoticed. He didn't want to give himself away just yet. As the music of the ballroom number that Sarah was dancing to was building up, she performed three amazing pirouettes, one after the other. Nick got excited and joined in on the last turn with her from his hiding place in the shadows. He kicked the wall in the process, which made him swear. He clapped his hand to his mouth, hoping Sarah hadn't heard him. Luckily she had the music on louder than he usually did, and she was in her own little world, so she was still blissfully unaware that he was there. The music started to slow and quieten down. Nick froze when Sarah turned to face where he was standing. She turned gracefully and lowered herself to the floor, not realising she was directly in front of him.

When she bowed her head and closed her eyes, Nick saw his chance. He tiptoed out of his hiding place and knelt down in front of Sarah. He took hold of her hands softly, and she jumped at his touch. She opened her eyes and looked straight into his but did not say a word. He had captivated her just from the look he was giving her. He stroked her lips with his thumb, and together they got to their feet. Nick pulled Sarah towards the centre of the studio, not taking his eyes off her. He twirled her around under his arm like a prince would with his princess. He moved in close to her body, put both of his hands on her face and placed the softest kiss on her lips. Sarah stood completely still, eyes closed, hoping he would be coming back for more, but instead, she felt him hold one of her hands with his and place his other hand on her back. He was holding her in a dancing frame. She put her hand on his shoulder, and the next thing she knew, Nick was whirling her around the floor in a waltz whilst adding a bit of his own style. He lowered her down and moved his face close to hers. She puckered her lips just as he swooped her up and carried on twirling around with her again. *Why is he teasing me?* she thought.

A few minutes later, she was starting to get very dizzy when Nick stopped dancing and stepped backwards away from her, singing the song that was playing in the background to her. Her dizziness was easing when she saw Nick slowly drop to one knee. He was holding an open box out in front of him with a gorgeous platinum and diamond ring inside. Sarah stared at the ring, then at Nick and back again. He was grinning at the look on her face, shock written all over it.

"Come here then!" Nick told Sarah, laughing. She ran over to him and squeezed him so tight. She let go and knelt on the floor in front of him.

"Will you marry me?" he asked her.

"Yes, I will!" She burst into very happy tears as Nick took the ring carefully from the box and slid it down her finger. The square diamond suited her finger perfectly, and the smaller diamonds on the band caught the light beautifully, making it sparkle and shine around the room. Now Nick kissed her properly, showing her how much he wanted her to be his wife. He picked her up and spun her around in his arms. He put her down gently and they swayed together to the music.

"I love you, and I have been so desperate to do that all day!" he said. "As soon as the director said we were done, I ran back to my car so I could come back to you."

"I love you too, and is that why you are still wearing the

clothes from your music video?" she laughed.

Nick looked down at himself. He was indeed still wearing the white leather trousers and silver shirt.

"Err… yeah. I was going to propose to you this morning while you were in bed, but you looked so peaceful sleeping, I didn't want to disturb you… plus, I wouldn't have gone to work if you had just agreed to marry me." He winked and had a very cheeky look on his face and a glint in his eye.

"Mmm, I think you should have done it this morning then," Sarah purred.

She sashayed to the doorway, turned back to Nick and with a sultry look of her own in her eyes, she gestured with her finger for him to join her. He didn't need asking twice. Nick ran to the door, faster than he had ever moved before.

Chapter Sixteen

The screams that emanated down the phone from Suzanna and Katy the following day nearly pierced Sarah's eardrums.

"So you're both happy then?" Sarah asked, laughing as she saw their beaming faces on her phone screen.

"Sarah, we are ecstatic!" Katy shouted in reply. "Does this mean I will be meeting my soon-to-be brother-in-law very soon?"

"Definitely, yeah!"

Suzanna suddenly moved away from Katy's side, and Sarah could no longer see her.

"Are you happy, Mum?" she shouted, hoping that it would make Suzanna come back to the call. "Mum? Katy, where's Mum gone?"

Katy looked behind her then turned back to the screen, rolling her eyes and grinning.

"She's crying, Sar; she can't speak!" she laughed. "She's gone to get tissues. Mum, come back here."

Suzanna appeared in front of Sarah once more with both hands full of tissues.

"Are you okay, Mum?" Sarah asked. "You are happy, aren't you?"

Composing herself, Suzanna answered. "Of course I'm happy, darling. I was secretly hoping this would happen soon. I told Tim about it when I was over there with you. He told me he had a feeling it would happen sooner rather than later."

"Are you forgetting we are on a video call, sis? Show us your engagement ring!" Katy demanded.

Sarah held her left hand up to the screen to show off the new rock on her finger.

"Wow, that is a beauty!" Katy seemed entranced by it.

"It certainly is!" Suzanna agreed.

"Well, thank you very much!" Nick made them all jump as he sneaked up behind Sarah to join in the call.

"Nick, oh my goodness! Hi, I'm Katy!"

Now she was beside herself. Sarah could have sworn Katy had just tried to shake Nick's hand through the screen. Sarah looked away in an attempt to hide her laughter and to save her sister the embarrassment. If Nick had noticed, he didn't let on.

"Hi Katy, it's great to see you! How are you and Suzanna?"

"We are great, especially now since this call! We're so happy for both of you!"

"Thank you. I'm a very lucky man; your sister is an incredible person." He put his arm around Sarah's shoulder and pulled her close to him. "We will be throwing an engagement party really soon, so you can come over here and we can finally meet in person. Oh, excuse me a second." Nick got up and walked away from the screen.

"Oh man, Sarah, I can't believe I've just spoken to Nick Taylor!"

Sarah laughed at this. "Katy, you do realise he will be your family soon, don't you?"

"Yeah, but, wow… Nick Taylor. It's just weird going from only seeing him on TV and in celebrity magazines to then talking to him on a video call in real life!" Katy was majorly starstruck. "To be honest, I didn't expect him to be so friendly because he never looks happy in magazines, but he seems like a normal person!"

“I’ll let you in on a little secret,” Sarah said. Katy edged closer to the screen in anticipation. Suzanna sat back stifling a giggle, knowing what Sarah was about to say. “He is a normal person!”

“You fool!” Katy roared. “I thought you were going to say something really juicy then!”

Suzanna and Sarah couldn’t contain themselves any longer. Their raucous laughter burst out of them.

“I’m sorry little sis, but did you expect him to be some kind of alien or something? Just because he’s famous doesn’t mean he isn’t a human being. I was nervous around him too when I first met him, and I’m talking about when it was just me and him. Obviously, I was petrified about the thousands of screaming fans I stood up in front of beforehand! He isn’t the stuck-up celebrity that the magazines make him out to be. He just likes his privacy. I’m looking forward to the day when you meet him properly; then you will see what the real Nick is all about.”

Nick came skidding into view again. “Sorry about that, ladies. I’ve just come back to say goodbye and to say to you Suzanna…” he looked over his shoulder, then back to the screen and whispered, “… Tim can’t wait to see you!” He winked and disappeared again as quick as a flash. Tim could be heard shouting “Oi!” in the background, followed by Nick’s distinctive laugh.

Suzanna started to fan her face whilst trying to look unbothered. She failed miserably.

“Mother, as if you’re not thinking the exact same thing as Tim!” Katy said, chastising her. “We aren’t stupid, you know.”

Sarah pointed to Katy and nodded, showing that she completely agreed with what she had said. “As much as I love you, I’m going to have to leave you now. I’ll be in touch with the deets of the party when I know more. I love you and I'll see you soon." Sarah blew kisses at the screen.

"We love you too. Bye."

Sarah looked up and saw Nick standing in front of her with a mischievous look.

"You little tinker, teasing my mum like that!"

"Oh, I'm not teasing," he told her. "I just told her what's written all over Tim's face."

The next day, Nick plonked himself down on the sofa next to Sarah and showed her his laptop screen.

"How magnificent is that?" His eyebrows were raised; he was pointing at a stately manor set within stunning grounds.

"Wow!" Sarah exclaimed, pulling the laptop towards her. "Is that a wedding venue?"

"Yep. Fancy taking a look? Shall I book an appointment?"

"Yes, book an appointment. It looks like a lovely place to get married in."

He leapt up and ran back to his office, laptop in hand. Sarah could hear him talking on his phone within seconds of him being in there. She popped her head inside the door and found him scribbling on a piece of paper hurriedly. He spotted her and pumped the air with his fist, confirming to her that he had indeed booked an appointment to have a look around the amazing place. He ended the call a few minutes later and looked serenely happy.

"Well, you're planning things quickly, aren't you, Mr. Taylor?"

"Can you blame me?" He got up from his desk and sauntered over to Sarah. He tucked his arms under hers and stroked her back. "I can't wait for you to be my wife."

Sarah was amazed at how many different appointments Nick had booked and how many different websites had been bookmarked on his laptop since they had viewed and paid for the manor house a few weeks before. He had made enquiries with venue dressers, a photographer, a videographer and lots more that Sarah wouldn't have even thought of.

"Gosh, Nick, is wedding planning actually your day job? Do you only moonlight as a singer?" She laughed as his head popped up behind stacks of paper. He had a pencil sticking out of one side of his mouth.

"No, I definitely don't plan weddings for a living. I'm just a lot more into this than I thought I would be!" He smirked, then looked back down at whatever it was that he had been scribbling before Sarah had come into his office.

"Hmmm. I thought famous people hired wedding planners," she teased, leaning on the mountain of paperwork on his desk. Nick's face looked panicked when he spotted Sarah doing this.

"Okay, I'll move, don't worry," she said, holding her hands up.

"Thank you," he said. "And no, I didn't want to hire a wedding planner. I didn't want somebody coming in here telling us how to plan our wedding day." He held his hand out to Sarah and sat her down on his lap. "This is our day and it should be personal to us. I want us both to choose everything from the colour scheme, flowers, food, the cake. I do have a couple of small requests, though?"

"Go on," Sarah said, intrigued.

"It should go without saying that I want you to choose your dress and the bridesmaids' dresses, and I would like to choose the guys' suits. That way, we will all be surprised when we see each other on the day." His face lit up with happiness, imagining everybody dressed up to the nines.

"Okay, what's the other request?"

"I would like to choose your entrance music when you walk down the aisle, and I would like to keep it a secret until the day."

"I think that's a lovely idea! I'm happy with that."

Nick's eyes danced with glee, and Sarah could only guess what he had in mind.

Over the following few weeks, Sarah and Nick had attended the appointments that Nick had made with various places and had made decisions quite quickly. They set their wedding date for the following April, just six months away. Sarah had been to a bridal boutique by herself and, to her surprise, had found her wedding dress already. She had chosen dresses for her bridesmaids, Katy and Rachel, who had been ecstatic when Sarah and Nick had asked them to be their bridesmaids, so Sarah couldn't wait to see their faces when they laid eyes on their dresses.

Suzanna and Katy arrived in Los Angeles on the morning of the engagement party. Just like she had been on the video call, Katy was undeniably starstruck when she met Nick. Sarah was dumbfounded that her sister was actually capable of being rendered speechless! Katy held her hand out nervously towards Nick, who shook it and then welcomed his future sister-in-law to his house with a peck on her cheek.

As a special surprise, Nick had treated Sarah, Suzanna, Katy and his own mother and sister to a spa day at the most luxurious place ever. They spent the morning having massages, facials and being pampered in every way possible. They indulged in the many sandwiches, cakes and drinks on offer when their afternoon tea had arrived at midday. They were all still wearing the soft, snuggly robes that the spa had provided as they tucked in. Sarah had not yet informed the ladies where they were off to next.

"So Sarah," Rachel said, sipping her wine. "Have you been recognised yet?"

"No, not really. Nick is trying to be smart." Sarah giggled at a memory. "Not long after I moved here, we went out together. He spotted a camera from quite a way away, so he strode ahead of Tim and me, so it looked like he was just walking past somebody he didn't know. Tim was wearing shorts, a T-shirt and a cap, so he looked more inconspicuous than he usually does. Anyway, Nick's plan worked and they did follow just him, but they managed to get me in the shot as he was walking past me. Come to think of it now; I'm astounded that nothing appeared in the paper from the performances at The Diamond Lily when I came back here."

"Nobody from the media was allowed in, and I think the venue had an extremely strict no phones policy in place that night. Hmm, I wonder who asked them to do that?" Rachel put her finger and thumb on her chin in a thinking gesture and then winked.

"You?" Sarah and the others laughed as Rachel nodded.

"I don't think you'll be so lucky when you're married to him. He gets hounded if he's ever spotted," Gloria piped up. She looked a little bit worried.

"I know, Gloria," Sarah said in a soothing voice. "But Nick is trying to prepare me as best he can, and I know it will probably happen sooner rather than later because I will be going to events and things with him. I do feel safe, though, because Tim is with me. I'm sure Nick has secretly made him my own personal security guard because he sends him with me if I go out anywhere. Like now, for instance." She giggled and looked across at Tim reading a newspaper at one of the tables nearby.

"How are you feeling about the party today, sweetheart?" Suzanna asked.

"To be honest, Mum, I'm a mixed bag of emotions. I'm happy because it's my engagement party, I'm nervous because there's going to be loads of people there who I haven't met yet, and at the same time, I'm sad because the rest of my family aren't here."

Suzanna stroked the back of Sarah's hand. "I know, but it's hard for them to fly over just for a couple of days, but they will all be here for the wedding."

"I know. I just miss them."

"I know you do, darling." Suzanna reached out and cuddled her eldest daughter.

"Okay, ladies, enough feeling sad for now. Let's get dressed. I have a surprise for you!" Sarah said mysteriously.

She had wanted to keep the trip to the bridal shop a secret for as long as possible. They were all happily chatting in the car when Tim pulled into a car parking space behind the shop and announced that they had arrived. All five ladies started to scramble for the car door handles when they realised where they were.

"Ahh!" Katy screamed. "We're going to see your dress!"

They walked into the bridal boutique beaming with joy, Sarah clinging onto Suzanna and Katy's hands, and were greeted by a very friendly lady who introduced herself as Stephanie. Her blonde ringlet hair was pinned back with two bright red slides that matched the colour of her plump lips, and her tight-fitting shirt was tucked into her black pencil skirt. Tim pushed the door open a few seconds later, shut it quickly behind him and gave Stephanie the thumbs up. Stephanie returned his gesture with a smile and glided across the floor towards the door. Katy almost choked on Stephanie's strong perfume as she walked past her. She locked the door of the bridal shop behind Tim. Sarah was the only one of the ladies who noticed this silent conversation between them and realised that this was Nick's idea. He had requested that the shop be closed once they were inside so nobody could take pictures of her if she were to be recognised by any chance. The last thing he or Sarah wanted was for her wedding dress or Katy and Rachel's bridesmaids' dresses to be plastered all over the front pages of the newspapers the following morning.

"Follow me, ladies!" Stephanie said gleefully.

She led them upstairs to a room that was bigger than Nick's dance studio. It had many changing rooms all around the edge with floor-to-ceiling mirrors inside. There were rails upon rails of dresses here for every occasion, but all eyes fell on the many rows of wedding dresses. Stephanie had stood herself next to a podium covered in a silk sheet, waiting for their attention to return to her. She picked up a mirrored, silver tray from the podium and handed each of them a glass of champagne from it. She then held the tray in front of her face to check her reflection. She patted her hair, smiled at herself, then put the tray carefully back down onto the podium.

"Darlings!" Stephanie said loudly, clapping her hands twice. "Come this way."

Stephanie strutted across the room in her sky-high stiletto heels, making her way over to two long, pristine white dress bags. She checked the names on the bags, then handed one to Katy and one to Rachel. With confused looks on their faces, Stephanie ushered them inside two changing rooms next to each other. There was silence in the room apart from the unzipping of the bags. Then both sets of curtains were yanked open. Katy and Rachel stood with their mouths wide open in shock.

"What?" Sarah teased, trying to look serious.

"Sarah, this is the most beautiful dress I've ever seen!" Katy exclaimed.

"Mine too, Sar, I mean, we are going to look damn fine in these!" Rachel added, laughing.

"Go back in and try them on then, girls. I've been waiting ages for this!"

"Let me know if you need any help, and please be careful with my curtains." Stephanie's voice, although soft, oozed danger. She stroked the velvet curtains almost seductively and gazed at them as if she was spellbound by them.

Katy cleared her throat, snapping Stephanie out of her weird daydream and edged back into the changing room to try on her dress. Stephanie shook her head and adjusted her glasses with one finger. She grabbed a glass of champagne for herself and glugged it down in one. Sarah focused solely on the curtains willing them to open to relieve the awkwardness of the situation. Then, obviously not having paid any attention to Stephanie's feelings towards the curtains, Katy yanked them open once more and stepped forward, out of the changing room with tears welling in her eyes.

"Sarah, I can't believe you chose this for me; it's gorgeous!" Katy shouted the last two words. She whirled around to face the mirror beside Sarah and gasped when she saw herself. The calming, blue colour of the dress made Katy think of the sea around a tropical island. The corset bodice had a sweetheart neckline and was a mixture of soft silk and pretty lace. The lace, which sat over the top of the silk, had been flawlessly sewn into lots of delicate flowers. Small silver and blue sequins sat neatly in the centre of the flowers, making the bodice sparkle when the light reflected off them. The skirt of the dress was made from silk and tulle material and had more flowers cascading down the front and back. Katy swished the dress back and forth, unable to tear her eyes away from it.

"So you like it then?" Sarah laughed.

"I love it, I absolutely love it, Sar," replied Katy, still swishing in the mirror. "It's beautiful!"

"That's why it suits you so well." Katy clutched Sarah's hand. Suzanna, overcome with emotion, burst into loud sobs.

"Mum!" Both girls said together, concerned.

"I'm sorry," Suzanna choked, waving them away. "I'm just so happy! Every mother looks forward to this day, looking at dresses in a bridal shop with her daughters, but nothing can prepare you for how it makes you feel inside!" She stood and engulfed both of them in a smothering hug just as Rachel's curtain was drawn back. Stephanie eyed Rachel suspiciously, watching her every move as she poured another glass of champagne.

"Oh my goodness, Rach!" Gloria cried. Her own happy tears were forming in the corners of her eyes.

Rachel's dress was the same as Katy's. Sarah had been curious, wondering how they would look on both of them, especially with them having different body shapes, but she needn't have worried because the dresses suited them both perfectly. Sarah was thrilled.

Now she was ready to move on to what she anticipated would be the biggest surprise of the day. It was time to show the ladies her wedding dress! When Sarah stood, Stephanie stopped filing her nails and power walked across the boutique. Sarah winked to the ladies as she strolled into a changing room with

Stephanie behind her.

"Sarah, what are you doing?" Katy asked in a questioning tone.

"You'll see," she sang.

When she came back out five minutes later, there was silence. Suzanna, Katy, Rachel and Gloria were speechless. The biggest compliment as far as Sarah was concerned. Sarah had never liked being the centre of attention before but, after Tina's death, Sarah saw how much love people had for her, so she felt ready to relish this moment. She stepped up onto the box that Katy and Rachel had used and admired her reflection. She smiled at the elegance of herself. The dress was a classic A-line style, although it did have some princessy elements to it, such as lots of sparkle, sequins and pearls on the bodice and a stunning lace back. The shoulder straps were bedecked with more sparkly stones that shone as Sarah moved around. The lace hem ran all around the bottom of the tulle skirt and all the way along the cathedral length train.

She let out her breath and a small giggle and turned fully to face her family.

"You look absolutely stunning," squeaked Suzanna, tears choking her slightly.

"You do. You look well fit!" Katy laughed.

Sarah stood between her two bridesmaids and allowed the very proud mums to take a photograph, with a promise not to show anybody else.

Stephanie was near enough galloping towards them with refilled glasses of champagne for all of them on her mirrored tray again. Her eyes had a glazed, glassy look to them that was not there when they had come into the shop.

"That woman's balance is impeccable!" Sarah whispered to

her bridesmaids, stunned that Stephanie hadn't spilt any of the drinks.

"Who wants champagne!" Stephanie cried extremely loudly.

"No, we're fine, thank you very much!" Gloria snapped. "I think the girls had better take those dresses off before any drink gets spilt, and you…." she gently pulled the tray out of Stephanie's hands, "… I think you have had a bit too much to drink. Why don't you let us out and then go home?"

Very shortly after that conversation, they were back in the safety of Tim's car and on their way back to the house. Sarah made a mental note to herself to pick up the dresses a few days earlier than planned just in case they might need to fix any *mishaps* that the dresses may have acquired at the hands of Stephanie whilst under the influence of champagne. Sarah hoped that Stephanie had heeded Gloria's advice and gone home immediately.

Chapter Seventeen

Sarah, Suzanna, Katy, Rachel and Gloria arrived back at the house later that afternoon. Each one of them was laden with several enormous shopping bags in hand, thanks to Nick's credit card and his insistence that they all go shopping and treat themselves. Tim, who was bringing up the rear, looked like a circus artist walking a tightrope, balancing a stack of boxes that were precariously swaying in the wind. The ladies were astounded when they saw that in true Nick Taylor style, the garden had been transformed into a five-star restaurant! Sarah was gobsmacked when she saw the huge rectangular dinner tables placed just as they would be if they were in an actual restaurant. Nick was already dressed in his impeccable black tuxedo, with a crisp white shirt and black bow tie. Sarah licked her lips at the sight of him.

"Whit woo, Mr. Taylor!" Sarah purred as she sidled up to him.

He snaked his arm around her back and kissed her neck.

"I was thinking exactly the same thing."

Sarah looked down at herself in her vest top, old grey jogging bottoms and battered trainers. She gave him a baffled look.

"Oh yeah, I look gorgeous!" Sarah laughed sarcastically. "Thank you for treating us, you generous thing." She kissed him on his lips.

"You're welcome. I hope you had fun?"

"We did! It was great to have some time with Mum and Katy, and it was a really nice opportunity for them to get to know your mum and Rachel better." She smiled at them all huddled together, laughing with each other. "I'm going to take the girls upstairs to get ready before everybody arrives."

Sarah finally had a minute to herself after greeting around a hundred people. She gazed around the garden, with a glass of wine in her hand, watching the guests greet each other with air kisses and handshakes. All of the guests had adhered to the dress code listed on their invitations, which was '*formal wear*'. Sarah noticed how their faces changed from when they walked through the gates to when they walked into the garden. They looked equally as awestruck as Sarah had been, wearing smart tuxedos and beautiful ball gowns or pretty dresses. Sarah had chosen to wear her floaty, cream dress that she had been wearing when Nick had invited herself and Suzanna over for their two-week visit. Sarah remembered that night extremely well, first the luxury hotel with the huge bouquet of flowers from Nick, then the performance at the club, him kneeling in front of her and singing in his extremely sexy falsetto voice, then finally….

"I hope you're thinking about me!" Nick whispered to Sarah as he pinched her bum.

"What?" She said, startled.

"You looked like you were miles away with a dreamy look on that gorgeous face of yours." He grinned. "So tell me, what was I doing in your head?"

"I was just thinking about the first night we er…." Sarah winked.

"Oooo, saucy! Hmm, yes, that dress makes me think about

that night too. I recognise it as the one that was thrown onto my bedroom floor," he giggled.

Katy's voice came from nowhere. "Yeah, thanks for that, guys! Next time, I'll definitely be making my presence known!" She walked off with her camera in her hand, shaking her head in what Sarah guessed was disgust, muttering as she went. "Trying to get a natural-looking shot, overhearing things I definitely didn't want to hear, won't be doing that again!"

"Sorry, Katy!" Sarah shouted, blushing slightly.

"Ah well, she should just be thankful she can't read my mind right now!" Nick teased. "Then she would be disgusted!" He nuzzled into her neck, kissing her softly.

"Put her down, Nicholas!"

Sarah jumped.

"Chad, Cole, hi! How great to see you!" Nick said, but not actually sounding at all like he was pleased to see them.

"Dad sent us over to ask you when the food's being served. Says he's hungry." Cole laughed.

"We don't think Mom feeds him," Chad added to Sarah.

Nick rolled his eyes, held Sarah's hand and headed towards the gazebo where an orchestra band was setting up their instruments for the party. Nick took hold of the microphone.

"Good evening, everybody! Sarah and I would like to thank you all for coming tonight." He turned to Sarah and smiled, feeling the tension radiate from her due to all of these people's eyes on her. He squeezed her hand, silently giving her reassurance.

"We have a three-course meal organised by my very dear friend Miranda along with the talented chefs of Freshwater Springs restaurant." Everybody applauded enthusiastically. "Now, I have something to say that quite frankly, I am a little afraid of telling my fiancée." Sarah stared at him, suddenly petrified. "I left my brothers in charge of the entertainment that you may or may not enjoy tonight, and I have no idea what they have planned." Laughter broke out at the uncomfortable look Nick was now sporting on his face. The welcoming tone of Rachel carried through the warm air.

"Don't worry, Nick, I supervised. There's nothing dodgy!" Sarah visibly breathed a sigh of relief.

"I will thank you on behalf of my fiancee whose heart has just started to beat again!" There was gentle laughter from the guests. "Well, I'm going to sit down now before Dad comes up and drags me off. He's hungry, poor guy. Everybody enjoy your meal and have a fantastic night!"

Before Sarah and Nick had even taken their seats with their parents and siblings, Andrew had his hand in the air beckoning one of the waiters to their table so he could place his order.

"I was wasting away whilst you were rabbiting on Nick!" Andrew exclaimed.

"I highly doubt that, Dad, but I have to thank our guests. It's a polite thing to do."

"Oh, ignore him, Nick," Gloria smiled. "I must have forgotten to point out where the kitchen was before I left the house today. Your dear old dad hasn't eaten a single thing all day!"

Andrew folded his arms and sulked as laughter around the table erupted. His mood did not shift into a much happier one until a plate full of steak, vegetables and mashed potato was put in front of him. He devoured his main meal and his dessert of apple pie and ice cream and was the first one at the table to finish. Soon after, with his belly full, he was back to his usual merry self.

"I'm sorry, I should have warned you before now, Sarah,"

Gloria began. "These Taylor men are grumpy when they're hungry!"

"What's that, darling?" Andrew asked, in a state of pure joy.

"Oh, nothing." She stroked his hand then turned back to Sarah with a look on her face that said, *trust me.*

Sarah noticed some whispering and pointing going on between the twins towards the end of the meal. She eyed them suspiciously and received two bright, megawatt smiles back in return.

"You two are being rather shifty," she stated.

"We're not," insisted Chad. "We're just making sure your night goes perfectly."

"Hmm, okay."

"Right, come on, let's go!" Cole backhanded his twin in his chest and raced towards the gazebo. The orchestra came to an abrupt end as he roared down the microphone. "Let's get this party started!"

Upbeat, party songs suddenly started to blast from two gigantic speakers. They had been hidden behind a decorative wooden fence which was covered from top to bottom with lots of pretty white and blue flowers. The fence doubled as a background for photographs which the guests had posed in front of when they had arrived.

Chad strutted and danced back and forth through the gazebo as if he was in a boyband from the nineties! He snatched another microphone from a stand as the music was lowered.

"Yo yo yo, my people!" The guests stopped dancing and smiled at the twins. "I'm sorry to interrupt; I just really need to say something." Chad looked over his shoulder at his twin who was covering his mouth, looking fit to burst with laughter. Then he pointed straight at Sarah. "Sarah, you didn't really think you would be having an elegant and sophisticated engagement party with me and my twin bro in charge of the entertainment now, did you?"

Nick shook his head as the twins laughed hysterically. Sarah shot a panicked look at Rachel whose expression mirrored her own. Clearly, the twins had kept her in the dark with some of the details of the entertainment.

"What have you done?" Rachel shouted at them, not needing a microphone.

"Woah woah, steady, Rach! Don't worry; there's no strippers or anything." Cole insisted. A gasp echoed through the crowd of guests. "We just have some games to play, and we have a lovely cake for the bride and groom. Sarah, Nick, please go over to the table with the pink box and open the lid."

Nick stayed rooted to the spot staring at his brothers, daring them to upset Sarah. Sarah, on the other hand, did as she was told and gingerly crept towards the cake that she was afraid to look at. She opened the lid, inhaled sharply and then burst out laughing. The twins and Nick ran over, the twins gleefully, Nick curiously.

"Sarah, please could you describe your beautiful cake to these lovely people?" Cole asked, holding his microphone to her mouth as if he was interviewing her.

"I think… I think…," Sarah could hardly speak, she couldn't stop laughing. "This is supposed to be Nick and me looking very loved up in a bed, doing what appears to be naughty things under the covers!" The crowd roared with laughter, all except Nick, Gloria and Suzanna, who were shellshocked. The next person to run over was Rachel, who was also laughing whilst trying her best to scold her younger brothers.

"Well, let's get it out of the box and put it on this lovely cake stand, shall we, so everybody can see!" Cole laughed down the microphone.

The guests ran forward and crowded around the table all together to take a look at the rude cake. Nick pulled Sarah aside, away from the commotion.

"I'm really sorry about this, babe. I had no idea they'd done this. I warned them not to embarrass you. Idiots, they are!" Sarah was taken aback by how mad yet hurt he seemed to be.

"That's okay, they haven't embarrassed me. To be honest, I expected that all would not go to plan or something along these lines would happen as soon as you announced that they were in charge of the entertainment. You should have known that putting those two in charge is like letting children plan a party. But this is what a party should be – fun. Look at everybody's smiles, Nick." She waved her arms in the air and gestured to the crowd of people; many of them were still huddled around the cake table with their mobile phones in their hands, taking photographs of the cake. Nick looked back at her with a grin now fixed on his face. "We've had sensible and sophisticated with the meal, which I loved, by the way, but now in the twins' words, let's get this party started!" Sarah kissed Nick hard on his lips and dragged him back to the guests.

Chad was working his way through the crowd with enough flowery Hawaiian garlands for the whole guest list hanging from his neck. Each person that crossed his path had one of the garlands unceremoniously slung over their heads. He followed this with a cheery thumbs-up to his surprised victim. Cole jumped back onto the gazebo and was gearing up the crowd with chants and hoots, getting them into the party spirit. The party was well and truly in full swing, champagne flowed freely, and every guest was dancing, whether it be on the dancefloor, by their tables or even while sitting in their seats, as was the case for Nick's elderly grandparents. There was a pile of high-heeled shoes tucked into a corner of the gazebo where lots of ladies had kicked them off so they could dance joyfully.

The twins were leading the guests in a party dance. Everybody's eyes, including Sarah and Nick's, were fixed on them as if they were award-winning teachers!

"Oh man, I'm going to have to stop for a minute!" Chad announced to the guests after half an hour of party dances back to back. He bent over dramatically, clutching a pretend stitch in his side. "I may not be as energetic as I used to be, but at least I'm still very good-looking!"

Cole sniggered down the microphone and shook his head, seeming to forget that he was Chad's twin. "It's time for the games to begin! You may be disappointed, but some of them are quite tame, thanks to our sister, Rachel." He pointed straight to her in the crowd as if nobody knew who she was. He started to pace across the gazebo. "Much to our amusement, we've already shown our naughty side once tonight. But! We don't think that's anywhere near enough."

Both twins shook their heads as the devilish looks were firmly back in place on Rachel and Nick's faces. Sarah cheered and clapped along with the rest of the guests, slightly scared but excited to find out what else they had planned.

"Now, don't worry, Sarah, these games aren't just aimed at you. Everybody can get involved." Chad opened his arms wide as if he was embracing the whole crowd. "Let's start with one of Rachel's games, shall we? We'll get the boring ones out of the way first." He whispered into the microphone, obviously meaning for everybody to hear this. Cole stood next to him, patting his mouth in an exaggerated yawn.

Rachel folded her arms and shook her head at her brothers.

"Man, we'll be in trouble when this party finishes, bro," Cole told Chad. "Check out that frosty glare from our sister!" The twins hugged each other, pretending to be scared as Rachel tried to hide the smirk on her face. "Everybody, please come this way."

Both twins led the guests to the flowery wooden fence, then disappeared behind it. When they re-emerged, they were holding between them a life-sized cardboard cutout of Sarah! It was a photograph that Nick had taken of her, looking giddy with happiness, holding her left hand out to show her engagement ring. Sarah soon realised that it must have made its way to Rachel, and this was the reason why. Crazy images flashed through Sarah's mind of what they might be doing with this, and about the state it would be in by the end of the night.

"Don't look so worried, Sarah!" Cole insisted.

"That's impossible when you two are in charge!" Sarah exclaimed.

"Let me explain. This game is called 'Pin the ring on Sarah's finger'." He draped his arm over the cardboard Sarah's shoulders and paused until the laughter from the guests had settled down. "Rules are simple. Very similar to another well-known party game. I give you one of these," he picked up a cardboard engagement ring, "blindfold you, you then walk over to this lovely cardboard cutout and place the ring on your finger. We are very safety conscious, so…"

"Ha!" Gloria's voice carried over everybody's heads at this obvious lie.

"Thanks, Mom! Anyway, as I was saying, we are very safety conscious, so there are no actual pins involved here; we've gone all out and used sticky tack."

Chad stood next to the real Sarah with the blindfold clutched in his hand. “As you’re the bride, we think it’s only fair that you get to go first,” he told her.

Without waiting for an answer, he slid his microphone into the pocket of his jacket and threw the blindfold in front of Sarah’s vision. Very tightly, he tied it into a knot at the back of her head, managing to tangle some of her hair within it. To say she felt vulnerable being blindfolded by Chad was an understatement. She expected to suddenly get pushed into a paddling pool or something else ridiculous like having a drink served to her by a naked waiter when she took the blindfold off. Thankfully, nothing of the sort happened. Chad guided Sarah by her shoulders to a short way in front of the cardboard cutout and passed her a cardboard engagement ring.

“We forgot to say before that this game is just for the bridal party due to how many are here tonight,” Cole told everybody, “but fear not my party people, we have games which are much more fun than this for you beautiful lot!” Another stern look from Rachel. “Sarah, off you go!”

Sarah’s attempt at pinning the ring on her cardboard cutout finger was atrocious. She had pinned, or tacked, the ring to her knee. Nick’s wasn’t much better. He had put the ring on Sarah’s stomach. Katy’s was by far the closest as she had managed to get the ring onto Sarah’s hand. The twins waited until each member of the bridal party had taken part before grabbing their own cardboard engagement rings. The twins were both spot on and managed to get the ring on the cardboard Sarah’s finger perfectly. However, they had both run straight up to the cardboard cutout with their blindfolds sitting blatantly on top of their heads. Rachel had told them that due to their obvious cheating, their attempts didn’t count, and she announced Katy as the winner.

After the many complaints and whines from the twins had

finally stopped, Rachel stepped onto the gazebo by herself and informed the guests that she would be hosting the next game. It was a game just for Sarah and Nick but one that would be incredibly fun for the audience to witness. A classic Mr. and Mrs. game!

Rachel invited Sarah and Nick onto the gazebo where a table, complete with a divider across it, had been set up. Sarah and Nick took their places on either side of the table whilst Rachel glanced down at her question sheet. She immediately looked up and threw a death stare in her younger brothers' direction. They were rucked up with laughter, reminding Rachel of when they were children, giggling uncontrollably, usually at inappropriate times. She angrily scribbled out the question that had been *edited* by them and scanned the rest of the sheet. Her head shot up again as she came across another one of their *special* questions. Chad and Cole's whole bodies were shaking from laughing so much and their eyes were streaming with tears. Once again, Rachel scribbled out the rude question while still shooting them daggers with her eyes.

"Rach?" Nick whispered. "We're ready."

She plastered a smile on her face and tried to put the thoughts of her doing some serious damage to Chad and Cole at the end of the party to the back of her mind.

"Hi, folks! Here we have a Mr. and Mrs. game!" Rachel cheered. "We have twenty questions for our bride and groom to answer, and the aim is for Nick and Sarah to match as many answers as possible." She spoke to Nick and Sarah. "Use the boards and pens you have here in front of you and keep your answer hidden until you have both finished writing. Okay, let's get started. Question one, where was your first date?"

They both smiled at the memory as they wrote out the same

answer.

"Oooo, Nick's hotel in London. Nice!"

A wolf whistle pierced the ripple of applause. "What did you get up to there then?" Chad shouted, giggling.

"Things that you have probably never done or will ever do, now shut up, Chad!" Rachel shouted back. Nick burst out laughing at his brother's embarrassment. Rachel cleared her throat and continued as if there had been no interruption. "Question two, who's the best at cooking?"

Sarah smirked as she wrote her own name on her board. Nick did the same.

"Obvious," Rachel said. "I think a lot of people here tonight knew the answer to that one if they have ever been subjected to Nick's cooking. Or even if they have been in Nick's house when he attempts to cook, in fact!"

"Come on now, move on," Nick said, jokingly.

"Question three, which song of Nick's is Sarah's favourite?"

Instead of using his board to answer this question, Nick started to serenade Sarah with the chorus of 'All My Love'. She nodded to show that it was the correct answer. The guests clapped loudly when Nick had finished. He turned and gave them a low bow.

Nick and Sarah had done rather well by the time Rachel had got to the final question by writing different answers only once. On question five, each of them had written the other's name when Rachel had asked, 'who is the most attractive?'

"Okay, last question, guys," Rachel said in a serious tone. "The important one. Who said 'I love you' first?"

They both scribbled Nick's name onto the board, but underneath his name on her board, Sarah added, 'But I said it back right away!'

"Aww, that's sweet! Nineteen questions correct out of twenty, well done, guys! Woo!" Rachel and the guests clapped as Sarah and Nick hugged each other and giggled about some of their answers. They looked around the garden at the excited faces, some of which were looking eager to find out what the next game was going to be.

Chad seemed to have fully shaken off his earlier embarrassment as he made his way back to the gazebo with Cole in tow.

"Friends!" Chad exclaimed. "Cole and I have put a large envelope on each table. Inside the envelope is the next game that we are going to play. When you open them you will find a bunch of blank bride and groom trivia sheets, one for each person sitting around your table. We would like you to fill them in within the time limit that we set, and please don't share your answers with anybody else. Nick and Sarah will provide us with the correct answers to each question, and we will read them out at the end of the time limit so you can check your answers. Fire away, peeps!"

Lots of shuffling ensued as the guests reached for the envelopes and handed out the sheets around their tables. The music started up again in the background whilst everybody was filling in their answers to the trivia game. There was lots of laughing and interacting coming from the guests as they peeked at each other's sheets, against Chad and Cole's rules.

At the end of the thirty-minute time limit the twins had set, they were back on their microphones, calling for quiet around the garden and for the music to stop. Nick made his way onto the gazebo and handed the correct answers to Cole in his own sealed envelope. He looked pleased with himself as he jogged back to Sarah and put his feet up on an empty chair.

"As you have all just witnessed, Nick has handed us the

correct answers. This envelope is sealed, so there's no cheating going on here. As well as our own sheets, we have been given our parents' sheets to mark, bit lazy guys," Cole added to Gloria and Andrew. "So let's see, whose bride and groom trivia sheet shall we read a few answers aloud from? Ah yes, we'll use this one – Mom's answers."

"Go ahead!" Gloria shouted, waving her hands in a relaxed way, showing that she was not bothered in the slightest about the twins picking on her. Cole passed Gloria's sheet to Chad.

"Well, this is an interesting answer, complete lie, no less." Chad raised his eyebrows at his mother and read. "What annoys the groom the most? Mom's answer – his twin brothers! What was the groom's first job? Mom's answer – an unwilling wrestling opponent of his twin brothers! Ladies and gentlemen, Mom's added underneath this question… usually the twins in a tag team versus Nick. And it goes on and on like this," Chad told the guests, rolling his eyes. "Needless to say, Mom, those answers will be incorrect. Now let's have a look at the questions and the real answers, shall we?"

Chad ripped open Nick and Sarah's envelope and read a few questions out loud.

How long have Nick and Sarah been together?

Where did Nick propose?

Where did Nick and Sarah meet?

He paused between each one, allowing time for himself, Cole and the guests to mark their answers. They finally arrived at the last question, which was, *what annoys the groom the most?* Chad read Nick's answer to himself and shook his head. He put his hands on his hips and looked at Nick, who had a naughty grin on his face, arms folded across his chest and his feet still on the empty chair.

“What a ridiculous answer!” Chad laughed. “The correct answer to this question, folks, is… his twin brothers!”

Many people stood as they clapped and cackled at the twins. Gloria was the loudest of all. She shrugged her shoulders dramatically as if that answer could and would ever be the only logical one.

“Yes, well done, Mother. And thank you, Nick and Sarah!” Sarah scowled and opened her mouth at the cheek of being blamed for this. She pointed to Nick, making it known that he was the only one behind it. “Now, finally, here comes the really fun bit of this party!” Chad exclaimed.

Two very burly men appeared carrying what looked like a gigantic rolled-up, white plastic sheet which seemed to be really heavy. Interest definitely piqued. The curious guests were silent, wondering what was going to happen next. The two men dropped the plastic sheet onto the centre of the dancefloor and started to roll it out. As they unfurled each layer, the penny dropped as the guests started to recognise the colourful circles on the mat. It was a massive Twister mat the size of one-half of a football pitch! Immediately around the garden, the guests who still had their shoes on were now kicking them off under their tables and rushing over to the huge mat with excited grins on their faces.

“Woah, people! Hold up now!” Chad told them, holding his hand in the air. “Now, as you can see, this mat is mega! There is plenty of room for everybody here, although I know not everybody will take part. Cole and I have decided that everybody moves on each turn because of the number of people here; you cannot have your turn individually. Our lovely sister will be spinning the arrow and telling us where to put our hands and feet.” Chad passed his microphone to Rachel then joined the other shoeless guests who were standing around the edges of the mat. The older generation of guests had, rather sensibly, decided to sit this one out. Their entertainment would be watching the carnage and chaos inevitably unfold.

After Rachel had shouted, "Left hand blue, right hand blue," then "left foot red," the guests who were playing all looked like they were runners waiting for the 100m sprint to start. Rachel had to pause at this point, she was unable to stop laughing at her uncle, who, instead of resting his free foot at the edge of the mat, had lifted it into the air and was now balancing precariously, trying to keep as still as he could. Rachel shouted, "Right foot red," and instantly started giggling again as her balancing uncle toppled over as he tried to swing his foot underneath him. He had taken down two other people on either side of him as he went. As laughter rippled around the mat, a few others lost their balance and had either ended up face planting the ground or ended up on their backs. Each turn that passed had at least one person falling to the floor in bouts of giggles. Gloria's cheeky tickling of some of the remaining players as she tiptoed around the mat claimed a few of them who weren't expecting to be sabotaged.

Suzanna found herself next to Tim, who had removed his jacket and tucked his tie into his shirt for this occasion. Rachel bellowed, "Right hand, yellow!" Tim, who was in a crab position, quickly placed his hand on the only yellow spot that was available to him. Suzanna looked around and realised, and was secretly excited, that in order to get to the only yellow spot that she could possibly put her right hand onto, she would have to lean over and across Tim's body. In one swift movement, she put her hand firmly onto the yellow spot and was face to face with Tim. In close proximity, Suzanna had to fight the urge to land a huge kiss on his lips and was disappointed but relieved at the same time when Rachel shouted out that they were all to put their left feet on a blue spot. As Tim attempted to move his foot, he caught Suzanna's leg and caused her to fall completely on top of him. Nick, who was still going strong, peeked beneath his arm and wolf-whistled as he spotted Suzanna and Tim together in a heap, making no attempt whatsoever to move from the mat. With the realisation that they were now being watched, Suzanna jumped up innocently and skipped quickly off the mat. Tim got up with a look of euphoria on his face and sauntered off in Suzanna's direction.

A few players remained, including Chad, Cole, Nick and two of their cousins. Rachel had abandoned the spinner board and shouted out random commands trying her best to make the rest of them fall. She had even added different body parts into the mix, and it worked immediately as Nick and one of the cousins fell at her first shout. They were then followed right after by the other cousin, which left only Chad and Cole. With one final shout of, "Right foot, blue!" Chad had intentionally chosen a space that would require him to stretch across into Cole's space. Reminiscent of a bull in a china shop, Chad barged into Cole, knocking him flying a fair distance across the mat. Cheers sounded and the music that had been playing in the background was cranked up a notch.

Chad stood and treated the audience to a deep bow, then dropped to the floor and performed a breakdancing move, as if the Twister mat had suddenly become a breakdancing one. He spun on his back and his head and leaped around the mat, exciting the guests more and more with each move he performed. The guests, including Sarah, reacted as if they were Chad's adoring fans.

"Well, well. I hope you're not falling in love with my brother's moves?" Nick teased.

Sarah jumped and swung around to face Nick. "Don't be silly," she chastised. "There's only one Taylor's moves I'm interested in. Now I don't need to ask you who the boy in the photograph is."

"What boy in which photograph?"

"The photograph in your trophy cabinet when you won the street dance championship in 1999. It's Chad!"

"Oh," Nick laughed. "Yes, it is Chad. He started street dancing lessons at a very early age. I used to watch him when he practiced at home, and he started to teach me some of his moves. It's down to Chad why I love performing; he gave me the bug. I think it's times like this when he forgets why he stopped dancing." He looked longingly at his older brother who still had the crowd in the palm of his hand. "Just look at the way he captures an audience. He's a natural talent."

"Why did he stop dancing?" Sarah asked.

"He didn't think he would be able to make money out of it and didn't dare take the risk, so he decided to look for a job away from dancing and then he got too busy to keep up with it. Although he doesn't seem sensible a lot of the time, Chad is the type of guy that needs to feel secure money-wise, so he chose to follow what his head was telling him to do. I've offered him a job numerous times as one of my dancers, but each time he said he's settled in his job and didn't want to 'upset the apple cart' as he put it. Looking at him now, you can clearly see that dancing is in his heart. He puts it into every move or step he performs."

"Maybe this will make *him* get the bug again?"

"Yeah maybe?" Nick sighed. "I hope so. It would be a shame to see such talent go to waste." He shrugged his shoulders and put his head down. Sarah steered the subject away from Chad and instead asked about Cole.

"So, does Cole have a hidden talent no one knows about?" Sarah asked, curious to know more about the secretive and sneaky twins.

"As a matter of fact, he does." Nick smiled.

"Oh please, do tell, Mr. Taylor."

Nick pointed at the rude cake that the twins had ordered her to open up in front of everybody. "See our very special engagement cake over there?"

"Yeah?"

"Cole made it!"

"What?" Sarah was gobsmacked.

"Cole bakes."

Sarah laughed, imagining Cole with an apron around his waist and bits of flour and icing sugar in his hair.

"Hey, hey, don't laugh!" Nick scolded. "He's an incredible baker!"

"Wow, what a talented family. I have a lot to live up to!"

"You'll fit right in!"

After nearly fifteen minutes of non-stop dancing and sweating profusely, Chad made it back to his seat and very kindly had a cold glass of water thrown over his head by Cole.

"That was amazing, bro!" Cole told him, acting like he hadn't just drenched his brother with water.

"Thanks, man, I don't know where that came from. I thought my dancing days were done," he added to Nick.

"You know I could always use dancers, brother. Just something to think about." Nick winked at him as he lifted his drink to his lips and sipped. He could see the cogs turning in Chad's head. Nick wondered if Sarah could be right and the dancing bug would indeed bite his brother again some day soon.

With the twins' entertainment done for the night, a buffet of sandwiches, cakes and lots of nibbles was served to the peckish guests. Many were glad to be sitting in their seats once again after being twisted and turned all sorts of ways. The look of joy on their faces was evident through their huge smiles and tears of laughter.

The party came to an end with a humongous conga line that nearly every person at the party joined in with and a game of limbo that lasted nearly forty minutes. Tim, who was crowned the winner, revelled in the joy and cheers that blasted out from the guests.

Although the second half of the party had been wild and extremely surprising, thanks to her two cheeky future brothers-in-law, Sarah had laughed harder than she ever had before, and she had loved every second of it.

As the last of the guests left the garden, Sarah wandered around collecting keepsakes for herself. She picked up some of the sparkly gems off the tables, a few petals from the wooden fence and the guest book that had been signed in by everybody who had attended the party. She laughed to herself again as she stopped in front of her naughty cake.

"So you've enjoyed yourself tonight then?" Nick asked, sneaking up behind her.

Sarah was munching on one of Nick's icing legs from the cake.

"Yeah, I've had loads of fun. I don't think I could have planned a better night myself!"

"Well…" Nick purred, with a smouldering look on his face. He put his hands in his trouser pockets and moved his shoulders in such a way that a small part of his chest was exposed through the open top button of his shirt. Sarah licked and bit her bottom lip – he looked delicious. "There is still lots of fun to be had."

Nick cupped Sarah's chin, lifting her face to his. "So why don't you finish the cake version of me so you can taste the real me?"

He winked and sauntered away, leaving her standing there in front of the cake, still holding her keepsakes, with her mouth gaping open.

Two days later, Sarah felt her heart break a little as she watched Tim drive away with Suzanna and Katy waving sadly to her from the back seat of his car. Just a couple of days with them was nowhere near enough time for Sarah, or Suzanna and Katy for that matter. The wedding seemed so close before, but now she knew that she wouldn't be seeing her mother or sister again until then, it seemed like it was a lifetime away.

Chapter Eighteen

Sarah was still on cloud nine a week after the engagement party, although she missed Suzanna and Katy like mad. She still couldn't believe she was going to be Mrs. Sarah Taylor! She had just climbed out of the shower and was choosing what to wear when her phone started to ring.

"Hello?" she answered, not looking at the number on her screen.

"Hi Sarah, this is Detective Althorp from Middlesbrough Police Department. I need to speak to you regarding Tina Lynch's car accident." Sarah's blood ran cold. "I went to your house but your mother told me that you are living in America now?"

"Yes, I do. Why do you need to speak to me about the accident?"

"It would be best, if possible, that I speak to you face to face. Is there any chance you would be able to return to England for a few weeks? This is really important." Sarah's heart was hammering in her chest.

"Yes, I'll come. I'll book the next flight out and call you when I've arrived back at my mother's house."

"Thank you, Sarah, see you soon."

Sarah did book the first flight available for herself, Nick and Tim. Nick was worried about them being recognised, so they boarded the plane before all of the other passengers and hid their faces with caps, sunglasses and scarves. The flight back to England was horrendous; there was terrible turbulence and an argument on board between a passenger and a crew member, which caused the pilot to threaten to land the plane halfway through the flight. Throughout this, surprisingly, Sarah remained calm even though she did need to squeeze Nick's hand a few times. The bravery that she had felt on the flight over to America and starting a new life had evaporated completely. Now she could feel herself shaking inside uncontrollably. *Snap out of it*, she scolded herself. Something told her that she would need to stay focused whilst she was in England.

Sarah marched through the airport like she was on a mission, Nick and Tim were several paces behind, struggling to keep up with her. She almost bumped into her mother, who was running at top speed and trying her best to dodge the other people milling through the place. They embraced but nobody said a word as they all climbed into Suzanna's car, wondering what was so important that they had to fly thousands of miles to be here.

Sarah called Detective Althorp from the car on the way to Suzanna's house and told him that she had arrived back in England. He immediately dropped everything and rushed to the house, pulling up outside just as Suzanna was reversing into the driveway. Sarah did not offer Detective Althorp a drink, instead asking him to 'spit out' what he needed to tell them so urgently.

"Sarah," he began slowly. "You may need to sit down for this."

"No, I'm fine standing, thank you." Sarah was not just standing but pacing around the room, feeling extremely irritated.

Detective Allthorp stared at her, wondering if he should insist but judging from the look on her face, he thought it best not to argue with her. He sighed loudly and began.

"We are going to be investigating Tina's car because we have reason to believe that the accident may not have been an accident. We would like you to collect her belongings from the car before we start so we don't have any contamination once we have started to look further into it."

Sarah looked at him gobsmacked. She felt herself shaking and held her hand out to Nick for support. "What reasons do you have for not believing that this was an accident?"

"Unfortunately, we can't share that information with you. We will need you to collect Tina's belongings at some point tomorrow so we can get started on this investigation as soon as we can. I've spoken with her husband, who has agreed to accompany us there."

"Great," said Sarah sarcastically.

Detective Althorp handed Sarah a business card. "My phone number is on there. Please call or text me when you know when you will be free, and I will collect you from here. I'll leave you alone now. Bye, Sarah."

Suzanna saw him out as Sarah stood rooted to the spot, not knowing what to think. There were so many questions in her head. A text message came through to her phone making her jump. It was from Bill.

Have you heard from Detective Althorp yet? Let me know!

She messaged him back.

Yes, he has just left my mum's house. Are you free at nine a.m. tomorrow morning? If you are, come to my house because Detective Althorp will be coming here to take us to Tina's car.

Bill answered straight away.

Yes, I am. I'll see you tomorrow.

Sarah texted Detective Althorp with the arrangements and tried to take her mind off everything to do with the investigation and Tina's death, but she could not shake off the uneasy feeling in the pit of her stomach.

Nine o'clock arrived on the following cold November morning. Detective Althorp knocked on the door on the dot. Suzanna opened it slowly and moved aside so Detective Althorp could come into the house.

Bill was already there; he had arrived half an hour earlier than planned with Gemma hanging off his arm. Sarah tried to ignore the fact that Gemma had tagged along. *Why is she here?* she wondered to herself. Sarah didn't think Gemma had any right to be near anything of Tina's when she and Bill had caused the breakdown of their marriage. Keeping the many thoughts about Gemma to herself, she wandered to the door.

She reached for her gloves which she had put on the shelf in the hallway, but the only thing her hand felt was thin air. She could not see them anywhere. She was still searching when Nick appeared behind her.

"What are you looking for, babe?" he asked.

"My gloves, I'm sure I brought them with me, but I can't find them."

"You were in a panic when we left so you could have easily forgotten them. Here," he held out his own leather ones to Sarah. "You can have mine."

"Thank you."

"Are you sure you don't want me to come with you?"

"No, I want to do this myself. I've told Bill the same, so he's promised to stay out of my way while we are there." Nick kissed Sarah on her forehead and she followed Detective Althorp out of the door without looking back.

The car journey was a quiet and very awkward one. Sarah was sitting in the front of the car with Detective Althorp, who was trying to have a cheery conversation with her but gave up when she only responded to his questions with grunts and muttered one-word answers. What made the journey all the more annoying was the constant whispering that was coming from the back seat. She had been biting her tongue most of the way, but she couldn't any longer.

"Will you shut up!" she shouted, still facing the front.

She could feel Gemma's glare burning into the back of her head but she didn't care. Her face was burning with rage. Bill and Gemma were silent for the rest of the way, as was Detective Althorp.

Thankfully five minutes later, he turned left into the car pound. Sarah craned her neck, trying to spot Tina's car as they drove towards the garage area. She finally spotted it tucked around the back of the garage away from all of the other cars. She burst into tears at the sight of it. The front of the car was beyond recognition. It had been caved in so far. Sarah knew that even if Tina had made it out of the car alive, she would still have passed on.

She got out of Detective Althorp's car and followed him to the garage. Bill and Gemma followed, walking quite a way behind them. They waited while Detective Althorp went into the office in the garage to collect some paperwork. He emerged with several sheets of paper on a clipboard, two empty bags and a pair of latex gloves each for them. He handed a bag, and a pair of gloves to both Sarah and Bill and the four of them walked slowly towards Tina's car. The tears were still streaming down Sarah's face and with each step closer to the car that Bill took, his chin wobbled more and more with emotion. Gemma stepped back while they worked, finding and loading Tina's belongings into the bags.

Nobody spoke a word until they were in the office together, going through the contents of each bag. Detective Althorp had Sarah and Bill empty each bag so he could jot down on the paperwork what they had taken from the car.

Gemma was outside smoking a cigarette while they did this, which Sarah was happy about. She did not want Gemma looking through Tina's personal property. She felt she had already done far too much of that. They were signing on the bottom of the paperwork when Gemma breezed into the office, reeking of cigarette smoke and looking impatient.

"Are you nearly done, sweetheart? I have a few errands to run today," she said to Bill in a bossy tone.

"Er, yes..." Bill began.

"You do know you didn't have to come here, don't you?" Sarah cut across him. She was incensed with rage. How dare this woman invite herself here, knowing this would be incredibly hard for both herself and Bill, then make it sound like it was inconveniencing her.

"Well, obviously I'm here to support my little munchkin," she answered in a sweet voice that made Sarah feel sick.

Gemma put her arm around Bill's waist and pulled him in close to her. Sarah turned away so she didn't have to look at that stupid smile on her face any longer. She marched over to the police car and stood with her arms folded until Detective Althorp ran over so she could get into the car. She looked around to see where Bill and Gemma were and saw Gemma dragging Bill along by the hand, looking impatient once again. Sarah noticed the way Bill kept looking back at Tina's car with his hand on his forehead as if the reality of losing her had only just hit him.

"Well," said Detective Althorp, not looking very comfortable at all after the silent car journey back to Suzanna's house. "I'll be in touch soon when I can tell you a bit more of how the investigation is going."

"Thank you," Sarah said. And with that, she got out of the car and slammed the door shut behind her.

Several days later, Sarah was drinking coffee with Suzanna and Nick in the house when she received a call from Detective Althorp asking if he could come over. Sarah agreed and waited anxiously for him to arrive, hoping that he would give them some information as to how the accident had happened. She was surprised to see him with another colleague when he knocked on the door.

"Hi, Detective, please…" He cut her off.

"Sarah Bailey, I am arresting you on suspicion of the murder of Tina Lynch," he said sadly, as he put handcuffs on her wrists.

"WHAT!" Nick roared.

"No," Sarah protested. "No, I didn't do this. Please tell me what's going on!" She started to cry as she was led out to the same police car she was in a few days ago. Nick was attempting to push past the mean-looking police officer that was blocking his way to Sarah.

"Mr. Taylor, you cannot speak to Sarah now. You need to stay here whilst we question her," he said nastily, showing Nick his yellowing teeth.

"No, this isn't right. You're making a mistake. She didn't do this!"

"And how can you know that for sure, Nick?" He asked, grinning. "You didn't even know who Sarah was when the crime was committed. Now you stay here like a good boy and let us deal with this." He smirked.

"I know she is innocent; she hasn't done this!" The police

officer continued to smile horribly at Nick. "I'll wipe that smile off your face!" Nick spat through gritted teeth.

The nasty police officer soon stopped grinning when he saw the fierce look in Nick's eyes.

"If you threaten me again, Mr. Taylor, I will arrest you," he said, sounding braver than he looked.

"Nick, come sit down. The last thing we need right now is you being arrested as well." Suzanna's calming voice snapped Nick out of his temper. The police officer made a beeline for the door when Nick turned his back on him.

"We need to figure out how to sort this mess and get our Sarah back." She patted his shoulder with a comforting hand.

Nick had Sarah's phone in his pocket, and the first thing he did was dial Bill's number.

"Hi, Sarah," Bill answered, expecting to hear her voice.

"What the hell is going on, Bill? Sarah has been arrested! They think she murdered Tina!" He was shouting again now.

"What! She would never do that. I'll go to the police station and find out what's going on." Bill said, flabbergasted.

"Good. Make sure you do, Bill, because if I go down there, I will be arrested for murder as well." He clicked the phone off angrily.

Sarah sat in the back of the police car, sobbing and pleading with Detective Althorp to tell her what was happening, but he did not say anything. He hadn't spoken to her or made eye contact with her since he had arrested her. The nasty police officer, who was called PC Moran, laughed at this.

"Oh deary me, Sarah. You are in trouble, aren't you? And your mega-famous boyfriend will be in a cell next to you soon enough if he can't control his temper," he said happily. He waggled his finger and tutted.

“Enough!” Detective Althorp suddenly shouted at PC Moran. He jumped, threw a dirty look at Detective Althorp and spent the rest of the car journey to the police station sulking.

At the police station, Sarah was shown to an interview room that was freezing inside. The only things in the room were a table, four chairs, a microphone screwed to the table, a computer and a set of drawers. Sarah sat down, shaking and crying.

Detective Althorp walked around to Sarah’s side of the table and removed the handcuffs. She immediately put her arms around herself, trying her best to keep warm. Detective Althorp looked at her with a sorry expression on his face. Though he didn’t usually do this, he left the room and came back in minutes later with a steaming mug of coffee for Sarah. She was glad to see that PC Moran, or PC *Moron,* which she thought suited him better, would not be joining them.

“I can tell you that our conversation will be being recorded here today, and I have to ask if you would like a solicitor present?”

“No, I don’t want to wait to find out what’s going on here. How can you think I would do something like this to my best friend?” she asked quietly.

Detective Althorp let out a huge sigh. “We believe we have evidence which points to you being involved in this.”

“No, please, you’re making a big mistake. I would never hurt Tina; I miss her every single day. It hurts my heart knowing that I will never see or speak to her ever again.”

“Sarah, I don’t want to believe this either, but as I said, the evidence is pointing at you,” he said softly. “I’m sorry, but we need to get started.” He reached for the set of drawers, opened the top one and pulled out a disc in a case. He loaded it into the computer, watching Sarah bury her face in her hands and sob. His voice broke slightly as he pressed the record button and started to speak.

"This is Detective Althorp of Middlesbrough Police Department and I am here with Sarah Bailey. This interview is regarding Tina Lynch's suspected murder case. The date is Friday, 9th November 2018, and the time is 11.14 a.m. Sarah, please state your name."

"Sarah Bailey," she croaked. She broke into tears again as the Detective read out her right to silence.

"Thank you, Sarah. I'm going to ask you some questions and please answer them as truthfully as you can."

"Yes, okay, I will." She wiped her eyes on the sleeve of her jumper.

"How long have you known Tina Lynch?"

"Around twelve years. We went to college and university together."

"You worked together in a hospital. Is that correct?"

"Yes, we were both nurses in the accident and emergency department."

"I need to ask you some questions about the night this incident happened. We know that you were the last person who saw Tina before the accident. What were you doing that night?"

"We were at Tina's house. I was comforting her because she had been given her divorce papers by Bill earlier on that day."

"How long had she been married?" asked Detective Althorp.

"Almost six months. She thought she would be with Bill forever, so she was devastated." Sarah answered sadly.

"And why did the marriage end?"

"Bill met someone else and cheated on Tina. I didn't know

who she was at the time, but I know now that it was Gemma. She's his boss's daughter."

"Was Tina drinking alcohol at all that night?" he asked, frowning.

"She wasn't while I was there, no, but she mentioned that she was going to have a drink after I left." Sarah started to feel confused. It felt like Detective Althorp was implying that Tina had driven under the influence. "Why are you asking me that?"

"We thought at first, given the circumstances and the state of mind that Tina was in, she may have made the wrong decision and decided to drink and drive in order to end her life."

Suddenly, Sarah was on her feet.

"What?" she shouted. "Tina was not thinking that way, I can assure you. Yes, she was extremely upset, but anybody would be if they were in her situation."

Detective Althorp tapped the table. "Sarah, please sit down so we can continue with the interview." She sat down slowly, feeling like a naughty child.

"I'm sorry, I just didn't expect you to think that about her."

"In cases like this, we have to explore every possible avenue; however, when her toxicology report came back clear, we ruled that one out. There was no alcohol or drugs at all in her system, so she couldn't have had an accident caused by being under the influence. She obviously got into the car before she had anything to drink."

Sarah frowned. "So why did you ask me if she had been drinking if you had proof that she hadn't?"

Detective Althorp looked down at the paper in front of him. "Just answer the questions, Sarah." He cleared his throat and continued. "The road was examined, and we found no skid marks from her brakes which is why we believed that she had intentionally crashed, but we did find brake fluid on the road. Do you know what time you left Tina's house that night?"

"It was around eleven thirty p.m. I arrived home at eleven fifty."

"Was anybody else at your house when you arrived home?"

"No. My mum and sister were out at a charity event for the hospital."

"You had been at Tina's house all day. Is that correct?"

"Most of the day, yes. She called me when Bill had dropped the divorce papers off to her in the morning, so I went straight over."

"Okay. We have strong evidence which shows that Tina's car had been tampered with. There was a cut in her brake line, which caused her car to leak fluid each time she pressed her brakes. She could only have gotten so far before her brakes would inevitably fail and would cause her to crash."

Sarah was shocked, and she stared at Detective Althorp as he spoke.

"We have CCTV footage of somebody messing with her car." He slid a photograph of a person dressed in a mechanic's uniform across the table. "Can you explain this?"

Sarah stared at the photograph. "No, I can't, but I can tell you for definite that Tina never had any work done on her car that day."

"Did you leave at any point during the day?"

"Yes but only to go to the shop. I was out for around twenty minutes."

"We have looked at the CCTV footage. We see you leave, and then we see this person approach the car and mess around underneath it. The mystery person leaves, then you come back. Are you sure you can't tell me what is going on here?"

"No, I can't," Sarah insisted. "Tina never mentioned having any work done. I'm sure she would have told me about it if there was an issue with her car."

"Can you explain how we found your fingerprints on the brake line on her car and a hair that looks like yours attached to it?"

"What? No! I didn't do this!" She started to panic.

"I'm sorry, Sarah, but because of the evidence against you, you will be remanded in custody." He pressed the stop button on his computer and the recording came to an end. Sarah sobbed louder than ever. Detective Althorp waited until she had calmed down.

"We will be looking further into the evidence, but at the moment, things don't look good for you. Please come with me."

He led her down a narrow corridor that was even colder than the interview room. It was eerily quiet. There were grey metal doors down one side of the corridor with a small window in each one. All Sarah could think about was Nick, Suzanna and Katy and hoped with everything she had that they would be here soon with a way out of this nightmare.

Detective Althorp unlocked one of the doors and led her inside. It had a creaky bed with a thin blanket and pillow, a metal toilet that smelt like sewage and a metal sink with dents and blood stains all over it. She lay down on the bed and didn't say another word to Detective Althorp as he left. As soon as the door closed, she let out all of the feelings she felt inside and screamed uncontrollably.

Detective Althorp stood with his back against the door, listening to Sarah's screams, feeling his heart break a little. He had shivers running up and down his spine. The feeling that something wasn't right here would not leave him. He made a decision and headed for his desk. He had to make a phone call.

Just as he was pelting past the front doors of the station, he spotted the very person he wanted to speak to. He rushed over and yanked the doors open.

Chapter Nineteen

"Bill!" Detective Althorp shouted. "I need to speak to you now."

"Detective! What the fuck is going on here? Why have you arrested Sarah? Where is she?" Bill was livid.

"Bill, please follow me. This is really important."

Bill sat in the same seat that Sarah had just minutes ago. Detective Althorp repeated what he had done with Sarah and pressed a record button on his computer. After introducing himself once again on the recording, he faced a very angry-looking Bill across the table and started the interview.

"Bill, you were married to Tina, correct?"

"I am still married to Tina," he answered.

"How were things between you the last time you saw or spoke to her?"

"To be honest, not good. I had just given her our divorce papers, so she was really upset. I couldn't stand watching her cry like that so I bolted from the house and drove away," he said quietly. He looked down, seeming as though he was ashamed of himself.

"What about the time before that? Did you argue with her at all?"

"Yes, because the time before that, I told her that I was leaving her because I had met somebody else. Then she told me to leave and not come back to the house."

"And how did you take that?" Detective Althorp had a strange look on his face which made Bill start to feel uneasy.

"Obviously I was angry. I told her that she was not keeping the house because I had pumped just as much money into it as she did."

"You were going to fight her for it?"

"I wouldn't put it like that, but I would have taken her to court, yes."

"So you wouldn't have tried to remove her from the house yourself then?" Detective Althorp asked calmly.

The realisation of how this conversation was going hit Bill like a tonne of bricks. "Hold on! You think I had something to do with this now?"

"Where were you on the night Tina died, Bill?"

"I was at work."

"Can anybody prove that?"

"Yes. About a hundred people! I work for a TV company, and we were filming a show through the night."

"And where were you during the day?"

"I was at work then too. I started work that day on a different project at ten a.m. I delivered the divorce papers to Tina on my way to work. I went home to rest for a few hours when I finished at three p.m., then I returned to work for a seven p.m. start that evening and worked all the way through to seven a.m. I found out about Tina's accident when I finished work in the morning. I had ten missed calls and loads of messages from Sarah on my phone telling me what had happened." He was getting exasperated and lowered his face and closed his eyes in an effort to calm himself.

"How did you feel when you found out?" Detective Althorp asked.

Bill's head snapped up, and he looked straight into the police officer's eyes.

"Is that a real question, Detective? How do you think I felt? I had just been told that my wife had died in a horrific car accident. I was completely broken. How would you feel?" Bill felt his blood boiling.

"So if you still felt like this about her, why did you cheat on her, Bill?"

Bill deflated instantly. "I can't answer that because I don't know. At the time, I suppose I thought I didn't want to be with her any more. I thought that Gemma would give me more, a better life." Bill started to cry. "I did not have anything to do with this Detective, and neither did Sarah. Why are you keeping her here?"

"I'm afraid I can't say, Bill, I'm sorry. End of interview."

Detective Althorp pressed stop on his computer. He then discreetly pressed a button on his bodycam. He stood and opened the door of the interview room to allow Bill to leave ahead of him. They walked outside in silence through the car park until they got to Bill's car near the entrance gates.

"Sarah's fingerprints have been found on the brake line of Tina's car."

Bill was fiddling with his keys but stopped abruptly and stood with his mouth hanging open.

"Just that evidence alone is enough to convict her for Tina's murder, but we do have other evidence that we can present. We have CCTV footage of somebody dressed in mechanic's overalls tinkering with Tina's car on the day she died. We have found a hair that we will be testing for DNA which looks remarkably like Sarah's." He looked apologetic. "My issue is, I don't think she did this."

Bill came out of his trance and his face changed. "How can you say that after telling me about all that evidence? Did you not hear what you just said? It seems so obvious that it was Sarah now!"

"Well, you've changed your tune towards her."

"How can I not? There are numerous pieces of evidence that point to Sarah!"

"As I said before, we haven't tested the hair for DNA yet, and I want to take a closer look at that CCTV footage. We will keep you informed of any developments. In the meantime, here's my card. If you have any information about this, please don't hesitate to call me."

Detective Althorp reached for Bill's keys, unlocked the door and held it open for him. He could hear Bill muttering under his breath as he got inside, the odd phrase clear enough to understand... *you think you know someone... could do better police work myself... how could she?*

Bill shut his door so forcefully that the window jumped inside the frame. Detective Althorp watched him drive away then made his way back inside to see if his gut feeling could be proven right.

While Detective Althorp was writing up the paperwork to send off the hair for DNA testing, a team of officers had been sent to Suzanna's house in search of the mechanic's overalls or any other evidence they could link to the accident. They returned to the station later that same day and presented Detective Althorp with nothing.

The police officers had searched through the whole house and had ransacked Sarah's bedroom. They had even broken a few items in their mad search and had been shouted at by Suzanna because of this. They told Detective Althorp that the only thing they had left the house with was a promise from Suzanna that she would be sending the bill for a very expensive vase to the police station! Detective Althorp was both angry due to the recklessness caused by the officers and happy because his instinct seemed to be right so far. He sent the very confused officers away while he worked on Sarah's case.

It was later on that day when Detective Althorp had packaged up the hair sample, filled in all of the paperwork and sent it to the laboratory to be tested. He had made sure to state that it was to be fast-tracked and returned to himself only. He left the station that day with a heavy heart. Even though the thought of Sarah locked away in a jail cell made him want to cry, he so desperately wanted to find the conclusion either way, so he didn't have to work on this case any more. It was one of the worst cases he had ever worked on and it was incredibly draining.

Weeks passed and Detective Althorp had received no end of phone calls from both Nick and Bill. Nick, eager to find out when Sarah would be being released and Bill, calling to make sure that she would be staying in jail for years to come. He noticed a thin envelope on his desk when he walked into his office that morning. It was marked 'private and confidential' and was addressed only to him. He ripped it open as fast as he could. The paper inside shocked him more and more the further down he read. He reached behind him for his chair and fell into it.

His phone started to ring, and a number he now knew off by heart was flashing up on the screen.

"Nick," Detective Althorp said quietly.

"What's going on, Detective? Why is Sarah still locked up?" Nick had asked this question a thousand times already.

"I've received some results back from the hair," Detective Althorp replied.

"And?" Nick raised his voice.

"It's inconclusive."

"What? What does that mean?"

"There isn't enough DNA on the hair." He sounded close to tears now.

"What do you mean? It's a sample of hair! There's bound to be…."

Detective Althorp interrupted him. "Nick – the hair is from a wig."

There was silence from both sides of the phone. After a minute, Nick spoke.

"So you have to let her go then. There's no DNA tying Sarah down to this crime," he insisted.

"You don't know how sorry I am, but I can't do that. Just because there is little or no DNA on the hair, it doesn't mean that Sarah didn't do it."

Nick roared down the phone like an angry animal. Then, the phone cut off.

Detective Althorp's tears started to fall onto the paper. He was sure these results would be the answer to finding something else. Something that might not point to Sarah being guilty. He was starting to wonder if the gut feeling he had was wrong for the first time in a long time. *Maybe she did do this*, he thought. He would need to question her again.

The following day, Detective Althorp drove to Lakewall Prison, where Sarah was being held. He had with him the CCTV that he had watched about a hundred times and the DNA result from the hair.

He felt uneasy and extremely nervous as he walked through the doors of the vast prison. He was shown to a tiny room, which was more like a concrete box, with a rickety old table, four uncomfortable-looking chairs and an obvious camera that was screwed to the ceiling inside. The only splash of colour in here was from the cheap plastic chairs, which were lime green. He sat down in one of the ugly chairs and felt like it was going to collapse underneath him. He could see his breath and could feel the goosebumps on his arms beneath his shirt.

Then the door opened. Sarah was led in by a prison guard, who resembled a gargoyle, with her hands in handcuffs. She looked like she hadn't slept a wink since she had been arrested. Her eyes were so swollen with tears that Detective Althorp could hardly see them. His heart ached at the sight of her, but he knew that he could be dealing with a murderer so he needed to keep his head together. Sarah sat down in one of the chairs opposite him and did not say a word. The prison guard stood next to Sarah, watching her like a hawk as if she expected her to attempt an escape. She had a look of pure hatred for Sarah in her eyes. Detective Althorp wondered if this was how the guard looked at every inmate who crossed the threshold.

Sarah bowed her head so low that she was nearly touching the table. She stayed this way until Detective Althorp cleared his throat and pulled all of his equipment from his bag. He tried to speak to her whilst he was getting everything ready for the interview, but she just stared blankly at him, as if she couldn't understand him. He could see her shivering and could feel her legs shaking against the table.

"Sarah, are you okay to do this?" Detective Althorp asked her softly.

"She's fine!" The horrible guard shouted. "Look at her, so pathetic! If you hadn't murdered somebody, you wouldn't be in here!" She bent down, so she was right next to Sarah's ear. Sarah tried to move away from her but the guard got closer still.

"Do you need to be in here?" Detective Althorp asked, irritated.

"I need to keep my eye on her!"

"Could you please wait outside the door? I need to speak to Sarah alone."

"I need to keep my eye on her," the guard repeated.

Detective Althorp rose from his chair, opened the door and ushered her out. He saw Sarah relax a bit once the guard had left the room.

"Thank you," Sarah mumbled.

"That's okay. I think we had better get started then before she comes barging back in."

"What is this about Detective? I thought you had asked me all your questions before." She sounded completely drained of energy.

"I need to show you the CCTV footage from that awful day. I know I showed you a photograph the last time we met, but I would like you to see the video."

He pressed play on his portable DVD player. Sarah's eyes were fixed on the screen, a look of concentration on her face. Her interest in the footage was apparent as she leaned in close to the screen.

When it had finished, she asked Detective Althorp if she could see it for a second time. He watched her curiously. She squinted her eyes as she pointed at the screen and her lips moved, but no sound came out. She sat up when the CCTV ended again and opened her eyes properly. A light seemed to have come on behind them. She had come alive.

"Sarah?" he asked. "Can you explain why you were so interested in that?"

"Detective, you can clearly tell that the person in that video is not me."

"How so?"

"Whoever that person is, they are shorter than me, and I don't mean to be rude, but that person is wider and certainly more rounded than me at the front."

Detective Althorp started to scribble ferociously on his notepad. Then he turned the DNA result over and showed it to Sarah, who scanned the page quickly.

"The hair is from a wig?"

"Apparently so. Do you know where that wig is from, Sarah?"

She frowned at him now. "You still think it's me after seeing that footage? Detective, as I said before, Tina was my best friend, and I would never have done anything to hurt her. On that footage, you see me leave, and if I am not mistaken, it seems like that person keeps looking in the direction that I went in. Almost as if they are checking to see if I am coming back and…" She looked him straight in his eyes, "I do not, and have never, owned a wig in my life. You have the wrong person, Detective. Please, I am begging you to look closer at that footage and find the evil person who did this to my best friend. I need to be back with my family." She started to cry. "I am so scared here. Every day I feel myself break a bit more. Please help me."

He closed the DVD player and put all of his equipment back into his bag.

"I will have a much closer look at the footage. I will promise you that."

"Thank you."

The prison guard suddenly burst into the room.

"Are you done with her? There are toilets that need scrubbing!" She laughed a hideous, gritty laugh. She yanked

Sarah up from her chair, but Detective Althorp gently pulled her from the mean guard's grasp and spoke to her quietly.

"Hold on a little longer, Sarah. I'll speak with you as soon as I can."

Sarah managed a small smile and then dodged the guard's clawing motion as she tried to grab her once more. This small gesture made Detective Althorp's heart lift again. He could tell that she was stronger than she looked.

He arrived back at the station just as the evening was starting to draw in and called Nick. He answered on the first ring.

"Nick, it's Detective Althorp. I'm calling to let you know that I have been to see Sarah about the DNA result, and we have reviewed the CCTV footage together. Sarah is adamant and very confident, I might add, that the person in the CCTV is not her."

"She's told you that a million times already," Nick said, exasperated.

"Yes, I know. I have promised her that I will have a closer look at the CCTV. I am ashamed to admit this as a long-serving police officer, but there are things that Sarah has pointed out in the footage that I have missed."

"So what happens now then? When is she coming home?"

"We need to study the footage more closely and check the evidence again. Until that has happened, she will have to stay where she is because we cannot rule her out yet."

Nick's sobs echoed down the phone.

"I'm so sorry, Nick. I'll speak to you soon." He ended the call.

Detective Althorp felt so frustrated and confused. As Sarah had said, it did indeed look like a different person in the footage, but the evidence they had against her was staggering. He rubbed at the throbbing ache in his head, pulled his portable DVD player towards him and watched the mystery person on the screen for the third time that day.

Chapter Twenty

Nick couldn't sit and wait for news from Detective Althorp any longer. It had been an agonising two days since he had been to interview Sarah in prison. Nick and Suzanna hadn't heard a word from him. Nick grabbed his coat and phone and marched to the front door.

"Nick, where are you going?" Suzanna asked.

"The police station. I want to speak to Detective Althorp face to face and find out what's going on. I can't just sit here and wait."

Without another word, Suzanna picked up her car keys and tossed them to Nick.

He drove to the police station with a million thoughts going through his mind. His phone startled him when it started to ring. He frowned when he saw it was from a withheld phone number. Since Sarah had been arrested, Nick had become suspicious of everyone and everything. He pulled the car over and pressed record on his phone before he answered it.

"Hello?"

"Hi Nick Taylor," the voice said nastily.

"Who is this?" he asked, fear gripping him.

"Never mind that, just listen to me!" Nick stayed silent. "Your precious Sarah isn't safe within those prison walls. The evidence is piling up against her Nick, so it looks like she will be in there for a very long time. Of course, I could help you if you give me what I want!"

"Please," he begged. "Just tell me what it is and I will do it. Just don't hurt Sarah."

"Oh, I won't hurt her. Unfortunately, with her being locked away, I can't. But I have friends who can. I will send you the details of a bank account. You will send ten million to that bank account today because if you don't, that means Sarah will have to pay – with her life. I made Tina's death look like an accident, just like my friends inside will do with Sarah's. Get on it, Mr. Popstar!"

The phone clicked off. Nick sped to the police station with the evidence that they finally needed to clear Sarah.

Bill had not stopped thinking about the interview with Detective Althorp since it had happened. The anger he felt towards Sarah was immense. The question constantly gnawing at his brain was, 'why would she do this?' He needed to clear his head. He decided to go out on his own for a relaxing game of golf. That always helped him to unwind. He wanted to go now whilst Gemma was out of the house. She had been so moody as of late and had started to lash out at him.

The last time it had happened, he had ended up with a black eye, a bloody nose and scratches all over his face. Gemma had given her father some excuse as to why Bill needed time off from work. He shuddered at the memory. He didn't want to be hit by her again. He had come to realise that he wanted out of this relationship, but he was too scared about what she might do to him if he tried to leave.

Bill tried to calm his nerves by busying himself with finding his golf clubs. He searched all over the house but he couldn't find them anywhere. He checked in the two places they were most likely to be, his car and the garden shed, but he still had no luck.

He flitted from room to room, trying to remember what he'd done with them the last time he had been to the golf course.

Then he remembered.

Gemma had forced him to take her with him the last time he went golfing. She hadn't even let him have a proper game. She told him that he was only allowed to practice his swing, so she had made him do just that. She had sat behind him in the seating area, huffing and puffing each time he took a golf ball from his basket and placed it on a tee. Bill had tried his best to keep her happy. He constantly offered to buy her refreshments, and he even tried to involve her in golf by asking if she would like to practice her swing. Each time she refused. Her huffs and puffs had grown louder and more vicious as time went on, and Bill decided that he could no longer ignore her. He let out a huge sigh and handed his basket over, with most of the golf balls still inside, to the gentleman who was playing next to him. Without a word from Bill and a grotesque smile from Gemma, they left the golf club.

Gemma had driven that day, and she had made him leave his clubs in her car when they had arrived back at Bill's house. He had since seen her dragging them into the house but had no idea where she had put them. He decided to check through her wardrobe while she was safely out of the house.

He padded up the stairs, feeling deflated but hopeful that a game of golf would cheer him up before he had to return to Gemma's wrath, which he knew would come once she found out he had gone out somewhere on his own. He opened the creaky wooden doors of the ancient wardrobe and saw his golf clubs standing there as if this was where they belonged.

His sad eyes moved slowly down the immaculate red and silver bag. He choked back his tears when he saw that the message he needed to see at this moment was gone.

To my lovely husband, Bill
Happy Wedding Day!!
I Love You, Tina xxxx

Tina had sewn it onto his golf bag so neatly and carefully in midnight black cotton. Now there was nothing but the outline. Gemma had hacked through Tina's embroidery so callously. He could just imagine the spiteful look on her face as she did it.

This is why she made me leave them in her car, he thought. *She did this because she was mad at me.*

In his anger, he wrenched the bag of golf clubs out of the wardrobe so hard that he also sent a small bottle green bag from the wardrobe flying across the room. He stomped through the bedroom and bent down to retrieve the bag. A few things had fallen out when it had landed with a thud next to his bed. A sudden fear gripped Bill, and he felt like he couldn't breathe. *What was all this? Mechanic's overalls? A brown wig?*

Bill rummaged through the bag and found several pairs of latex gloves, a mini hacksaw and… Sarah's gloves? Lots of different thoughts started to swirl in his mind and his heart was hammering in his chest.

"No," he muttered, tears welling in his eyes. "Tina."

He heard a key in the lock… Gemma. He shoved the bag and the golf clubs back into the wardrobe and wiped his eyes. He needed to call the police.

"Bill, darling!" Gemma shouted in a sing-song voice that made Bill want to vomit.

"Yes, I'm here." He appeared at the top of the stairs and looked at her, hoping that she wouldn't see that he had been crying. He looked at her in disgust, but she didn't seem to have noticed.

"Good. I have had a terrible day, so I would like you to run a bath for me, sweetums."

"Yes, I will do, sweetheart. I just need to get something from my car." Bill dashed outside with his phone in his hand and dived into his car. He snatched Detective Althorp's card from the centre console and dialled.

Nick arrived at the police station and punched the buzzer on the wall to get in. The intercom buzzed and a man spoke slowly as if he had all the time in the world.

"Hello? Do you have an appointment?" he drawled.

Nick was really agitated. "No!" he shouted. "I need to see Detective Althorp, now!"

"Can you tell me what this is regarding, please?"

"Man, open the door. It's about Sarah Bailey!"

Detective Althorp had heard Nick's shouts from his office window. He was walking down to the reception area at a brisk pace, but upon hearing Sarah's name, he charged towards the doors. He nearly swung them off their hinges in his hurry to get Nick inside. Together, they sped through the police station and were in Detective Althorp's office in less than a minute.

"I have evidence that Sarah is innocent!" Nick held his phone up. "You need to record this."

Detective Althorp invited Nick to sit on the chair on the other side of his desk and grabbed the recording equipment from his drawer.

"What do you have, Nick?" Detective Althorp asked as he was getting a disc ready.

"I've just recorded a phone call from a man telling me to

deposit ten million into a bank account or else some friends of theirs will kill Sarah in prison!"

Nick's anger turned to tears. Saying it out loud himself made it more real.

"Oh, come on, please!" Nick was pulling at his hair in his angst, begging Detective Althorp to hurry.

"Okay, it's ready, fire away."

With his phone firmly in his hand, Nick played the recording of the conversation he had just received from the withheld number. Detective Althorp was silent and had not moved at all since the recording had begun. His phone started to ring just as the recording came to an end. He listened, looked at Nick and held his finger up to his lips, ordering Nick to stay quiet.

Detective Althorp shouted, "I'll be right there!" He got up as fast as he could, thanked Nick and asked him to return to Suzanna's house and wait for his call. Nick was confused, but he could tell this was important, so he did as he was told and drove back to Suzanna's house. He told Suzanna and Katy about the mysterious phone calls and the abrupt end to his and Detective Althorp's meeting.

Chapter Twenty-One

While Bill was waiting for Detective Althorp, he made the decision to keep Gemma sweet so she wouldn't suspect anything. He went back inside the house and straight upstairs to the bathroom. He started to run the water in the bath and poured in the foam that smelt like out-of-date strawberries. He couldn't understand why Gemma loved it so much. He was sprinkling Gemma's rose petals in the bath when he felt her arms snake around his waist. He plastered a fake smile on his face as he turned around to face her. She had an evil-looking face; how had he not noticed this before?

"I'm going to change into my dressing gown, angel. Would you bring me a glass of *your* wine upstairs when the bath is ready?"

"Certainly dear, anything for you." His voice was shaking. Her hands left his waist and he heard her footsteps in the bedroom.

Gemma searched around the room for her favourite dressing gown. She opened her wardrobe and froze. Her hacksaw was lying at the bottom of the wardrobe, and she could see her wig sticking out of the bag. She had made sure that everything was inside and the bag folded over. She cursed herself. *Why didn't I get rid of this stuff?* Then, the realisation hit her. Bill had seen it. *This is why he's acting strange,* she thought. *Well, I'd better go and make sure he never breathes a word of this!*

She put on her vile green dressing gown and slipped the

pocket knife that she had taken with her on the night that Tina had died into the pocket. She crept downstairs to lock the front door just in case Bill tried to escape, then she tiptoed back upstairs to the bathroom where he was bending over the bath. He stood just as she approached him.

"Oh, you made me jump, sweetheart. Are you ready to get in?" he asked.

"Yes, but I wanted to ask you something first," she answered with a sick smile on her face. Bill started to back away from her but he had nowhere to go. Gemma was blocking the doorway. Bill continued to smile at her and tried to keep calm. He started to sweat.

"Ask away, darling."

"So when exactly did you realise that I was behind your precious wife's death?" She said this through gritted teeth and Bill's face turned green.

"What… what do you mean?" he stammered.

"Oh, don't play dumb with me, you idiot, I know you've seen my goody bag." She made a terrifying cackling noise that sent chills up Bill's spine. "The plan was going exceptionally well up until this point." She bared her teeth at Bill. "I was amazed at how easy it was to get *poor little Sarah* arrested. All I had to do was take her gloves. Simple, eh? Dear old Nick is about to part with his money to save her life, and I am not going to let you stand in the way of that." She poked him hard in his chest with her finger.

"Oh, and what are you going to do if Nick does pay? Go to the police station and tell them it was you? Yeah, right!"

"No, of course not. My very willing accomplice told Nick that he would help him if he gave us what we wanted, but I have no intention of doing that. Sarah can rot in there for all I care."

She laughed. "Oh well, it's a shame Bill, but…" She slid her hand into her pocket and pulled out the knife. She waved it threateningly in his face. "You put an end to my plan, and I put an end to you!" Gemma dived at Bill. He had been prepared for this, so he ducked under her arms and pulled her legs from under her. She whacked her head on the toilet. Blood started to seep from the wound on her head.

Bill could hear Gemma tearing after him down the stairs. He got to the front door and turned the handle. It wouldn't open. The laugh that came from behind him made his blood run cold.

"As if I would be that stupid Bill. Do you think I would make it that easy for you to go blabbing about me?" She inched closer and closer to him, holding the knife up so he could see it clearly. She was enjoying the look of terror on Bill's face. "My dad told me not to bother with you, you know. He said I needed somebody more like myself, clever, powerful and gifted in being able to get exactly what I want in life. I saw something in you. It must have been your pathetic nature and your willingness to do everything I said because, let's be honest, it certainly wasn't your looks, was it?" Bill's eyes left the knife and stared straight into her evil ones. "Oh, what's the matter, Bill? Did you think you were a catch? Did you think I was lucky to have you? Please. I could tell you were an easy target. I could use you for what I wanted and then get rid of you when you were no longer useful to me. I didn't imagine I would be getting rid of you like this, though, but…." She shrugged her shoulders and laughed. "I thought you would be happy when you found out that Tina was dead. You said you wanted her out of your house one way or the other so I thought I would make it easy for you. I went to visit a couple of friends in the prison where they are probably getting really close to Sarah at this point." She chuckled and winked at Bill.

"They came up with the fabulous idea of doing away with your wife so I could get my hands on your house and your money. The best part… they told me exactly what to do to make it look like an accident. I had been watching her for a while so I could figure out when to strike when you made that even easier for me. You gave her the divorce papers. I knew that she would be heartbroken, god knows why though, I mean, look at you." She looked at Bill with a disgusted look on her face. "I watched you from a distance. You nearly threw them at her and ran off. Then Sarah came over and nearly ruined the whole thing! She stayed with Tina all day, mopping up her tears probably, so I didn't think I would have a chance to do what I needed to, but then, she came out of the house and walked off down the road. I waited for a bit and then took my chances. It was all done and dusted by the time she came back." Gemma patted herself on her back. "I went to run a few errands afterwards, but I made sure I was home before you came back for your rest time, thereby making you my unknowing alibi. Yay to me! I went back to Tina's house when you had gone to work that evening so I could watch the show." She giggled.

Bill glared at Gemma, a look of hatred on his face. "How dare you refer to my wife's death as a show!" He said this through gritted teeth.

Gemma rolled her eyes and carried on as if they were sharing a nice story over tea and cake. "I saw Sarah leave quite late that night, she was trying to convince Tina to go with her, but she refused. I thought she might end up going to Sarah at some point so I waited. It worked a treat!" Gemma said excitedly. "The little cut that I put in her brake line only let her drive halfway to Sarah's house before she crashed. It looked like a freak accident." Bill had tears flowing down his face now. "Aww, what's the matter, Bill? Is my story upsetting you or are you missing your dead wife? I saw you at her funeral sobbing like a baby. I've never seen anything more pathetic in my life!" She faked a dramatic yawn and took her eyes off Bill.

He saw his chance. He dived through the living room door and then ran as fast as he could into the kitchen. He grabbed a knife and pointed it at Gemma as she skidded into the kitchen.

"This ends now, Gemma," he told her menacingly. "You are going to hand yourself in to the police and tell them exactly what you did. You won't be able to wriggle out of it because you are so stupid as to leave your, what was it you called it, your 'goody bag' upstairs in the wardrobe! Did you really think you wouldn't get caught with that lying around? Did you think idiot Bill wouldn't dare to open your wardrobe? Did you want to keep the evidence as a souvenir? I don't know why you kept it, Gemma, but now you have completely screwed yourself over." He started to laugh.

"It doesn't matter because I will soon be getting what I want from Nick, and then I will be leaving the country. I might find a house near Mr. Hotshot," she grinned wickedly. "I am never going to hand myself in!"

Just then, they heard a gigantic bang on the front door which sounded as if it had come off its hinges.

"Ahh, you won't need to after all. They have come for you!"

Gemma pretended to cry, and she discreetly put her knife back into her dressing gown pocket. She ran through the kitchen door towards Detective Althorp in the living room.

"Oh, thank goodness you're here! Bill was going to kill me!" she cried.

Bill put down the knife and joined them in the living room. He watched as Detective Althorp slapped a pair of handcuffs on

Gemma's wrists.

"No! What are you doing? You've got this all wrong. He was going to kill me!"

A female officer searched Gemma's pockets and pulled out the knife. She held it up to show her colleagues, then placed it in an evidence bag. Bill watched the scene unfold in front of him, wondering how close he had come to death, how close he had come to joining Tina as one of Gemma's victims.

Another officer appeared in the living room carrying the bag that Bill had found in the wardrobe. He placed the lot in another evidence bag.

Gemma did not say a word as she was led outside to a waiting police car. Bill noticed her crying for real in the back of the car. *Good*, he thought. *I hope she gets what she deserves.*

Four hours later, when the police had finally finished taking his statement and searching the house, Bill had a knock on his newly repaired door. He peered through the peephole timidly and swung the door open when he saw who it was.

"Suzanna, what are you doing here?" Sarah's mother was the last person Bill was expecting to see.

"I came to thank you profusely." She placed her hand on her heart as Bill stepped aside to let her in. "You have just saved my baby girl from that wretched place, and judging by what that evil witch said to Nick, you have saved her life too!"

She started to cry and threw her arms around Bill. He hugged her as she cried and waited for her sobs to subside before he spoke.

"I'm so sorry about all of this, Suzanna. If I hadn't brought her into our lives, none of this would have happened. I wish every day that my Tina was still by my side, brightening up all of our lives." He managed a very watery smile.

"Don't be silly, Bill, you didn't know Gemma was capable of this. You don't realise what some people are hiding. Nick was going to come over, but as soon as the police knew that Sarah was innocent, they let her out of prison straight away. They've taken him to fetch her and bring her home where she belongs. I can't wait to see her; she's been through hell. How are you doing after all this?"

"Have you got time for a coffee?" Bill asked her.

Suzanna checked her watch. "Yes, I have."

"Please have a seat. I'll put the kettle on and tell you everything."

Suzanna listened intently and stayed silent throughout as Bill started from how he had met Gemma, right up until the point when the police had left a short time ago after searching his house. Suzanna was gobsmacked and was open-mouthed by the time Bill had finished.

"How did she expect to get away with this when she gave Nick bank account details? Surely, the officers would track her down through those?"

"The police suspect fake names, fake documents and disguises. She may have been caught by them investigating that, but I found the bag pretty much at the same time that she had an accomplice call Nick. They got her before any of that needed to be done. Oh, one thing I forgot," he added, "Gemma and a friend came to Tina's funeral. She was teasing me because I was crying and completely heartbroken. I wondered if this was when she took Sarah's gloves, but I don't know for sure if she came to the wake."

Suzanna snapped out of her trance-like state. "What?" she gasped. "She has Sarah's gloves? Why does she have Sarah's gloves? She thought she'd lost them. She was looking for them in my house." Bill looked nervous now.

"When I went to the police station, Detective Althorp told me that her DNA had been found on Tina's brake line. I'm ashamed to say this, but I did believe that Sarah might have had something to do with it. I'm sorry, my head was not with it, and I wasn't thinking straight during my interview with Detective Althorp. When I found the bag in the wardrobe and noticed Sarah's gloves in there, I realised that she had been framed. Gemma knew that the police were investigating the possibility that Tina's death wasn't an accident. She made me take her with me when we went to collect a few items that Tina had left in the car. She must have seen Sarah's gloves in your house then and seized her opportunity because she knew that the police would find the damaged brake line. She obviously used them to plant evidence on Tina's car, knowing that Sarah would get the blame. I'm so sorry that I ever doubted her, Suzanna, please forgive me." He was pressing his hands together, begging her.

"I forgive you," she said, smiling. "I suppose when your head was still in the shed, you were bound to believe what the police told you. I will always be grateful to you for getting my girl back home again and exposing that nasty piece of work." She held his hands as he thanked her over and over again. "Well, I had better be going. I want to be at home when Sarah gets back." She stood and hugged Bill. "Thank you again," she whispered.

Detective Althorp and Nick had travelled to Lakewall Prison with the blue lights flashing and the sirens blaring. Neither of them wanted Sarah to be in there a second longer. They arrived just as Sarah was being given back her things in a massive see-through plastic bag. Nick threw himself through the doorway as soon as a prison officer had opened it and hugged Sarah harder than ever. Tears fell down both of their faces instantly.

"Nick, I'm so glad to see you!" Sarah was struggling to speak through her gasping sobs.

"I'm so glad to see you too. I love you so much." He kissed her face over and over again. "Come on, let's get you out of here."

Detective Althorp followed behind them and didn't speak until they climbed back into the police car. He turned to Sarah.

"Well, I did promise you I would look at that footage again." He said this with a smile on his face but then looked very serious. "I'm so sorry, Sarah. I should have believed you."

"I understand that you were just doing your job, but… I wish you had believed me!" She giggled. Detective Althorp was happy to see that she hadn't lost her sense of humour whilst she was in that awful place.

"Come on then, let's get you back where you belong."

He started the engine and pulled out of the car park smoothly. Sarah appreciated being able to ride in a car again, even if it was in the back of a police car! She thought she would never be in a car ever again. She settled into Nick's shoulder in the back, trying not to think about what could have been.

She realised when they pulled onto Suzanna's drive that she had fallen asleep on the way home. The weeks of stress and worry had finally caught up with her. She started to sob again as soon as she set eyes on her mother and sister, who were rushing out to greet her with wide-open arms.

Chapter Twenty-Two

Returning to America just after Christmas felt bittersweet for Sarah. Although she was glad to be home in the surroundings that had quickly become so familiar to her, she missed Suzanna and Katy more now than ever. Her time in that wretched prison cell had made her think about her family a lot more. Just the thought of being away from them forever and not having a choice in the matter had made her anxiety levels go through the roof. She vowed to see them as much as possible from now on, even though she was thousands of miles away from them.

The wedding was fast approaching, and it gave Sarah something to occupy her mind and finally take it off the horrendous ordeal that she had endured over the past couple of months. She set about writing her vows as she and Nick had agreed, and she poured her heart out onto the paper. With a week to go, every small detail had been organised and Sarah started to feel herself relax a bit. She was eagerly awaiting Suzanna and Katy's arrival back at the house. She was so excited to have a decent amount of time to spend catching up with her mother and sister, especially after not having had much time with them after everything that had happened. Nick had invited them to stay at the cottage on the grounds until the day before the wedding. Sarah was more than happy with these arrangements, and she had even stayed in the cottage with them for a couple of nights, sleeping next to her sister in one of the double beds.

Back in her own bed on the morning before the wedding,

Sarah was woken by Nick's soothing singing voice, flowing into the room like waves, as he walked into the bedroom with her breakfast on a tray. He had tried his best to arrange her runny scrambled egg into a love heart shape on top of her burnt toast. Sarah looked at the tray, then back to Nick. He had the cutest smile on his face, clearly proud of the effort he had put into this.

"Thank you!" Sarah said genuinely. "Is, er, Miranda not working today?"

"Yeah, she's here, but I wanted to make your breakfast. I'm sorry about the toast. I got distracted by the egg," he said sheepishly.

"Oh, don't be silly, I don't mind burnt toast. I'm sure it will taste lovely, and besides, it's not how it looks…"

"It's how it tastes." Nick finished.

"Exactly," she said as she popped some egg on toast into her mouth.

"You can say it's gross if you want; I don't mind." Nick pretended to look hurt.

"It's not gross… but I can definitely tell that Miranda hasn't cooked this!" Sarah teased.

"Luckily for you and everybody else here at the moment, I'm taking us all out for dinner tonight so you can eat something a bit more edible!"

The afternoon spent in the garden with her and Nick's family was joyous. Their mothers were chatting as if they were best friends and their sisters swapped many stories in whispered tones so Suzanna, Gloria and Andrew wouldn't hear, Sarah suspected.

Nick, Tim, his father and brothers had disappeared with what looked like silver guns in their hands and goggles on their faces. They came back an hour later covered in lots of different coloured paint! Sarah's expression was dangerous. Chad and

Cole scarpered at the fire in Sarah's eyes.

"Nick, what the hell?" she cried.

"Calm down, babe, it's fine!" he laughed.

"Don't laugh! We're getting married tomorrow, and you're all going to be covered in bruises on the wedding photos!"

"Don't worry. I made sure we only aimed for legs… and chests… and arms." He got quieter with each word he spoke.

"So basically then, everywhere but the face!"

"Nick, I'd stop messing with her if I were you, or else I will be pushing you around in a wheelchair tomorrow." Tim interrupted.

"Okay, okay." Nick lifted his polo shirt and showed Sarah his padded vest. He leant forward to kiss Sarah on her nose, then trotted off and sat down next to his mother, while still smiling cheekily at Sarah. She stood still, feeling very relieved and then giggled when Gloria playfully swiped Nick on the back of the head whilst she was still in a full flow of conversation with Suzanna.

The day had flown by. Everybody was extremely jolly and full of merriment after the luxury meal they were now digesting. Gloria and Andrew bade everybody a good night, warned their sons to behave and to keep the noise level to a minimum, then hitched a ride with Tim in one of the golf carts down to the cottage. Nick was joining his brothers in one last drink in the garden before they said their goodbyes until the next morning.

Sarah had taken this as a welcome distraction and had sneaked off up to her bedroom, unnoticed by anybody. She slid several items of clothing along the rail in her wardrobe and pulled out the only box she hadn't unpacked that had been shipped over from England when she moved here. She stood quietly for a few seconds, listening out for any potential incoming interruptions. When she could hear nothing apart from loud laughter coming from one of her future brothers-in-law, way out in the garden, she carefully tore the tape from the top of the box. She reached inside and transferred the bag she was looking for from the box to her overnight bag that was currently stashed under the bed. She smiled to herself as she imagined her wedding day, then zipped up her bag, carried it downstairs and added it to the mountainous pile of items that were already waiting in the boot of Tim's car. In just a few short hours, she would be walking through the doors of Blossom Spring Manor House, where she would be spending her last night as Miss Sarah Bailey.

"All right, blushing bride, up you get!" Rachel shouted as she charged into Sarah's room the next morning, in full bridesmaid mode. Her hair was already in rollers, and she had donned her special dressing gown, which had 'Bridesmaid' sewn on the back of it in bright pink neon cotton and 'Rachel' sewn onto the front in the same eye-catching shade.

Sarah jumped and pulled her earplugs out. "Bloody hell, Rachel, you scared me even with these in! What time is it?"

"Time to get up," she answered simply.

"Come on, Sarah!" She heard her sister's screechy, excited voice echoing from her and Suzanna's room two doors away and got up at once.

"Umm… you might have gathered that your sister is already awake?" Rachel said sarcastically.

"Hmm, I thought so. I'll go and tell her I'm up now before she screeches again, otherwise I might not be able to hear Nick's vows later!"

She wandered off to Katy's room with her fingers in her ears.

Rachel could tell as soon as Katy had clapped eyes on Sarah from the tell-tale scream that had resounded from her room.

Sarah had been pulled clumsily into the room by Katy, who was also wearing a 'Bridesmaid' dressing gown with her name on the front. Suzanna was sitting up in her bed holding a cup of tea in one hand and a newspaper in the other. She looked up at all the commotion.

"Ah, good morning, sweetheart!" Suzanna said merrily.

"Morning, Mum. How can you possibly be reading the newspaper with all the racket going on?" She jerked her head towards her sister, who was now holding her bridesmaid dress up to her body. "Oi, put that back on the hanger. I don't want any creases!" Katy did as she was told immediately. The stare that Sarah had still scared Katy more than she cared to admit!

"She's been screeching and squealing all morning. I've got so used to it now I've been able to ignore her. I did tell her to keep it down so she didn't wake the whole house." She glared at her youngest daughter. "I'm surprised you didn't hear her."

Sarah held up a pair of earplugs. "I couldn't hear her. I heard Rachel barge into my room, though! Speaking of Rachel, she came into my room wearing one of these." Sarah said, pointing to Katy's robe. "Where have they come from?"

"Rachel had them made for us!" Katy answered excitedly. "Here's yours!"

Katy hurled what looked like a fluffy white ball straight at Sarah's face.

"Thanks, you moron!" Sarah scolded, although jokingly. She held it up and let it unfurl in front of her. There in glittery silver cotton was the word 'Bride'. She turned it around so she could see her name on the front. Instead of 'Sarah', like she expected to see, it was 'Mrs. Taylor' that had been neatly sewn onto the front of the robe.

"Wow, this is great!" Sarah beamed as she put it on.

"Right, enough chit-chat, get dressed, I'm starving! I'll meet you downstairs for breakfast."

The four ladies ate breakfast together around a white and glass table with a huge parasol above their heads, set within the manor's grounds. It made Sarah think of a meadow with vibrant, green grass and tall trees as far as the eye could see. There was even a lake that had swans and ducks gliding through the water.

"Are you ready for this then, Sarah?" Rachel asked, beaming.

"Yeah, I can't wait to marry Nick. I would marry him right now if he came out here!" She laughed. "He's been an absolute dream with the wedding planning because he knows more about how weddings are done over here, and I didn't know where to go for anything. I didn't realise how many differences there were between English and American weddings either! We kept confusing each other when we first started to plan everything, so we decided to incorporate both sides."

"Oh, that's so nice," Rachel said. "It will be lovely to see how things are done across the pond!" Rachel raised her glass of fruit juice. "To you, you gorgeous lady and my baby brother!"

"Cheers!" They repeated.

It was at this moment when Suzanna pushed a small but beautifully wrapped present across the table towards Sarah.

"What's this?" Sarah asked.

"It's your something new, open it," Suzanna whispered, full of emotion.

Sarah took the box and pulled gently at the soft, silky pink ribbon. She looked at her mother wonderingly as she tore the wrapping paper. It was a smooth, black suede box. Inside it was a large silver heart-shaped locket with roses expertly engraved into the precious metal.

"Look inside," Suzanna nodded.

Carefully, Sarah unclipped the locket and gasped as her father's face looked back at her. She covered her face with both hands as she cried. Suzanna, Katy and Rachel enveloped her in a huge cuddle and they cried together. When they returned to their seats, the locket was admired by each of them as it was passed around the table.

"I'm sorry, darling, I didn't mean to upset you," Suzanna said softly.

"Ahh, that's okay, Mum," Sarah replied as she dabbed at her tears. "I do miss Dad, especially today, but I feel like he will be walking down the aisle with us now." She smiled.

"He would have loved Nick," Suzanna stated.

Sarah nodded and touched Suzanna's hand, then for the first time that day, she checked her watch. It was ten a.m.

"Okay, ladies, I think we need to go and start getting ready!"

Chapter Twenty-Three

"Tim, come on, man!" Nick shouted through the house.

"Nick, chill!" Tim appeared behind Nick and put his hands on his shoulders. He shook them lightly. "The ceremony starts at three p.m. It is only ten thirty a.m. We have plenty of time to get to the manor and get ready. Besides, your parents aren't here yet."

Nick shot out of his front door and threw himself into one of the golf carts in the garden. Before Tim could get to the front door, Nick had already driven off in the direction of the cottage where Gloria and Andrew were staying.

"I hope they're ready to go," Tim muttered to himself.

A few minutes later, Nick and his parents reappeared in the golf cart, looking happier than ever. Nick pulled up behind Tim's car. He took his mother by the hand and helped her out of the golf cart, then immediately ushered her into the car.

"Come on, Dad, hop in!" Nick told his father sternly.

Andrew slapped Nick's cheek lightly. "Have patience, Nicholas and enjoy this day."

Nick, completely ignoring his father's advice, impatiently closed the car door behind Andrew and jumped into the front with Tim.

"Okay, Tim, let's go."

Just under an hour later, the glorious, sprawling grounds of Blossom Spring Manor House came into view. Tim drove through the majestic iron gates after chatting briefly with the security guard. Gloria gave a small 'oh' and put her hand to her mouth at the sight of the manor. Andrew stared out of the car window, mesmerised, and Nick smiled from ear to ear. True to the name of the manor, the trees in the grounds were blooming with pink blossom, and the flowers on either side of the long, sweeping driveway were bursting with different colours. The neat lawns seemed to stretch on for miles and miles. The manor house was an extremely old building but still looked incredible with its pencil grey brickwork, many impressive chimneys and too many square and arch-shaped windows to count. On the right of the house sat a hand-carved, three-tier white marble and stone water fountain with lots of vibrant coloured flowers growing from the stone pots around the edges. The scene in front of them reminded Nick of a landscape drawing. It was perfect in every way.

As they got closer to the manor house, Nick's heart dropped into his stomach at the sight of a person with a camera, manically taking pictures. Instinctively, he put his hands up to his face to shield himself from view.

"Er Nick," Tim said. "I don't think Sarah will be very happy if you're covering your face in your wedding photographs."

"What?" he asked, baffled. Then he looked at the man's beaming face that had appeared from behind the camera. It was Dirk, one of the two photographers that Sarah had insisted on hiring. Nick giggled with relief as Tim parked his car.

Standing at the window, Katy squealed, making the rest of the ladies turn their heads sharply in her direction.

"What?" Rachel asked.

"Nick's here!"

"Oh man, I'm nervous now," Sarah told Rachel, who was

applying her eyeliner like a professional makeup artist. Rachel stepped away from Sarah with the eyeliner pencil still in her hand. She grabbed her phone to check the time.

"Eleven thirty," she stated. "I knew he would be mega early."

"I think it's cute," Katy smiled. "He wanted to get here as soon as he could."

"I suspect he's been rushing my parents. He's probably had, '*slow down and enjoy the day*' from my dad." Rachel and the others laughed. Her impression of Andrew was uncanny!

After lots of champagne-sipping, hair curling, makeup applying and the snapping of Vivian, the second photographer's camera, two o'clock arrived, and Sarah could wait no longer. She stepped carefully into the delicate fabric of her wedding dress. She gently pulled the dress up her body and placed the straps onto her shoulders. She stood quietly in front of the mirror as Suzanna zipped up the lace back. Sarah felt too overwhelmed to speak at this moment. Seeing herself in her wedding dress, knowing that this was her wedding day, felt surreal to her. Suzanna reached up to place the embellished, floor-length veil into Sarah's beautiful, wavy hair. Then she straightened the stately diamond tiara that Sarah had borrowed from Gloria. It made her feel like a princess the instant it touched her head.

Sarah had fallen in love with the tiara as soon as Gloria had shown it to her and carefully removed it from the emerald green velvet box a month before the big day. She was honoured to be wearing something as breathtaking as this, and the fact that it belonged to Nick's mother really touched her heart. Sarah knew that this was Gloria's way of welcoming her into the family.

"All done, sweetheart," Suzanna smiled.

"Thanks, Mum," Sarah replied.

Suzanna walked over to the dressing table, which was laden

with makeup, jewellery, hair clips and several boxes of tissues. Suzanna grabbed a tissue from the open box and handed it to Sarah.

"It's okay to cry on your wedding day, and I know you're nervous but don't forget…" Suzanna lifted the locket with the photograph of Stan inside and fastened it around Sarah's neck. "Me and Dad are both with you."

Sarah embraced her mother and closed her eyes. Images of Stan and Tina played through her mind like an old movie. She could see their smiles, the look of joy on their faces. She imagined them in the wedding outfits they would both be wearing right at this moment if tragedy had not struck twice over. Tears sprung to her eyes, but she dabbed them away with her tissue.

"I'll go see if the girls are ready," Suzanna said.

She left Sarah alone in the room, still standing in front of the mirror. She ran her hands down the bodice of her wedding dress, feeling all of the immaculate detail with her hands. She lifted her bouquet of white roses from the bed and held them as if they were a precious newborn baby. She turned the bouquet round until she could see the small blue photo frame that was tucked safely inside.

"Let's do this, Teeny," Sarah whispered to the photograph of a very happy, smiling Tina.

The hours leading up to this moment had dragged by but now, through the open and ornate wooden door, Sarah heard the seven-piece orchestra start to play a familiar song. Her eyes filled with tears immediately; she could see Nick so clearly in her mind down on one knee before her in the dance studio.

Sarah closed her eyes, lifted her locket to her lips and whispered a prayer to her father. She gently linked her arm through Suzanna's, then looked back at Katy and Rachel.

"Ready?" Sarah asked them.

"Ready," they answered in unison.

They slowly walked into the room, which had been beautifully decorated. The scent that emanated from the delicate white roses all around the room was soft and sweet. The crystals, set into the centre of each rose, made the room sparkle. Each golden chair had a floaty sky blue sash draped over the back of it, held into place with four more fresh, white roses. A pristine, ivory carpet had been placed from the top to the bottom of the aisle, and Sarah felt like she was walking on a cloud as soon as she stepped foot on it.

Sarah started to walk down the aisle with Suzanna next to her and her bridesmaids behind her. She heard gasps from the guests as they looked her way, but her eyes fell only on Nick. He was standing at the top of the aisle, the sun glaring in through the window shone on him from behind, lighting him up. Even though he looked a little teary himself, the smile on his face went from ear to ear as he watched Sarah walk towards him. He looked so handsome in his navy blue suit, stunning silver waistcoat and silver tie. The smart black shoes that he was wearing were so shiny they could have been used as a mirror. Tim, who had the honour of being Nick's best man, stood beside him wearing the same suit but a slight difference in tie. His was sky blue, the colour matched Katy and Rachel's dresses perfectly.

Sarah had to fight the urge to run to Nick, she felt like she was walking at a snail's pace. She couldn't wait to get her hands on the man that would very soon be her husband. Instead, she continued to walk in step with her mother, and finally, she clasped hands with Nick at the top of the aisle.

Suzanna kissed her eldest daughter softly on her cheek,

relieved her of her huge bouquet of roses and took her seat next to Katy. They joined hands as the music faded into the background and watched as Sarah and Nick started the next step into their future together.

"Good afternoon!" The registrar announced. "We are gathered here today for the coming together of Nick and Sarah in marriage. Love is a celebration. It is heartwarming to see all of you marvellous people here to witness this joyous occasion. Nick and Sarah have written their own vows. Nick, please proceed."

"Thank you." He reached into his jacket pocket and pulled out a piece of very neatly folded paper. "Sarah, I'm really nervous. Sorry, that's not part of my vows."

The guests and Sarah laughed.

"Sarah," he started again. "I love you. I know we haven't been together for years and years, but it feels like I've known you forever. The month we spent apart before you came here to live with me was like torture and every day without you was a struggle because I missed you so much. We have faced challenges together already, challenges that are now firmly behind us. To me, this proved that together we are a powerhouse, and we will always be able to get through anything. I never want to be without you ever again, and I am so happy that you agreed to marry me." He smiled cutely and pretended to wipe sweat from his forehead.

"Thank you, Nick," said the registrar. "Sarah, please proceed."

"Nick," she started. "I still feel like the luckiest girl in the world. We met when you chose me to share the stage with you and now look at what that has led to." She gestured around the room as Nick started to well up with tears. "Waking up this morning, I had never felt so much joy in my heart. Just being able to get to this day fills me up with happiness inside. I promise that we will never be apart again, so bad luck if you start to get sick of me," Sarah laughed, and Nick playfully rolled his eyes, his grin still fixed firmly in place. "I love you and I can't wait to spend the rest of my life with you."

Nick lunged forwards and kissed Sarah full on the lips.

"Nick, too early, mate! You're supposed to wait until you're pronounced husband and wife!" His brother, Cole, shouted.

Laughter erupted all around the room. The registrar was trying but failing to hide his own laughter behind the book that he was holding.

"I'm sorry, I couldn't resist," Nick told the registrar.

"That's quite all right. Let's continue. Tim, could we please have the rings?"

Tim, still laughing silently, stood and placed Nick and Sarah's rings onto the table in front of them. He patted Nick on his back and returned to his seat next to Nick's mother.

"Nick, please place Sarah's ring on her finger and repeat after me. Sarah."

"Sarah."

"I give you this ring as a token of my love, honour and respect."

"I give you this ring as a token of my love, honour and respect," Nick repeated.

"It is a symbol to show my promise to be by your side for as long as I live," the registrar finished.

"It is a symbol to show my promise to be by your side for as long as I live." Nick slid the plain platinum wedding band down Sarah's finger and looked straight into her eyes.

"Sarah, please repeat after me."

Sarah repeated the same words that Nick had spoken and

carefully slid his own matching wedding band down his finger.

"By the power vested in me, I now pronounce you husband and wife. You may kiss." The registrar announced.

As Nick and Sarah shared their first kiss as husband and wife, there was hooting and wolf-whistling coming from the groom's side of the room. They both highly suspected that those noises had come from Nick's mischievous brothers. All of the guests clapped and cheered loudly.

"I now present to you, Mr. and Mrs. Taylor!"

The cheering continued as Nick and Sarah shook the hand of the registrar and walked back down the aisle together, finally as a married couple.

Chapter Twenty-Four

"I'm pleased to announce the arrival of Mr. and Mrs. Taylor!" Pete boomed down the microphone as Nick and Sarah walked through the doors into their wedding reception, their photographers snapping away with their cameras. Just as Nick and Sarah had planned, the lights from the chandeliers faded, and the disco and spotlights lit up. Their guests had not yet seen them dance together, so Nick and Sarah had decided to treat them to a waltz around the dance floor to the song they had chosen. It was one of Pete's and was called 'Promise Me You Will Hold Me Forever'. It was a slow, sensual song and Pete sang it superbly down the microphone that he was still holding.

The room was so silent that you could have heard a pin drop. The guests gaped at the beauty of the dance that was being performed in front of their eyes. Some of them had tears welling, some had covered their mouths with their hands and others, like Katy, stood rooted to the spot with their mouths hanging open in shock. Halfway through the song, Nick and Sarah turned towards the crowd and bowed. Cheers from the guests rang out.

Nick saw his chance to whisk his new bride away from the centre of the floor as the guests who wanted to dance got up in their droves. Nick took Sarah to a dimly lit part of the room, pulled her close and trailed soft kisses from her forehead to her cheek and then finally to her lips. He pressed his body against hers as they kissed, breathing in her scent and loving the feel of her so close.

“I love you,” he told her.

“I love you too,” she answered.

He lifted her arms and placed them around his neck. He swayed slowly with her in his arms to their song that Pete was still crooning to, gently moving his body from side to side, perfectly in sync with her. They kissed again, losing themselves in each other once more.

“At least wait until your guests have gone home first, you two!” Pete shouted.

Nick and Sarah jumped apart laughing and found Pete and the rest of the guests looking in their direction. The lights had come back up as the song was finishing, and neither Nick nor Sarah had noticed.

“Shut up, you, a bride and groom are allowed to kiss whenever they want to on their wedding day!” Nick shouted back and grinned cheekily.

Pete chuckled and handed the microphone back to the DJ.

“Come on then, I can have you all to myself later,” Nick winked at Sarah. “Let’s get back to our guests.”

Holding hands, they came out of their spot and hugged and kissed their guests as they walked around the room together. They were flabbergasted at the sight as they took in their surroundings.

There were twenty large, round tables each laid out around the edge of the dancefloor. They had been covered with white cotton, and elegant lace tablecloths and the matching chair covers had a blue silk bow tied around the middle. The centrepieces looked even better than Sarah thought possible. She had chosen tall glass vases in honour of her and Nick’s first date back in his hotel in London. The cream roses reached out of the vase and above the guests' heads. Sarah had wanted lights incorporated into them, so she had instantly fallen in love with the way the manor house staff had hung cute lanterns from the roses and threaded warm white berry lights throughout the stunning centrepieces. The lanterns and lights created a calming, cosy atmosphere all around the room.

Sarah and Nick had decided against having a top table, opting instead for a sweetheart table just for the two of them. They had no table plans, they wanted their guests to sit with whoever they wanted. It came as no surprise to Sarah when she spotted her mother sitting at Tim's side with their heads close together, already deep in conversation. He had removed his jacket and hung it casually on the back of his chair. His arm was resting on the back of Suzanna's chair, and he was stroking her arm with his finger.

"Nick?" Sarah asked as they finally made their way over to their table after greeting all of their guests. "Why are there four chairs at our table?"

"Oh, you'll see," he grinned.

As she got closer, she noticed a glittery frame sitting on the table, with a photograph inside that she had looked at hundreds of times before. It was one of her favourites – Stan and Tina at Sarah's sixteenth birthday party just before he started to get ill. She dabbed at her eyes whilst trying not to mess up her makeup, as tears fell for what felt like the tenth time that day. She looked back towards her mother, who blew her a kiss.

Nick reached underneath the table and handed Sarah a small bag. She pulled out a set of cufflinks that read 'Father of the Bride' and a bridesmaid sash. She arranged them so they sat neatly in front of the photo frame. She stood for a few minutes in Nick's arms, doing nothing but staring at the photo. She felt so connected with her dad and Tina at that moment that she didn't dare move through fear of it breaking. The flash of a camera behind her let Sarah know that one of the photographers had perfectly caught this moment, and she couldn't have been more grateful.

Sarah sat next to the chairs that had been tucked beneath her and Nick's table for Stan and Tina, as she, Nick and all of their guests tucked into their mouth-watering five-course meal. Served first were their canape appetisers, which consisted of fresh ricotta cheese spread over a warm french baguette. Next, they enjoyed a wide variety of thick and rustic soups, all of which had a lovely, creamy taste. Sarah chose the tomato, she wasn't very adventurous when it came to soups, but Nick had chosen the Italian soup, which was full of different kinds of meats such as beef, pork and chicken. He ate it mega fast.

"Hungry?" Sarah asked him as he scraped his spoon against his bowl, trying to get every last bit out of it.

"Aww, man, that soup was delicious! I've gotta learn how to make that!"

"You? Really?" Sarah teased.

"Okay then, you. But only because I don't want to burn the kitchen down!"

They were still talking about the lack of Nick's cooking skills when the salad courses were brought out of the kitchen.

Sarah gasped. "Woah!" She exclaimed as the waiter placed hers down in front of her. "This doesn't look anything like any salad that I've ever made!"

On the plate were fresh onions, goat's cheese, crispy bacon, mixed greens and cubes of ham served with a lemon dressing. After this course, Sarah gazed around the room and was amused to see a lot of people loosening their belts to give them a bit of extra room. She, herself, was glad she had only eaten a small bowl of fruit for breakfast.

Nick's favourite part of the meal came next. Out of the four choices, two of which were vegetarian dishes – spring vegetable risotto or grilled salmon, Nick had chosen a rack of lamb with vegetables and potatoes and nodded in appreciation as he was eating. Sarah had opted for the smothered chicken and vegetables, and she enjoyed every single mouthful.

At last, came Sarah's favourite course, dessert. On everybody's plate were four mini desserts. A lemon meringue tart, a velvety chocolate cream tart with fresh strawberries laid neatly on the top, a creamy vanilla cheesecake and a strawberry cupcake topped with thick pink frosting and an edible red rose.

Sarah thought she wouldn't be able to move for a good half hour after the meal she had just devoured. She happily sat and scanned the room, watching everybody chatting, laughing and hugging each other. Suddenly, she shot up like a bottle of pop!

"Nick, look at the cake!" she gasped.

Sarah sprinted over to the table which held their towering six-tier fruit and sponge wedding cake. Nick was behind her, although he was walking rather slowly. They both gasped in amazement when they laid eyes on the cake properly. The pure white icing had been draped over the cake flawlessly and styled with a lace pattern on three of the tiers. Pretty light blue coloured ribbon had been wrapped around the bottom of each tier and a display of sugar paste roses, the same colour as the ribbon, sat on the top of the cake. Just like in Sarah's bridal bouquet, a small sparkly crystal had been placed in the centre of each rose. She walked around the table several times, viewing the cake from all angles.

"This is amazing, Nick! Is this Cole's handiwork?"

"No, not this time. He didn't dare in case he messed it up!" Nick laughed.

Sarah was still in full admiration mode when Katy came marching through the guests on the dancefloor with a determined look on her face. Nick made a hasty retreat.

"That was a secret you kept rather well, sister!" Katy exclaimed.

"What secret?" Sarah asked, baffled.

"I did NOT know that you could dance like that!" She jokingly held her hand up to Sarah's face, pretending to be mad at her.

"I can't dance that well on my own." Sarah insisted, playfully slapping Katy's hand down. "It's just that Nick dances SO well that he makes me look good! Come on, you, let me take you for a twirl!"

Sarah and Katy danced energetically to the many classics that the DJ played. They even busted out a few moves of their own that they had invented years ago when they used to put on shows for their mum and dad. They had been dancing for hours when Nick sauntered over to them, looking as sexy as hell. He'd removed his tie, unfastened two of his buttons and rolled the sleeves of his shirt up to his forearms.

"I've got another little surprise for you!" Nick purred in Sarah's ear.

"Another one?" She gasped.

She watched him walk backwards to the stage, not taking his eyes off hers. He picked up the DJ's microphone and put it to his mouth. A song that Sarah had played over and over again in her bedroom before she met Nick at his concert echoed around the room. 'Say Yes!' had a smooth, chilled-out beat, and Sarah started to sway her body in time to the music. She still had her sister tucked under her arm, and they stepped from side to side as Nick belted out the first lyrics of the song. The guests who had raced to the dance floor to get a better view of Nick had raised their phones in the air with the torches alight. The photographers looked as if they had won the lottery. They ran frantically through the room in order to put themselves into the best positions to capture this moment through their camera lenses. Dirk stood slightly behind Nick, and Vivian had squeezed behind Sarah and Katy, silhouetting them against the disco lights.

A few minutes later, Nick leapt off the stage and shimmied his ass to the beat of the music. He fixed his eyes on his bride, a smile teasing his mouth. Sarah giggled at the way Nick was moving his body, dancing vigorously, as he very quickly shortened the distance between them.

Katy shot off the dance floor like a rocket and landed next to Suzanna. She would have been far too close for her liking to the public display of affection that was inevitably about to happen. Within seconds, when Sarah and Nick were within touching distance of each other, the whole crowd erupted. Nick had bowed Sarah down in a dramatic way as if they were in a movie and kissed her full on her lips. Katy joined in with the cheering, whooping and clapping but was also genuinely worried about how her sister's back would be feeling after that!

Tonight had been the best night Katy had ever had, and she'd been a part of some very rowdy nights out with her uni pals on several occasions before! She had met and had long conversations with people she never thought she would meet in a million years. She had well and truly let her hair down and felt completely free as she threw some major shapes on the dance floor. She replayed the day over in her head and felt deliriously happy for her sister and new brother-in-law, as well as feeling rather drunk as she made her way up to her room later on that night. She had left Suzanna and Tim talking, drinking and eating wedding cake at their table downstairs. Without removing her shoes or her bridesmaid's dress, she collapsed onto her bed and fell asleep instantly. Soon after Katy had retired to her bedroom, the DJ announced it was time for a final dance from the bride and groom. Nick and Sarah took to the floor once more but decided that this dance would not be a rehearsed one. They held each other close, kissing and cuddling all the way through the song. At the end of it, the lights came up, and the guests came forward onto the dance floor, eager to get close to Nick and Sarah to wish them well one more time before they left.

Chapter Twenty-Five

Finally arriving at their honeymoon suite, Nick reached into his pocket for the key card and unlocked the door. He pushed it open then turned back to Sarah.

"As is tradition…" Nick paused and swept Sarah off her feet. They kissed as he carried her through the door and kicked it shut behind him. When they came up for air, they looked around them and were taken aback by this gorgeous space.

The round, king-sized bed was decorated with dozens of rose petals and pretty lights in the intricately carved oak headboard. There was a bottle of Nick's favourite champagne in an ice bucket located on a dressing table, along with a basket full of chocolates, strawberries and other goodies. Sarah inhaled sharply as she turned and noticed a jacuzzi the size of a small swimming pool, sitting atop three marble steps on the other side of the room. The soft lighting gave the room a cosy, romantic feel, and she couldn't have been happier that this was where she would be spending her wedding night with her new husband.

"Would you like some champagne?" Nick asked as he picked up the bottle of the very expensive liquid.

"Yes, please, I'll go and pull some of these clips out of my hair while you do that." Sarah smiled and felt a blush creeping up her face, then walked quickly to the bathroom, grabbing her overnight bag on the way. She had felt so daring and brave when she had packed her bag the day before. She definitely didn't feel it now.

Come on, she told herself. *Imagine the look on his face when he sees. I'll regret it if I don't, come on, do it!*

Hastily, she unzipped the back of her wedding dress and carefully took her arms out of the straps. She let the dress fall down her body and quietly opened her bag. She rummaged around inside it and felt a frisson of excitement just looking at the sexy black bra, panties and red sheer dress that Davina, the manager from 'Seductive', had thrown into her basket all those months ago!

She slid her arms through the bra straps and tucked the cups beneath her breasts. *Wow, push-up bra indeed!* Sarah thought. Next, she pulled the delicate panties up her legs. The material of the bra and panties against her skin was silky smooth. She unbuttoned the red dress and put her arms through the spaghetti straps, then buttoned it up at her middle. She grabbed the shiny black stiletto heels that she had bought a couple of days before the wedding and slid her feet inside, then stood and looked at herself in the floor-length mirror.

As she had told Nick, she pulled all of the clips out of her hair and ran her fingers through her long, wavy locks, letting it cascade down her back. She looked at herself in the mirror once more and smiled, feeling surprisingly confident.

With adrenaline pumping round her body, she slowly opened the bathroom door and peeked around it. Nick was lounging on the bed in a relaxed position, leaning back against the frame with his legs stretched out in front of him. The open buttons of his shirt and his hair damp with sweat from dancing made Sarah's knees go weak. He looked unbelievably gorgeous.

"What are you doing?" He purred.

"Oh nothing, I just thought you might like to see my new outfit." She pushed the door open fully and came back into the room so Nick could see her properly.

His eyes nearly popped out of his head. He sat up straight and leant forward with his mouth hanging open. His lips started to move, but he was unable to string two words together.

"Do you like it?" Sarah asked him breathily.

Finally, coherent speech returned to Nick.

"Yes, yes, Mrs. Taylor, I do." He stuttered.

He never took his eyes off Sarah as he sauntered across the room to her. She leant against the wall and fixed Nick with an intense stare. It drove him wild. He picked up his pace, threw himself against her and kissed her hard and passionately. She could feel his full-on erection through his trousers. He slid his hand inside her panties, rubbing and caressing her as she closed her eyes in enjoyment. He kissed and softly grazed her neck with his teeth, listening to her heavy breathing in his ear. Then he dropped to his knees. He stroked her legs as he tugged on her panties and slid them down. He removed them slowly, then looked up at her and bit his lip. He buried his face between her thighs and massaged her with his tongue, rolling it round and back and forth until her legs started to shake and her orgasm burst out of her body. Before Sarah had calmed down, Nick released his erection and thrust himself deep inside her while she was still standing up against the wall. He unbuttoned her dress and gently pulled her breasts out of her bra. He kissed them over and over while he had sex with her. He could feel Sarah starting to build up again and he held her as she let out a long, satisfied moan. His penis started to tingle and tense up as an amazing sensation of heat flowed throughout his body. He groaned and smiled sexily as he came into his wife.

A soft kiss woke Sarah from her slumber the next morning. She opened her eyes and smiled tiredly as she gazed into Nick's eyes. She could still feel the thrill of the day before in her stomach.

"Good morning, beautiful." Nick greeted her.

"Hi, handsome," she replied.

"I'm sorry to wake you so early, but we need to get ready to leave for our honeymoon in a few hours."

"We have something to do first," she told him, fixing him with the same intense look as she had the night before.

Chapter Twenty-Six

"Congratulations again!" Tim beamed a few hours later in the manor house reception area.

"Thanks, Tim!" Nick engulfed him in a huge hug, and Sarah kissed him on his cheek.

A raucous sound that reminded Sarah of a herd of elephants echoed behind them. Katy suddenly appeared, out of breath, through the doors of the reception area. Sarah guessed she must have run full pelt from her room.

"Don't... go ... yet..." she panted, holding the stitch in her side. "Mum's... coming."

Sarah guided Katy to a seat, pushed her down onto it gently and gave her a perplexed look. "Do you really think I would have gone to the airport without saying goodbye to you and Mum?"

Katy looked sheepish and finally got her breath back. "I heard Tim shout and panicked."

A second later, Suzanna, glowing with happiness, breezed through the doors looking like she didn't have a care in the world.

"Sweetheart!" she boomed. Sarah ran to Suzanna and held her tightly. "I'm so proud of you! Everything about yesterday was beautiful, and I'm so glad we were able to come and share it with you both. Call me when you get to Mauritius."

"I will, Mum, and you call me when Tim has taken you to the airport tomorrow." Suzanna nodded.

"I will. Nick?" Nick stopped loading cases into the car and jogged towards Suzanna. "It's so great to finally call you my son-in-law!" She reached for his face and pecked him on his cheek. "I wanted to thank you for paying for us to stay here another night. As I've said before, you are very generous."

"You're welcome, and you are worth it. I wouldn't have my sensational wife standing next to me right now if it weren't for you."

"You little smoothie!" Suzanna chuckled. "Have a fabulous time and I'll see you when you come to England soon."

"We will, Mum, bye."

"Is it my turn now?" Katy asked. "I want cuddles too!"

Sarah and Nick both put their arms around her, making her feel like a tinned-sardine.

"All right, that'll do, thanks," she told them, trying to shrug them off. "You," she pointed sharply at Nick. "You make sure you look after my sister or else!"

"Don't worry about Sarah, little sister; she's the most precious thing in my life!" He went back to the car to carry on packing the suitcases.

"Katy, why does Mum look so happy? I mean, I know she was excited for my wedding, but jeez, I didn't expect her to look like she's floating on air!"

"I'm pretty sure she spent the night in Tim's room," Katy said slowly.

Sarah giggled and put her hand over her mouth. "Really?"

"Yeah. I went up to bed and left them downstairs together – this is the first time I've seen her since then."

"Maybe she just got up before you did, which would explain why you didn't see her?" Sarah reasoned.

Katy shook her head and whispered. "No. The towel shaped like a swan was still on her bed this morning, and her shoes, dress and bag were nowhere in sight!"

They both glanced across at their mother. She was stroking Tim's arm and looking at him coyly.

"They definitely did it!" Katy said suddenly. Then she scuttled in the direction of the dining room, looking back to Sarah, waving as she went.

"Come on, wife!" Nick shouted. "Your carriage awaits!"

"Excuse me, Mr. Taylor, there will be less of that," she teased.

As they drove back down the winding drive, Sarah turned in her seat. She felt more thankful at this moment than she had ever been before in her life. Since losing Tina, her life had become a rollercoaster of emotions. The thought of never being as close to anybody else as she had been to Tina had made her desperately sad. Meeting Nick so soon after felt like it was Tina's blessing. Sarah liked to think that Tina had been watching from above, egging them on and pushing them forwards. Sarah lifted Nick's arm and put it around her.

"You okay?" he asked her.

"Yes, I'm fine. I was just thinking about when we met."

He smiled warmly and kissed her on her forehead. Sarah snuggled into Nick's chest and dozed off with lots of thoughts of Tina and Stan swirling around her head.

Chapter Twenty-Seven

Three weeks in Mauritius was exactly what both Sarah and Nick needed. The tormenting memories that Sarah had sometimes felt like she was drowning in finally left her mind. Listening to the calmness of the sea when they lay on the beach during the day and hearing the gentle breeze flowing through the leaves of the palm trees at night was almost like medicine for Sarah. They spent most days wandering along the golden beaches, feeling the sand between their toes. They relaxed each night on the porch of their secluded hideaway hut on the beach, wrapped up in each other's arms, having deep conversations as they watched the waves in the sea. They were more than happy in each other's company, away from the hustle and bustle of the real world.

Sarah felt a little glum on the last night in their private escape, but at the same time she felt excited to be seeing Suzanna and Katy again so soon. She triple-checked her suitcase and laid out the bridesmaid sash at the very top. She had somewhere she needed to put it.

Visiting Tina's grave was something that Sarah had dreaded each time she did it, but also something that she knew she had to do in order to fully come to terms with losing her best friend. She told herself over and over again that one day she would be used to seeing it, but deep down, she knew this would never happen. Now, here she was in England once again, standing in front of Tina's grave with Nick clutching her hand.

There was her fantastic friend's name written in gold lettering etched into the heart-shaped, grey marble. Sarah crouched down so she could lay the bouquet of roses she and Nick had bought from Betty, the florist on the ground in front of Tina's headstone. Betty had once again gifted Sarah with a huge bouquet of her own, free of charge. Sarah pulled the small framed photograph that had been attached to her bridal bouquet out of her bag and tucked it carefully inside of the flowers that were now laid in front of the headstone. Then she draped the bridesmaid sash over the headstone to look as though it was wearing it. Her eyes drifted up to the sky above, a picture forming in her mind of Tina happily prancing about in the sash. She wished more than anything that the image she could see in her head as clear as day had been a real one.

"Happy birthday, Teeny. I love you."

Sarah stood up slowly and wrapped her arms around Nick's waist. He kissed her forehead then tapped her on her shoulder. He nodded in the direction of Bill walking towards them with a huge bouquet of flowers in his hand. His face was gaunt. The stress of everything that had happened seemed to have aged him dramatically.

"Hi, Sarah, Nick. How are you?" he asked them. He looked drained but managed a small smile.

"We're fine, thank you. We wanted to come here so I could lay some birthday flowers for Tina." She gestured towards the stone and the flowers on the ground.

"They are lovely, and I'm so happy for you both."

Bill shook Nick's hand. He really was happy for them which made Sarah smile.

"Wow, those flowers are beautiful, Bill. You bought roses too," Sarah said.

Bill placed them down, touched his fingers to his lips and then touched the photograph of Tina, looking completely carefree, that was displayed on her headstone.

"Yeah, they were her favourite and beautiful just like her," he said, not taking his eyes off the photograph. "I always bought her a bouquet of roses on her birthday. She had a special vase just for them. She wouldn't put any other flowers in it. She said it was only for the roses that I got for her. I played a little trick on her once. I bought her a box of Roses chocolates instead of flowers… I laughed; she didn't. I got straight back in the car and drove back to the shop to get her the flowers! When I arrived back home, she was already working her way through the box of Roses. She told me that I wasn't allowed any because I should have got the flowers in the first place!"

They all laughed. Sarah was happy that Bill still had precious memories like that of Tina. It was obvious that he loved her even now.

After a while, Sarah told Bill that they needed to get going so they could have some more time with Suzanna and Katy before they had to leave again for Los Angeles. She hugged Bill because it felt like the right thing to do at that moment, although she did still feel a tiny bit of resentment towards him for thinking that she was involved in Tina's death at first. She let go of him and said goodbye, but he grabbed Sarah's hand as she was about to walk away with Nick.

"Sarah. I really did want to marry Tina." He nodded to emphasise the fact. "I'm glad I did and I never regretted it even for a second. She looked so beautiful on our wedding day, and I felt so lucky that she was my bride. She had chosen me. I couldn't believe that a stunner like her would ever see anything in me. I was glad that I was able to make her feel like a princess, and I picture her like that all the time. I still don't have an answer to why I did what I did to her. I think it was just pure stupidity. I knew she wouldn't have taken me back so I didn't even try for another chance with her. I did try to apologise to her, but every time I picked up the phone to call her or got in my car to drive to her, I chickened out. I don't know how I even managed to give her the divorce papers. Although, thinking about it now, it was probably Gemma making me feel like I had to get it done quickly. I didn't know what I could possibly say to make Tina feel better and I didn't want to see her cry. I hated seeing her cry. I love her with all my heart, and I regret every single day what happened between us. I didn't realise how much I loved her until she..."

Sarah stepped towards Bill and hugged him again, but this time it was different. She felt like a weight had been lifted off her shoulders just by hearing him say those words. Her mind wandered back to the day he had turned up at her door asking for help with Tina's funeral. He had run off when Sarah had asked him if he'd wanted to marry Tina. She had never known the answer to this until now, and by him saying this, he made it crystal clear that he had still been completely in love with Tina when she died. He had never stopped loving her.

Sarah understood now that Bill had needed to get his anger out to help him deal with his grief. When Detective Althorp told him his suspicions about Sarah, he believed him straight away because that was the easiest thing for him to do.

Sarah thanked Bill for sharing this information with her. She hadn't realised but she had needed to hear this from him. She no longer felt the resentment towards him that had been inside her for months. She hoped that it had made him feel better too. She thought it had because his face seemed to have brightened up, and he smiled just like he had on his and Tina's wedding day.

“Thank you for everything Bill. Please keep in touch with us and take care,” Nick said, shaking Bill’s hand again.

“I will do and thank you for always being such an amazing friend to Tina,” he said, turning to Sarah. She nodded, struggling to utter any words.

Sarah and Nick walked away from Bill hand in hand back through the cemetery towards Suzanna’s car. They turned to look back at Bill and saw him dabbing at his face with a handkerchief. He looked up at them and waved. They waved back as Sarah wiped her own tears away. She made a silent promise to herself that she would always be there for Bill, no matter what. He had saved her life!

“Let’s go home,” Nick said, putting his arm around his wife.

Sarah allowed him to lead her back to her mother’s car and was thankful that after the troubling times they had all been through, she finally felt at peace.